Cry of the Sea

by

D. G. Driver

To Ardon,
Have great adventures.
D. G. Driver

F&I
by Melange Books

Published by
Fire and Ice
A Young Adult Imprint of Melange Books, LLC
White Bear Lake, MN 55110
www.fireandiceya.com

Cry of the Sea ~ Copyright © 2014 by D. G. Driver

ISBN: 978-1-61235-786-7 Print

Names, characters, and incidents depicted in this book are products of the author's imagination or are used fictitiously. Any resemblance to actual events, locales, organizations, or persons, living or dead, is entirely coincidental and beyond the intent of the author or the publisher. No part of this book may be reproduced or transmitted in any form or by any means, electronic or mechanical, including photocopying, recording, or by any information storage and retrieval system, without permission in writing from the publisher.
Published in the United States of America.

Cover Art by Caroline Andrus

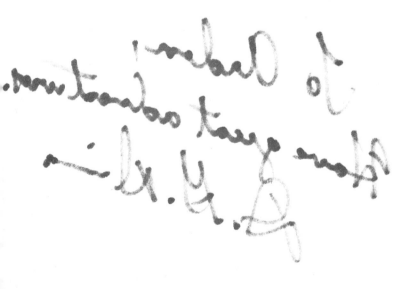

Dedication

*To my family for supporting me each time I dove into this project
and again when I occasionally came up for air.*

"The most haunting time at which to see [mermaids] is at the turn of the
moon, when they utter strange wailing cries..." J. M. Barrie, *Peter Pan*

Chapter One

"You ready to see how the next big change in your life is going to look?"

That was my dad, cheerfully holding the door open as he escorted me into the gym at school for College Night. He was excited to have me shake hands with the representative from Washington University and get that ball rolling. I didn't know then that the next big change in my life would happen in less than twelve hours—and it would have nothing to do with which college I picked.

When we first entered the room Dad immediately scanned all the booth banners to find his target. The moment he saw it, he grabbed my hand and yanked me in that direction. I actually wanted to look at some of the other booths, and I had told him that in the car.

His response? "Why bother?"

Full of smiles and giddy as if he were sending me to prom instead of a night of gathering brochures, he told me that once Mom got back from her business trip we'd all go to the University together and tour the campus. Maybe Mom would take me to some of her classrooms and old haunts. I told him I couldn't wait.

But I was lying.

Lucky for me, the path to the Washington U. booth was filled with half a dozen teachers I'd had at one point or another. We couldn't go more than a couple steps at a time without one of them accosting us and saying something obnoxious like, "You must be June's proud father!" I'd smile painfully and nod that it was indeed my father standing next to me. Then there would be lots of hand shaking and bragging about how their magnificent teaching skills motivated me to be such a great student.

Dad loved it and was happy to share with them how I was as brilliant as my mother, and that I shared all their interests.

I let him bask in all that glory on his own, using each teacher's approach as an opportunity to sneak in stops at booths and take hand-outs from happy, enthusiastic college representatives. These friendly people hadn't seen my grade average or SAT scores yet. They didn't need to with the big show of my dad and teachers going on behind me. Besides, when they took in my darker skin and straight, long black hair, their eyes got so big. Juniper Sawfeather would be a great addition to their campuses, because they could add my American Indian heritage to their statistics and boast about their diverse communities.

Everyone was so cheerful. So welcoming. They had no idea that I was a social outcast and that my dad, Peter Sawfeather, the most outspoken Environmental Activist on the West Coast, was to blame.

For one night, though, I put aside dealing with the reality of my life as I knew it. We were a happy dad and daughter dreaming about my future. Different dreams but both good ones. We both wound up getting what we wanted from the event and arrived home later that evening in pretty good moods, laughing about the chances of me attending Brown or Stanford or Yale. Dad teased me about sending me to an all-girl university.

"I'll kill you," I said to him.

"Why?" He laughed. "It's not like you hang out with any boys now."

"I just haven't found that special boy who likes to picket loggers at five in the morning."

He smiled broadly. "I don't see why not. What could be more romantic than an early morning protest? You get to shout and scream with each other. Show lots of emotion. Plus, you get to cuddle up to stay warm. That's what your mom and I do."

"Dad!" I whined at him. "So not cool to talk to your seventeen-year-old daughter about cuddling with boys!"

I smacked him playfully and chased him around the living room. I grabbed that long, black Willy Nelson braid he always has trailing down his back and pulled him off balance. He made a big show of falling onto the couch. I collapsed into the armchair.

"I win!" I shouted. We both laughed as we gasped for air. As he struggled back to his feet, I noticed for the first time how a little gray had started to streak his hair. Would I age as gracefully as he had over the years? Even with all his hard work and worry, he still looked really young for a guy in his fifties. He only had a few small wrinkles around those brown eyes and between his dark eyebrows. Since I was the spitting image of him, broad nose, dark skin and all, I hoped I wouldn't get a gray hair until later in life either.

The phone ringing interrupted our fun and games as my dad jumped up to answer it. He always tried to answer the phone before it rang a second time no matter where he was in the house. It turned out to be Mom calling from Alaska checking in for the night.

While Dad talked on the phone, I went into the kitchen and sifted through the college catalogs and pulled out the ones I knew I'd never attend. Princeton, Harvard, Yale, the all-girl schools, and Washington State University all found the trashcan a convenient place to hide from snooping parental eyes. I'd have put them in the recycle bin, but unfortunately (and hadn't I heard years of my parents complaining about this?) glossy magazines aren't recyclable. Plus, the trashcan has a lid, and I kind of tucked them way down toward the bottom.

With the remaining catalogs, I made piles of the places I really wanted to go, the places more likely to accept me, and the places I would go if no one else accepted me. None of my choices, even the most pathetic of them all, were within four hundred miles of Olympia, my lovely, cold, and wet hometown.

"June," my dad called. I poked my head around the corner and saw him holding out the phone with his hand over the mouthpiece. "Your mother wants to talk to you." He whispered, "She's had a long day."

Great. She'd want to talk to me about College Night, and she was already in a bad mood. With the catalogs pressed against my chest, I walked over to the sofa and took the phone from my dad. I sucked in a deep breath of patience and said, "Hi Mom."

Dad started preparing dinner while Mom repeated a lot of what she had just told him about her day. I pretended I didn't know what she was talking about, so she could keep going on about herself and stay away from the topic of my day. Of course I knew what she did for a living.

Everyone knew. She was on the TV news and in the newspapers all the time doing it. My mom was a lawyer, whose main objective was to fight environmental legal battles with CEO's of major companies all over the world. That was her mission in life—to destroy big companies to save polar bears, owls, whales and ancient trees.

"So wait, Mom, what company is this?"

Mom sighed and explained. "I'm in negotiations with Affron Oil. You know, from the commercials?"

"The ones where they're saving the environment one gas station at a time?"

Mom snickered. "Yes, them."

"Well, shouldn't they be willing to help out?" I asked, acting as if I were that naïve. "I mean, that's their ad campaign."

"Right," Mom said. "And the cigarette companies are paying for cancer studies."

I acted shocked. "You mean they aren't?"

I liked hearing Mom laugh. It was kind of rare. She's a serious lady.

Mom went on explaining, "They are the largest oil distribution company in America. They drill for oil in Alaska and ship it down the American west coast. Despite the billions of dollars in profit the company sees every year, they have never bothered to put any of it toward building better or more efficient ships. Instead, they ship oil in old, run-down, leaky vessels, which end up killing a huge amount of sea life and pollute beaches from Alaska to Baja, California."

I frowned. "But wasn't there a law passed about that? I thought you told me…"

"Yes," Mom interrupted. "You're right. You remember. That's good. I helped lobby for that."

I could actually hear the pride in her voice. Or was it amazement that I remembered something she had done. It made me feel a little guilty. A lot of the time when she talked to me about her work, I tuned her out, not caring at all about what she was saying and kind of wishing she'd stop. Apparently that was noticeable.

I made an effort to pull that information out of the recesses of my brain. "The law had something to do with how the tankers are built, right?"

I could almost hear her smiling. "That's right, June. In 2001 a law was passed that all oil tankers are to be constructed with a double hull to prevent oil leaks. But that doesn't have to be completed until 2015."

"So the problem is…" I wasn't quite sure I was following.

"Affron hasn't even started. Not one ship has been retrofitted."

"Oh, yeah. That's not good."

"It's been tough here. The whole community is fighting against me because they need their husbands to go to work on those tankers. There have been a few threats."

"Mom, are you going to be okay?" Both of my parents have been threatened before, and sometimes that meant damage to their cars or our yard. Mom was alone up there; would anyone dare to hurt her?

Mom didn't sound worried, though. "Oh, it's all just talk. And despite the guff I've been getting from these people," Mom's voice lightened, sounding almost giddy, "I finally got the executives at Affron to agree to a delay long enough for the inspectors to look at the ships and determine if they are legally fit for shipping oil! Success!" Mom squeaked on that last word. A different sound for her. I bet the Affron executives didn't hear her do that.

"Oh, that's cool, Mom. Congratulations." I knew I didn't sound overly enthusiastic, but I did mean it. My mom does great work. It's just that my mom has a lot of these victories, and it's hard to get too excited about them anymore.

"Thanks, honey," There was obvious disappointment in her voice, but it was kind of too late to do anything about it. If I got all excited now, it would sound fake or pushed. "So, tell me. How was College Night? Talk to any interesting people?"

I felt my heart start to pound, and my feet and hands went instantly numb as I tried to figure out the best way to let her down. I mumbled, "I got a lot of catalogs. Some look really great."

"Well, I don't even know why you went at all. Washington University has the best Environmental Studies program. Your father and I know several of the professors."

Ugh. Like I hadn't heard all this already from Dad. Dripping with impatience, I said, "Yes, Mom, Dad made sure I got a catalog from Washington University. It was the first booth we went to."

"Terrific. When I get back next week, we can look it over together."

"Yeah, Mom, but I…"

"Did I just hear you tell your mom that you have a catalog from Washington University?" Dad asked, stepping out of the kitchen, shaking coffee grinds and orange peels off the cover of that very same catalog. "Cause look what I found while getting ready to cook dinner."

Brilliant thinking, June. Why didn't I wait and throw it away at school or anywhere else?

"Sorry, Dad, I…"

He didn't listen. He stomped down the hall and picked up the extension in his office. "She threw it away," he told my mom.

"You what?" Mom asked, her voice hitting a chord that distorted the connection.

Did we have to do this over the phone?

I tried to explain. "I told you I didn't want to go to Washington. I want to go to San Diego."

"But their program isn't as good," my mom said.

My dad added, "Not to mention the cost of an out-of-state school."

"If it's a matter of living at home, we can help pay for a dorm or apartment."

"It's not that," I said, even though I knew going to any school this close to home would drive me crazy, "I don't want to major in Environmental Studies."

"Why not?" both parents asked, like they'd never heard me say that before.

"Why should I?" I came back. "I grew up in your house. You're both experts. Why waste money on a college education about stuff I already know? What good will that do me?"

"It'll get you a good job," Mom said.

"Like your mother's," Dad pointed out.

My dad always did that—made it seem like my mom's job was better than his because he didn't have a college education.

"I was thinking about doing something else, that's all."

That's when my mom said it. Those words that said everything about how much my mom cared about the environment and how little she cared about me. Because if I didn't want to grow up and be just like

6

her then nothing I wanted to do would be good enough. "You don't have the slightest idea what you should do with your life!"

And that's when I said my equally hurtful words. "No, I know what I want. I want to get away from you!"

No one spoke for a moment. I thought about saying something else, but I didn't want to make the situation worse.

"We'll discuss this more when I get home," my mom finally said in those even lawyer tones she had perfected over the years. "Just don't do anything. Don't fill out any applications, anything, until I get home. Can you handle that?"

I bit the inside of my cheek. "I think I can manage that."

Mom went on, "Now if everything goes smoothly with the inspection, I should be home by Monday. If not, it might be another week."

"That's fine, Honey," Dad said. "We'll talk to you soon."

My mom hung up without another word. Half a second later, I heard my dad hang up. Finally, I removed the receiver from my own stunned ear and placed it back on the hook.

When my dad came back into the kitchen he had a cocktail in his hand. He sipped what looked like a gin and tonic as he finished pulling vegetables out of the refrigerator. Clearly, he had no intention of talking to me.

"Dad?" I tried. He responded only by throwing an onion onto the counter next to me. "Dad?" I tried again. This time I got some parsley. "Dad, talk to me."

"I don't see why," he said, closing the refrigerator door with his hip. He dropped his load of cabbage and carrots on the counter without spilling his drink. "You don't care about anything I have to say anyway."

"That's not true."

"Isn't it?"

I really resisted the temptation to roll my eyes or raise my voice. "Honestly, I think it's the other way around. I think you don't listen to me. I'm not being an awful daughter just because I have different goals than yours."

"We raised you to follow in our footsteps," he said.

"That's not fair," I replied. "For seventeen years I have gone to all

your protests and rescue missions. I have helped right alongside experts. You know that I can do stuff that some college graduates can't.

"That's different," he said, throwing sliced onions into a hissing pan of butter. "Look, I didn't get a degree and can do things some college grads can't, but they still get paid more. They get more validity. Don't you want that?"

"Of course I want that," I said. "I'm still going to college, Dad. But not to do what you and Mom do, that's all."

His eyes got teary from the onions. I could feel the spicy waves stinging my eyes too. He didn't say anything, though. Instead he threw the rest of the vegetables into the frying pan. I listened to them hiss in the olive oil as I waited for him to continue the conversation. I watched him cook until the vegetables softened and the green smell permeated the room. As his sole interest focused on browning onions and peppers, it was clear that he didn't plan on speaking to me anymore for the evening.

I headed upstairs to my bedroom and shut the door behind me. Under my bed I kept a box stocked with snack cakes and candy bars. I ate two Ding Dongs and figured they would be more filling than my dad's meatless fajitas anyway. My parents would freak out if they knew I ate this junk. They never put a fraction of processed food in their mouths, nor meat, nor sugar unless it came from fruit.

I grabbed my phone and called Haley.

"Hey, turn your TV a little to the right," I said. I sat on my bed and looked out my window. Now I could see the screen across the fifteen feet that divided our houses and through her bedroom window to the far wall where the TV rested on her dresser. Some kind of reality show like *Dumbest Criminals* was on. The picture was tiny, but it was better than nothing. "What's happening?"

Even though we could both see each other and could talk from the windows without phones like we did when we were kids, we preferred to sit on our beds not looking at each other and use the phones as if we were miles apart. It was way more comfortable.

Haley groaned. "It's pretty boring tonight." Then she laughed really hard. "Well, that was funny!"

"What happened? I couldn't see it."

"I can't explain it, really," she said. "Your parents should let you get a TV for your room."

"Haley, you know they won't."

"I know," she grunted. "Do you know that they haven't even spoken to my mom since they found out she leaves the TV on all the time so our dog won't get afraid when everyone's gone or asleep?"

"It wastes electricity."

"Yeah? Well, they should see our clawed up kitchen door after the last time the dog freaked out when he was left by himself."

"Your dog is weird."

"Your parents are weird," she said. Then she added a quick "no offense" as if that made it okay.

I bit my lip. It's kind of one thing to insult my own parents; it always got on my nerves to hear someone else do it. I tried to play it off like it was no big deal. "They're just hippies at heart. They're harmless, really." I popped half the Ding Dong in my mouth.

"I saw you guys at the Washington U booth tonight. You change your mind?"

"No," I said, choking on the cake. "I just took the brochure to make him happy, but he's pissed now because I told him I don't want to go there and be a clone of my mom. He doesn't get that being a lawyer doesn't interest me."

"You can't help that."

"They make me feel so guilty, though," I told her.

"Don't," she said back. I watched her pick up the remote and turn the TV off. "It's your life, not theirs. And it's not like you want to do something crazy like drop out of school or spend the rest of your life working at the mall. You still want to do great work."

"I do. I want to do something that's my own, you know? Find my own cause to get behind, not just ride their coattails."

"That's why we're starting the Recycling Club at school," she said.

I laughed. "Well, that's hardly a new cause, but okay."

Haley came to the window and sat on the sill. I noticed that she had changed out of her school clothes and was wearing her pajamas. Her hair, usually up in a ponytail, was long and wet from a shower. It seemed more brown than blond that way, and I liked it better. Well, except for the frown she had going on under it.

"So I have to tell you this," she said. I leaned against my wall and thought how it might be easier to open our windows and talk directly at each other. She was kind of whispering, though, like she was telling a secret, and I guess I wouldn't be able to hear her without the phone. "I read what Regina posted on her wall. She said if *anyone* else in school wants to come up with a Recycling Club, she'd make sure it passed through the Student Council review, but she was not going to pass yours because you'd probably be running through the school snatching soda cans out of people's hands and tearing the pep rally posters off the walls while screaming about how much paper was being wasted."

It took me a second to process what she was saying. "Wait! You're 'friends' with Regina?"

Haley waved her hand like that wasn't important. "She 'friends' everyone because she wants to have the biggest number to show how popular she is. She never actually responds to anyone else's stuff."

"I can't believe you bother to read what she writes," I said. "She's an idiot."

"She's President of the Student Council, and without her support tomorrow we have no club. I don't think we're going to get it. She hates you." Then her voice weakened as she looked away from me, "Us."

I wished I didn't recognize the hitch in her voice. Poor Haley. I remember when she was ten and new in town. Cute, blonde, and bubbly. The kind of girl who could feel comfortable in any crowd and should have been popular. She should have had lots of friends. But she had the bad luck to stand up in class on her first day of school and introduce herself as my new next-door neighbor. Cursed forever by that mistake, she had no choice to be my best friend because if she didn't hang with me she wouldn't have anyone to hang with at all.

"I'm sorry, Haley," I said.

"When we do this presentation tomorrow, can you just try to convince them that you're not like your parents? That you're not going to do anything weird or obnoxious? We just want to put out some recycling bins and help people know what can and can't be recycled. We're not going to go rioting across campus and hijacking people's backpacks looking for recyclables."

My throat knotted up. Did Haley really see my parents like that?

After all these years, did she really worry that I would behave like that? I embarrassed her. "Tell you what. I'll let you take the lead on this. You do most of the talking."

Haley smiled and nodded enthusiastically. "That sounds great! Oh! And remember to wear your brown and green. We'll be Earth Sisters!"

"Got it."

"The Student Council might think we're dorks, but that doesn't matter."

"No, it does not," I agreed. "They're popular, mean, hateful, and selfish, but they're not entirely stupid. We—you—can convince them to let us have our club."

Haley wished me luck with my dad before hanging up and closing her blinds. I half wanted to go on the computer and see if Regina Williams would 'friend' *me*, but then I decided it wasn't worth it.

Dad never did call me to dinner or to "talk things out." Instead, he did one of his famous stand-offs, where he wouldn't speak to me until I apologized and gave in to his wishes. I didn't, though. I didn't feel like letting him win this time. I was mad too and could be just as stubborn if I wanted to be. I planned to wake up the following morning and leave for school without so much as a nod to the man.

Mom's frantic call in the middle of the night changed everything.

Chapter Two

No good calls ever came at two o'clock in the morning. Only ones that wipe out any hope of having a normal day. On this particular morning, it wiped out hope of anything ever being "normal" again.

The piercing scream of the phone yanked me out of my dream. One moment I was swimming with dolphins in the warm, blue waters of Waikiki. The next, I found myself on my stomach, arms above my head, sheets and pillows everywhere except covering me and keeping me warm.

I bolted upright and faced the clock on my bedside table. My movement was so quick, I wasn't even fully aware my eyes were open until I registered the digital numbers clicking into place. 2:03.

By the time my hand touched the receiver the phone had stopped ringing. My sleepy brain wanted to believe it hadn't actually rung at all, but the soft murmur of Dad's voice coming from his bedroom across the hall assured me that it had. He answered so fast, like he expected the call. When Mom was out of town, I think he slept with his hand wrapped around the phone in case it was her.

Getting calls like this wasn't that unusual. My dad's business was a nonprofit organization called EE Alerts, a website and call center for environmental emergencies that was basically a one-man operation run out of our house. What was the call about this time? Hurt animal? Fallen tree? Probably not. Even though we get those kinds of calls a lot, and I mean A LOT, those calls could usually wait until morning. Only big calls came this early. Forest fires. People chaining themselves to trees. That kind of thing.

Or it could be Mom calling from Alaska. She was okay when she called last night, but maybe the cold up there caused her to get sick, like "go to the hospital" sick. Anchorage in September has got to make the weather here in Olympia seem like summer. I pulled a blanket over my knees to warm up.

Or maybe…

Oh, the way my mind can go to the absolute worst thing at two in the morning. I hated myself for thinking it. This was my mom we were talking about, not a character from a primetime TV drama.

Melodramatic or not, though, I couldn't help thinking just then about how she told me that people from the organization she had been lobbying against had been harassing her. Maybe they did something to her. Something horrible that warranted a call hours before the sun came up. Maybe she was in real danger.

I couldn't wait the five minutes until Dad told me who called and what about, so I slipped my fingers around the receiver and used my other hand to cover the mouthpiece so no one could hear my breathing.

At the sound of my mom's anxious voice, I felt instantly nauseous.

"Peter! Are you awake? Are you hearing me?"

I wanted to scream into the phone, "Mom, are you okay?"

Luckily my dad asked for me.

"Calm down, Honey, what's the matter?"

Good advice, I thought. *Calm down. Just listen.*

"Affron's rolling," my mom sputtered. "Their ship was sighted off the Canadian shore three and a half hours ago! If they stay close to the shore, they'll be passing you any time now."

"I thought they were going to wait," Dad said.

My mom had no patience for this. "I thought so too, Peter, but apparently they didn't."

I carefully hung up the phone. Oh, that was all. Not that this threat from Affron Oil was a little thing, by any means. But Mom wasn't hurt. That was what really mattered.

Especially after the fight we had on the phone before I went to bed. I didn't want those stinging words to be the last one we ever shared with each other. How could I live with that?

Okay. No point in dwelling on it. My mom wasn't under immediate threat, so I would have time to apologize and maybe try to fix things with her later. Unfortunately, the news Mom relayed made going back to sleep an impossibility. She had called before dawn on purpose to let us know we had to get up and over to the nearest beach ASAP. And our Northwest American beaches weren't nice and warm like the one I'd been dreaming about. Odds were, too, that it would be raining.

I shut my eyes and listened for the familiar tap-tapping on my bedroom window. It rained so much here in Washington that I was used to tuning it out, and I had to really work to hear it. Just a drizzle, it sounded like. Enough to make the roads slick. The sand at the beach would be easier to walk on because it would be firmer. But it would be extra sticky and hard to get off our shoes and clothes, even without the oil that most likely would be splattered everywhere.

While rubbing the sleep from my eyes, I rolled out of bed. Like a firefighter to the beat of a pulsing siren, I jumped into my jeans, sweatshirt and rubber boots. I yanked my hair back into a ponytail and covered up the loose strands with a cap. It didn't matter what I looked like. No one who mattered would see me. Besides, what else could I do with my hair? It was long, straight, and black. No one has ever had straighter hair than me. I laugh at girls who use straightening irons on their hair. Honestly. Why would anyone erase her curls?

I headed down the hall as Dad hung up the phone. My father's groan let me know how serious the situation could be down at the beach. I knew Dad needed a couple minutes to get ready, so I went ahead and ducked into the bathroom to splash some cold water over my sandy eyes and brush my teeth.

I beat my dad downstairs to the study and began filling the duffel bags with equipment. We'd need to take pictures and video, so I packed the cameras and some lighting equipment. My dad had drummed the routine into my head. How many times had he told me, "Anything we get on tape will be enormously valuable to our cause. Years worth of damning press releases and propaganda brochures could come from this mission." So far, we had never gotten any pictures over the years that were impressive enough to do anything worthwhile for the many environmental causes we fought for except fill fundraising pamphlets.

I worked quickly and efficiently. Lighting equipment in the blue bag. Camcorder in the green bag, with extra DV cassettes for it and some

35mm rolls in the side pocket. The film camera I hung around my neck, and my cell phone was in a case attached to my belt. It took grainy pictures, but I liked to have it just in case. My dad would be taking the pictures, but I could carry the cameras for now.

Above my head, Dad stomped around his bedroom, probably looking for his boots. He wouldn't find them.

"They're in the garage, Dad. You left them there on Friday!"

The stomping ceased.

I dragged the bags out to the front door and was just dipping into the kitchen to grab some snack foods when my dad came down the stairs. I looked up and smiled. He did not smile back. In fact, by the way he sneered at me, it was clear that my attempt at a friendly greeting had insulted him.

"I've got everything ready," I said. "I'm pretty sure, I do. I double-checked. So, let's get moving." He didn't move or say anything. I noticed his shoeless feet. "Did you hear me about the boots?"

My dad just stood there. He didn't note the equipment ready to be carried out to the truck. He didn't seem to care that I knew where he left his boots. Instead, he stared at me coldly. "Where do you think you're going?"

After seventeen years of being *forced* to go to protest after protest, rescue mission after rescue mission, and so on, my dad asked where I was *going*? Was he *insane*?

Stumped by my dad's sudden lack of brain cells, I stood there in the doorway gawking right back at him. I couldn't find a way to answer his ridiculous question without being equally obnoxious. Impulses running through me urged me to shout, "You don't want me to help? Fine! I'll go back to bed!" But I knew better. Saying something like that would only make things worse.

Finally, I summoned up these words: "The phone rang, and I assumed there was a problem you needed help with since I heard you getting up."

He nodded. "It was your Mom. One of those leaky oil ships is headed this way. I'm going to see if it's causing any damage." His eyes drifted to the bags and then back to my face. "Go back to bed, June. I don't need you to help. I'll call Randy."

15

"I'm already dressed," I said. "I've got everything packed."

"I'm not going to make you do something you don't want to do," he said. "If you don't want to be a part of the work your mother and I take pride in, then that's your choice. Go back to bed."

Really? He was still hanging on to the fight from last night? Here we were at 2:25 in the morning with the possibility of a huge environmental emergency taking place off our coastline, and he was going to get all pouty because his feelings were hurt?

I wanted to scream some sense into him. Just because I wanted to major in a different area of study than my mother? Just because I wanted to go to a college in another place from the one my father's people had lived in for thousands of years? Just because I wanted to try something new, he didn't have to jump to the conclusion I wanted no part of his life.

But I didn't. I stayed as cool as I could. Someone had to, because Dad was clearly not interested in being sensible.

"I'm going with you," I said as evenly as possible through gritted teeth. I came up with a reason that he wouldn't be able to argue against. This tact was always important when dealing with my parents—they were activists, after all. Arguing was their life. "I want to go whether you want me to or not. This kind of operation goes right along with a Marine Biology major. If there's an oil spill, there will be hurt sea life. My volunteer work with them will help toward my college applications."

"I'm sure you've got enough volunteer work credits to get you into college without applications or even having to pay tuition," he said sarcastically, finally moving off the stairs and through the mudroom leading to the garage door. "You could wallpaper the house in recommendations from professionals."

Okay, that was rude. I followed my dad even as my face stung from that verbal slap. "That's true," I told him, working a little harder at maintaining my tone, "but since you and Mom only deal with environmental issues that affect the state of Washington, a lot of those recommendations won't do me any good in Southern California where I want to apply for school."

Dad shut the door in my face.

I leaned against the washing machine and waited. He had to come

16

back in to get the rest of his stuff. A beat later, boots on his feet, he stomped back through the doorway and whisked past me. I continued explaining myself.

"My plan is to submit work I've done specifically with rehabilitation centers, oil spill rescue, or anything related to helping sea mammals to demonstrate how devoted I am to my educational direction."

"Well said," he mumbled. "I'm sure you'll do well at your interviews." He picked up one of the duffel bags and grabbed his keys from the counter.

"Dad," I said. "Are you even listening?"

"Do I need to? Seems like you've got it all figured out." At the door he stopped and looked back at me. "Come or don't. I have to go."

I pulled the other bag over my shoulder and followed him out to the pick-up truck in the driveway. My dad helped me load the equipment into the extra cab, and then we buckled up and drove off. Thirty minutes had passed since my mom called. Too slow. Usually we moved much faster than this.

Those extra couple minutes shouldn't have made much difference, really. Nothing could stop the oil from leaking and the animals from dying. But if I had known what we were going to find on that beach, I'd have grabbed the keys and shoved my barefoot Dad and all his "poor me" attitude out the door so we could get there in time to help.

~ * ~

Neither of us spoke at all on the way to the beach. We didn't have to. We knew what we had to do once we got there, and if we spoke about anything else, we'd just argue. So we listened to the early morning news, wondering if the possible oil spill had been leaked to the press yet. It hadn't. Usually no one heard about these events before the so-called experts (who were secretly under contract with Affron Oil Company) came and declared that the situation "had only minimal impact."

Once Dad got on the highway going west, he floored it. At the speed he was going he'd cut a lot of time off our hour drive to the beaches at Aberdeen.

"Dad," I said, a little nervously, "don't worry, you'll be the first one there." Although, I felt pretty sure that his lead foot was more from anger than from his need to be first on the scene to get footage before anyone disturbed it. When he only shrugged, turned up the radio, and added another five miles per hour to the speedometer, I decided to shut up about it and let him drive. Hopefully, the death-defying speed would help get the drama out of his system and we wouldn't die before it happened.

I shut off the radio and said, "Dad, I'm sorry about last night. I didn't mean to make you mad."

The speedometer dropped back ten miles per hour as my dad sighed.

"No," he said, clearing his throat because he hadn't spoken in forty-five minutes. "I'm sorry. I didn't sleep well after we argued, and your mom's call put me on edge. This isn't the way to handle things."

I didn't say anything. How do you agree with your dad when he tells you he's being stupid? *Yeah, Dad. Get it together.* Ah, no.

"I still want to talk more about all that, but not now. Okay?"

I wasn't going to argue that. The last thing I wanted to do was launch into that topic again. Dad had finally reached a speed limit that didn't have me clutching the handle above the window.

"So, what do you think?" he asked. "It's Tuesday in September."

I stifled a smile and nodded thoughtfully. If he was going to play this like nothing happened and get right to business, I could go along with that. For now.

I drew in a deep breath as I considered what he was asking. "The weather's not too cold yet. There could be some die-hard nature-lovers. You know, the retired folks and beachcombers. No tents. Just mobile campers."

"That's what I'm thinking, too."

All of the main beaches were part of public parks with campgrounds, like Ocean City State Park.

"What about Grayland Beach?" I suggested. "It's south of town, away from the harbor and tourists. It's the one Haley and I usually hang out at because it's less populated. Odds are best that no one will be there."

"Good idea," he said, making a left turn at the off-ramp.

A few minutes later my dad pulled the truck into an empty public parking lot that led to the public beach at the base of the cliff. We leapt out of the truck and grabbed our equipment. The rain had stopped for the moment, leaving the air crisp and smelling of salt and sulfur. It was now about four o'clock in the morning, so the sky had brightened to a dull gray. In another hour or so we would be able to use the cameras without extra lighting equipment. By then, Affron's *people* would arrive, and it would be too late to get any pictures that truly captured the devastation. Those guys moved fast when it came to disguising their messes as "no considerable damage."

I hiked the asphalt walkway down the hill, carrying too much. With one heavy bag over my back, a tripod under my arm and a flashlight in the other hand, I didn't have a free hand to catch myself when I slipped on the wet sand. My legs skidded out in front of me. I skidded a half yard on my right thigh and then landed squarely on my rump.

"June!" Dad snapped at me. "Be careful!"

Like my dad even cared about me getting hurt. Even if I had, he'd just say, "Shake it off," because I was not allowed to cry. I hadn't been allowed to cry over a bruise or bump since 1 was six. He was only worried about the equipment. That's why he shouted. It stung a bit, to know that the equipment meant more to him than my leg, but I also knew my dad's reaction was the correct one. Scratches from a fall meant nothing, but if the lamp or bulbs in my bag broke, we wouldn't get any good pictures. I didn't hear a crack or break come from the bag. I was pretty sure it hadn't touched the ground, so hopefully everything was still in good condition.

Carefully, I stood up and continued down the path. My thigh screamed at me, and I knew an hour from now, I'd be looking at a heavy-duty scratch there.

When I caught up to my dad on the beach, he was already wrapping the 35mm around his neck and pulling the camcorder out of the bag.

"I'm going to need light, June," he said. "Can you hurry?"

"Sure."

But even without the light, we could both see that my mother's worries had been founded. Already a number of sea animals had beached themselves. Through the gray light of early morning, the sand was dimpled with objects much larger than broken seashells brought to shore by the high tide. Small creatures had crawled out of the surf to escape the film on the top of the water: clams, crabs, and a few turtles. I saw a lot of dead fish, a couple of sea otters and already dozens of birds—all of them far blacker than they should be for that kind of light. Some still struggled against the oil coating their bodies. Most were dead.

It never got better, seeing this kind of destruction. I could now bear the sight of it without breaking into sobs like I used to when I was younger, but that didn't mean I didn't want to fall on the ground and wail. I felt my throat close up and my body tense in the way I'd trained it so that I could stay cool despite the emotion rushing through me. My dad had taught me how to overcome the sadness. He had to stay calm and in control, and it didn't help him to have a slobbery daughter at his side to worry about.

Stiffly, I set up the lighting equipment that I would carry behind my dad from spot to spot.

"Come on, June," Dad called. "We're losing time."

I followed him down to the waterline and focused the lights on a porpoise. Its blowhole had been sealed shut by the oil and its eyes permanently closed. My dad snapped a few pictures and then switched to the camcorder. He held the camera, while I spoke into a microphone about how the oil was killing the porpoise.

"This porpoise was swimming in the ocean, eating fish this morning. It came up for air and couldn't get any. The oil spread across its blowhole so that it couldn't take a breath. Imagine trying to breathe through cellophane taped over your nose and mouth. In a panic, the porpoise swam to shore and beached itself, probably thinking that it could rub the oil away in the sand. Unfortunately, it can't get back into the water. It wouldn't matter anyway. The fish it ate were coated with oil too, and that oil is slowly poisoning his system through his kidneys. This animal will die in minutes, not hours."

Learning to talk through the knot in my throat had taken years of training, too. Usually I could keep it together if I could just stand and watch, but the second I had to say something and blam! Out the tears flowed. Just like a baby. But Dad preferred me to do the voice-over work, so he could focus on taking pictures, so I did the best I could.

Granted my vocal tones weren't smooth that morning. My words quavered and edged on losing it, but I knew we didn't have time for retakes, so I pulled out some inner strength and mastered it.

"As you can see, there are already a growing number of creatures here on the beach dying or dead because of the Affron Oil leak. The oil will begin to sink deeper into the ocean and will coat the scales of fish. The killer whales, sea lions, sharks, and dolphins will eat those fish and die. The oil will seep into the ocean floor and kill the coral, sea plants, and the creatures that live and feed on them. Thousands of creatures will be dead by nightfall."

We moved around the beach, getting shots of different kinds of animals and birds. I made sure to note on video which animals were endangered species. Dad complimented me on my growing expertise at making clear expository for the video clips and advised me about what to add as we walked away from yet another victim of the oil.

"I told you that I've learned a lot from you and Mom."

He smiled. Not in a whole-hearted happy way, but in that I-hear-you-and-appreciate-what-you're-saying way. "Yeah, I guess we've inundated you with this stuff. But look how good you are at it. You could really make a statement, if you'd just..."

"Follow in Mom's footsteps?" I finished for him. "I could, but I could also do a great deal of good with the animals themselves. Just think, I could know how to clean up these animals, get them healthy, and get them re-acclimated to the ocean. Wouldn't that be just as worthwhile?"

My dad put the camera down and rubbed his shoulder. "It's worthwhile, but..."

"But what?" I came back quickly. "How can you argue that animal research and rehabilitation would be bad?"

"I'm not saying it is. I'm saying that you wouldn't have to rescue any animals if people weren't hurting them in the first place. Your mother and I try to *prevent* things like this oil spill from happening. We need someone young and intelligent like you to keep our work going."

"You say that like you're going somewhere," I said. "You're not dying and you're not quitting, so why do you need me so much?"

"You're the voice of your generation, June. That's why."

I looked away from him back toward the water. The sky had lightened quite a bit, and now I could see two-thirds of the way down the beach. We had been there about an hour and already more pelicans and sea gulls had flopped onto the shore, their wings coated with oil so that they couldn't fly, their beaks stuck together so that they couldn't eat.

"Do we have enough?" I asked my dad.

"I think we've covered at least one of each type," he said. "We might as well keep shooting, though. The Coast Guard will be here soon enough, and we can stop then."

I scanned the beach for a particularly sad case that we could stick on the evening news when I saw something horrible down toward the far end of the beach. No, it couldn't be!

The sun was up just enough for me to be able to make out the silhouette of what looked to be a human being covered in oil. I took a couple steps to my left to see more clearly. No, I was wrong. It wasn't *a* human.

There were *three* humans struggling against the oil.

"Dad!" I screamed. "There are some people over there! We've got to help them!"

Chapter Three

They must be surfers, was all I could think as I ran toward the three squirming bodies. Who else would be in the water this early in the morning? But even for surfers, this was pretty early. They'd have to have been surfing in the dark. That didn't make any sense. Were they crazy? I knew some surfers at school, and they were definitely nuts sometimes, but surfing before the sun rose seemed extreme even for them.

Well, crazy or not, they didn't deserve to be caught in an oil slick. I crashed down to my knees beside the bodies and dropped my gear. I started to reach out my hand to tap them and see if they were all right without even stopping to get a good look at them. But before I touched any of them, my arm recoiled back to my side.

"Dad!" I screamed. "Oh my God! Dad!"

My dad rushed up behind me. "Are they alive?" he asked, trying to catch his breath.

"I... I..."

Words didn't come. I couldn't formulate a thought. I was too startled. These three figures lying in the sand in front of me weren't surfers at all.

They weren't even people.

From their facial features and upper torsos, they looked kind of like women, but all three of them had silver-colored skin. They were bald, with strange ridges marking their skulls. None of them seemed to have ears, only holes in the sides of their heads. No nose was visible, not even a bone or nostrils filled that space between their eyes and mouths. Although their mouths seemed to be moving, they were actually breathing through what looked like gills in their necks.

And if that wasn't weird enough, instead of legs, their upper torsos stretched out into long, scale-covered, silver fishtails. If I had to say what these things stranded in front of me, splattered with oil, appeared to be, I'd say mermaids. And no, they didn't look like they'd start singing songs or granting me wishes. They looked a little bit scary—but fragile too. Most of all, they looked like they were going to die, and no handsome prince was there to kiss them and keep them from turning into sea foam.

"June," my dad whispered. "Do you think they're real?"

"Yes," I whispered back. "Strange but very real."

"You don't think they're costumes?" he suggested. "Maybe some costume party on a yacht last night—they fell off."

Sometimes my dad's brain worked even more off-kilter than mine. I shook my head. "Those are not costumes, Dad."

Those beings lying there in the sand were not wearing anything that was cut or stitched together. What I saw wasn't material. It wasn't a lycra suit like on *Catwoman*, nor was it some kind of make-up like that chick from *X-Men*. Make-up would've been washed away.

What I saw was real skin. Or some kind of skin, if skin could be silver. And those were real scales, not some kind of pointy sequins. I'd been around enough fish to know the difference. Besides, if these were a couple drunk, rich women in costumes, they'd be dead already. I knew these creatures weren't dead, because the one closest to me suddenly opened its eyes and focused them right at me.

They were huge and midnight blue, almost like eyes from a Japanese Anime character but more oval in shape. The color was so deep, lacking any light, probably like the world the creature knew. In those eyes I saw such intense pain and desperation. The creature implored me with those eyes to do something to help. The mermaid raised its webbed hands to its throat. The other mermaids started doing the same action.

"I don't think they can breathe," I said. "They're suffocating."

My dad and I had been kneeling there in the sand, mesmerized by the creatures for far too long. I forced myself to my feet and sprang into action. Reaching into my pack, I pulled out a box of alcohol wipes. I used them to wipe the oil away from the mermaids' gills and faces. The mermaids cringed at the sting of the alcohol. While I attended to the mermaids, my dad got on the cell phone.

"Yeah," he said to someone on the other end. "It's Peter Sawfeather. We've got an emergency… Oil spill… How fast can you get the center ready? We've got a number of animals here, but we need to bring in three, um, fish, right away… We can't wait… Dolphin size… Saltwater… Give us twenty minutes. Maybe less." He closed his phone and came back to me.

By now the sun was fully above the horizon. The Coast Guard and Affron specialists should be arriving any moment to take over.

"We've got to get them out of here before Affron gets here," Dad told me as if I didn't know that already. "They won't be safe."

I chose not to take a moment to say, "Duh," even though I was thinking it. Instead, I slipped my arms under the cold, slimy body of the first mermaid. He didn't lean over and grab the tail. Instead, he was rummaging through his pack. "Dad," I said impatiently, "help me carry them."

"Wait," my dad said. "One second." He pulled out the video camera he'd stashed in there when he ran over to join me and aimed the lens at the three mermaids. "Hold that one up a little bit more, June," he ordered. "Let me get a good shot of her."

"Dad, we don't have time for this," I said. He didn't listen. He gestured for me to hold the mermaid up even a little straighter. "This might be hurting her." He put a 'stop' hand up. I guess I had her where he wanted. "Dad, am I in this shot?" I asked. "Please say no."

With the mermaid dying in my arms, I knew it was awful to think about how ugly I was at the moment. I mean, my hair wasn't brushed, and I didn't have a stitch of make-up on. A part of me realized that I shouldn't care about such things. I should only care about doing what was right—saving the mermaids and recording their plight for the world to discover. This was an unbelievable find that I could barely wrap my head around, and yet I knew it was more important than my stupid vanity. That was the thinking of the responsible person my parents raised, who understood the enormity of what was happening, what I was holding in my arms. The rest of me, however, was still a teenage girl with a few basic needs. One necessity was being given some kind of warning that I was going to be filmed, so I would not be completely hideous looking. Who knew where my dad might choose to send this footage? I didn't even have a free hand at the moment to tuck my stray hairs back up under my cap.

Dad put up a 'shush' finger in front of his mouth and then started narrating into the microphone: "We've found an amazing discovery at Grayland Beach in Washington today. What you are seeing are three sea creatures that appear to have human features such as arms, a torso, and a head. Based on these features being matched with fish tails, one might stipulate that these are the mermaids of legend. They have found their way to this beach because of leaking oil from an Affron Oil vessel. The mermaids have mere moments to live unless we can get them to a tank of water and get the oil cleared away from their gills." He leaned close to me to get a good shot of the gills on the mermaids' necks.

"Dad," I said urgently. "Stop taping. We don't have time. They're dying."

As he focused tightly on the face and neck of the mermaid in my arms, guess who else got a close-up on camera?

"Dad!" I shouted for two reasons. Do-gooder and teenage girl unite in protest!

My dad snapped up. "You're right," he said, backing up and turning off the camera. "I got carried away." He tucked the camera inside the bag on his shoulder and helped me lift the first mermaid.

Her skin had a spongy quality similar to the skin of a dolphin or seal, and yet it wasn't as thick as a sea mammal and not nearly as heavy. Some of the scales bent backwards and cut at my hands. I guessed the scales protected her like armor. As we carried her to the truck, I saw the mermaid's skin color darken. Her eyes fluttered, and her gills worked frantically. She had to get back into water—fast.

We put her down softly in the bed of the truck and covered her with some blankets. As quickly as I could, I ran back to the other two mermaids. What I saw when I got to them caused me to crumble to my knees and start to cry. I know I'm not supposed to cry; it makes my dad crazy when I do it. I just couldn't help it right then. When I looked at the mermaids in that early morning sun, the sadness took over so fast that the tears and sobs came out before I could control myself. Their gills had closed to slits and their strange fingers no longer clawed at their necks. The bodies lay completely still.

My dad caught up with me. "What's the matter?" he asked.

I opened my arms and gestured to them. "Can't you see?" I said. "They're dead. We weren't fast enough. Look at them."

"Come on, girl," Dad said. He wrapped his arms around me and helped me stand up. "I know it's terrible. It is, really. Just hold it together a little while longer. We still need to get them off this beach."

. My first impulse was to wriggle away from him, shocked by his words. I could feel my forehead creasing with the distrust filling my brain. Did my dad, always the warrior of creatures that had no voice, just tell me that these mermaid bodies needed to be taken somewhere?

"Why?" I seethed at him. "What are you going to do with them?"

"Calm down, June," he said. "Don't you know me better than that? I don't mean the bodies any harm. But I *do* need to keep them away from Affron. What do you think they would they do if they knew there were creatures like this in our waters?"

I felt stupid. Of course my dad wasn't thinking of diabolical plots to chop up the mermaids and study them for science. He'd never do that. He wouldn't even chop up already dead meat from the grocery store to eat for dinner. On the other hand, Affron scientists would have no qualms about exploiting the poor creatures if they knew about them. They'd hunt them down. Find their homes. Capture every last one of them. Not to mention just the testing and prodding they might do on these two cadavers.

"Sorry, Dad. I'm just feeling overwhelmed, you know."

"I understand," my dad said. "Now hurry. We still have a chance of saving the one in the truck. So, come on and help. Fast." He hefted a mermaid out of the sand and practically ran with it back to the truck.

I tried to be helpful by using all my strength and picking up the remaining mermaid by myself, only I quickly found out that was impossible. Although the mermaid appeared as thin and as slight as a supermodel, she must have weighed close to one hundred fifty pounds. With that being at least thirty pounds more than my own weight, all I could do was lift her up behind me and drag her over my shoulders by her arms. Dad came back after unloading the other body onto the truck and met me only a few yards from where I'd started. He took her upper body off my shoulders and helped me carry the mermaid the rest of the way. We put the two dead mermaids in the truck bed next to the barely surviving one.

"I hope she doesn't get creeped out by this," I said.

"Like she isn't creeped out already?" my dad pointed out. "C'mon."

We got into the truck and sped off. As we drove away from the beach, we passed four white SUVs with the Affron Oil logo painted on the sides heading the opposite direction. I don't know why I ever doubt my dad. When it comes to this business, he knows his stuff. We couldn't have stayed a breath longer without our mermaids being discovered.

No more than five minutes later Dad veered off the highway and pulled the truck into the nearly empty parking lot of the Aberdeen Sea Mammal Rescue Center, a large warehouse-looking place tucked between a pine forest and shore cliff. Dad had driven like the truck was on fire, and the center was only a few miles down the road from Grayland Beach. I jumped out of the truck before it had completely stopped and ran up to the door. At the same moment, a young man stepped out of a beat-up, used Civic and approached the door.

"You Sawfeather?" he asked me.

"Yes," I said. "I'm June. And that's Peter, my dad." I pointed back at the truck where my dad was still turning off the ignition.

The guy stood there, fumbling with the keys to the front door for an interminable amount of time. Did he even know which key opened the door? He didn't look much older than me, and the sight of this blond, shaggy-headed kid in his sweatshirt and jeans didn't impress me. Where were the marine biologists who were supposed to meet us? What good was this guy going to do me? He had to be too young to be of any real use.

"Excuse me," I said. "Do you actually work here?"

"Yeah," he said, not a drop of self-consciousness in his voice. "I'm an intern here. Name's Carter Crowe. I just got a call to come in for an emergency. You it?"

He finally got the door open.

"Well, not me personally," I said. "But we do have an *extreme* emergency in the truck and we need to get it into water fast. Is anyone else coming? Like someone who can actually help?"

Carter smiled at me. Straight, clean teeth. His eyes were bright. He'd had his caffeine on the way over, and it was working. I have to admit, his was the most dazzling smile I've ever seen. It made me slightly dizzy.

"No worries," he assured me. "I can help."

I can't say why, but all of a sudden I was absolutely sure that he could.

He flipped on the lights to the center, revealing a neat little room with a sign attached to the front of the information desk that denoted the space Visitor's Center.

I'd been to the Sea Mammal Rescue Center before, on a field trip in grade school and for a rescue I'd done with my dad after a construction crew left so much litter when building a new beachfront condo that it was killing the animals that relied on the water there. This place was a non-profit organization with some small aquariums and a tide pool in the front lobby. Tourists paid admission to see the tiny reef sharks and hold sea slugs in their hands. Little kids tortured sea stars, and everyone marveled at the jellyfish tank.

What the average person and school group didn't realize was that behind the double doors on the far side of the room was a warehouse facility. I could remember from the time I came a few years back being amazed at how much stuff was on the other side of those doors. And I felt so special being let in on the big secret of it all. The room itself was massive, and at the far end of it were two tanks large enough for dolphins to swim in tight circles, and they were set up side-by-side, filling the entire length of the wall, precisely for emergencies like oil spills or fishing disasters. Porpoises getting caught in tuna nets, otters stuck in plastic 6-pack soda rings, orcas maimed but not killed by harpoons. Along the right wall were sturdy shelves lined with more aquariums of varying sizes and some cages for rescued sea birds. Usually the pelicans and seagulls were sick from eating poisoned fish, and sometimes they had hooks stuck in their beaks. In the center of the room were some long, metal examination tables. Many cabinets, a sink, and all the tools of the trade cluttered the left side of the room, along with a door leading to a private office, and a hallway that led to an examination room and a locker room for cleaning up.

Carter flung open those double doors at that moment, giving me just a glimpse of the vast room of water and glass. I moved to follow him, eager to see if my memory of the room and reality were the same, but he stopped in the doorway and told me, "I'll set up a tank while you bring in the fish."

Stretching my neck to see past his shoulders, I asked, "Do you know how to do that?"

"Do you know how to bring the fish in?" he questioned in return, slipping through the doors and allowing them to shut with a bang behind him.

The challenge spoken, I retreated to the parking lot to hold the door open for my dad who had already unloaded the surviving mermaid. He carried her gently toward the center and had just passed through the door when another car skidded into a parking spot. The noise caught my attention, and I hesitated before shutting the door behind me to get a better glimpse of who had just arrived. It was just an ordinary, unmarked compact car.

"Dad, someone's here," I said to my father, who was already halfway across the room.

"I need your help, June," he said. "Come on."

"But what if it's Affron? What if one of them followed us?"

"Then close the door and help me move this body out of sight."

I shut the door tight and ran across the room to open the double doors to the warehouse for my dad. He was panting under the weight of the mermaid.

"What about the other mermaids?" I said, suddenly realizing they were still out there in the truck bed. My heart started beating really hard. "They'll see them."

"They're under a blanket," Dad said.

We kept moving inside, heading for the large tank at the end where Carter was adjusting temperatures.

"Over here, you two," Carter called over his shoulder. "Is that it? I thought there were going to be three of them."

"Two of them died," I said.

"That's too bad," he said sincerely. He faced my dad to help lift the creature up into the tank. When he saw the mermaid, he jumped back.

"What the hell is that?"

Dad didn't answer. Instead, he asked, "Where's Dr. Schneider?" By his tone, it sounded like he wasn't thrilled with the presence of this teenage intern either.

"Right here."

The new voice behind us startled me. I hadn't heard the door open over our talking. Dad and I both snapped our heads to see Dr. Schneider closing the double doors behind him. The thin, balding man grabbed a lab coat from a hook by the cluttered desk beside the doors and slipped it on over his wrinkled clothes. "I live a little farther away from here than your emergency allowed."

"You should move," I quipped.

I guess he didn't think that was funny, because Dr. Schneider ignored me as he headed across the floor toward my dad.

"So what have you brought for us, Peter?"

"I'm not sure," Dad said. "But I think it's something no one has seen before."

"It's a mermaid," I said. Carter and Dr. Schneider looked at me like I had three heads. "Well, that's what she looks like. You got a better idea what she might be?"

Carter shook his head. "Well, whatever it is, we'll have to get the oil cleaned off of it before we can put it in the aquarium, or it won't do any good at all." He directed my dad to place the mermaid on a large metal dissection table in the middle of the room.

"Okay. Do that," I said. "But hurry. She's at the end as it is."

The gasping mermaid was now almost a navy blue color, all the luster of her silver gone. Carter let out a long whistle at the sight of her once she was lying flat on the table and dad had backed away.

Dr. Schneider, who had been standing there sputtering as if the shock of seeing the mermaid had stolen his ability to speak, finally formulated some words. "Dear God! What have you found?"

I ignored all of their reactions. "I don't think we have time to clean her, Carter," I said. "She's dying. Let's get her in the tank now."

Dr. Schneider walked around the table slowly, giving the creature a long visual once-over. "No doubt about it," he said. I wasn't sure if he meant that there was no doubt that it was a mermaid or no doubt that it was dying.

"Sir?" Carter asked. "What do you suggest?"

"Yes, yes!" the scientist declared. "Into the tank. And fast!"

Carter moved fast to help my dad lift the mermaid and carry her to the aquarium. All the cockiness he displayed when we first got there evaporated with the task of handling this unusual creature. Now he was all business. He climbed the stepladder and pushed back the screen lid to the aquarium. Then he helped my dad and me guide the body up and over the edge. Gently, he let the mermaid topple from his hands and drift into the cold, salty water of the tank. He closed the top and joined us back on the cement floor of the warehouse.

All of us watched the mermaid as she sank lifelessly to the bottom of the aquarium. No one spoke. No one breathed. We waited patiently, each of us hoping the mermaid's color would return and that she would open her eyes.

Chapter Four

"Come on, girl. Breathe," I began to chant softly. "Come on."

At last, with great effort, the mermaid threw her head back and seemed to gulp in a large breath. She rolled in a small loop through the water before stretching upright again. It was as if she were standing, although her tail wriggled beneath her to keep her treading water in one place. Her large eyes were open, and I swear she was looking directly at me. Those giant blue orbs had softened away from the edge of fear and pain I saw in them earlier. I think I could understand what she was trying to convey to me through those eyes. She seemed *grateful* that we'd saved her life.

After a moment, when the mermaid decided she'd made her message clear, she began swimming around the tank to get her bearings. All the while, she swiped at her skin to try to remove some of the oil. Her efforts did no good. All she did was smear the greasy stuff around more. As she became increasingly agitated, her movements got more and more frantic. Her tail thrashed about wildly in the tank, causing water to splash over the top and making the screen cover slap up and down.

"We've got to get that oil off her," Carter said. "But I don't know how. If we pull her out again, she might die."

"Do you think she'd let us go in with her?" I asked.

"I don't know," Carter said. "She looks violent."

"Wouldn't you be violent if you were covered in oil?"

My dad interrupted us. "Perhaps we should wait for her to calm down a bit before making any decisions. She's got to get used to the environment, and she *is* breathing. Her life's not in jeopardy—"

Carter interrupted. "It is, sir."

"—at this second," my dad said, finishing his sentence. My dad's stony expression made it clear that he was not to be argued with or interrupted again.

Carter frowned but conceded to my dad. He backed up and sat on top of the metal table. I moved back, too, and leaned against the table next to him. Dr. Schneider, on the other hand, had slowly inched closer to the aquarium while we talked and was now practically pressing his nose to the glass to take in the mermaid's every action.

"This is the most amazing thing I've ever seen," he said. "You found this on Grayland Beach? This morning?"

"Yes," my dad said. "There were three of them."

That's right. I gasped, realizing that with everything we'd been doing, I had forgotten we left the other two bodies in the truck. I gestured at Carter for him to follow me, and he jumped off the table. As we headed toward the door, Dr. Schneider inundated my dad with questions about how the mermaid had looked when we discovered her.

"Did you find her face up or down? Had she crawled up on the sand with her arms? Or do you think she was pushed ashore by the tide? Were the mermaids horizontal or vertical to the shoreline?"

They were good questions, and as I walked away I tried to think if I knew the answers. I had been so shocked at discovering them at all and then overwhelmed by the need to save them, that I'm not sure I noticed all those details. I wish I had paid more attention. I knew they were face up, but I really couldn't remember any details that would have helped me to know how they got there.

Carter opened the double doors for me, and I passed through to the lobby. Once the doors were closed behind us, he said, "So, that's Peter Sawfeather. I've heard of him. He led that fight against Oceanside Construction a few years ago, right?"

"That's him. My mom, Natalie Sawfeather, was the lawyer on the lawsuit too."

"Yeah, my dad works for that company."

Great. Someone else who was going to hate me because of my parents. "Sorry."

"Oh no! It's not like that." Carter laughed, easing the tension that had instantly formed between us. "My dad works for Oceanside *now*.

After the lawsuit your parents won against the company, my dad got hired to oversee construction sites and make sure they are being left litter free and that the workers are following all the environmental guidelines. Your parents are heroes at my house." Carter held the front door open for me. "It's pretty cool of you to come out and help him like this."

I paused as I walked through the Visitor's Center. I looked back at his face and those nice blue eyes. "You think so?"

"Yeah," he said. "You know, there are girls that come in here all the time. They look great in their sundresses, perfect hair and makeup. They parade around and look at the tanks, but they won't even touch so much as a sea star because they're *slimy*." He pantomimed reaching his hand in the water and pulling it out with a shriek and a series of shivers. "Ew! Ew!"

I giggled in spite of myself. He grinned and shook his head.

"I know. Pathetic, right?"

"You could say that."

"You're different from them. You don't care how you look. You'll wake up before dawn and throw on whatever you've got 'cause you know you're going to get dirty with the fish and oil. I've never met a girl like you."

"Oh," I said, and continued toward the front door. I wasn't quite sure how to take that. I think he was trying to compliment me, but it didn't really work. All he did was remind me of how terrible I looked at the moment. Thanks for that. And why were all these girls coming to the rehabilitation center in their sundresses and make-up anyway? Ummmm, let me guess. It probably wasn't to look at jellyfish and sand sharks.

Outside, I unlatched the back of the pick-up and pulled the blankets off the mermaids. Carter took a step back. The smell of the bodies had ripened. They gave off a distinct dead fish odor mixed with sulfur that I knew would be in my pores and hair for days. I reached for the first body.

"They're heavier than they look," I said.

Carter got my hint and quickly stepped to my side to pull the torso out of the truck bed. I wrapped my arms around the tail. "I've heard your dad's name at school, too," Carter said, his voice almost too cheery. It seemed like he was trying to keep a light conversation going to avoid thinking about the grim thing we were doing. "My professor of Geology at Washington State is a friend of his. He's mentioned your dad a time or two during lab."

"You're in college?"

Dumb question. Of course he was in college.

"Aren't *you*?" he came back.

I felt my lips pull up into a wry grin. Well, that was something. I may have looked like Hell, but at least he thought I was older. That was cool. I kept my eyes diverted from his tan face.

"Well, actually, no," I said. "I'm a senior at West Olympia."

"That makes you even more unique, then. I can't imagine any high school girl doing anything but playing with her cell phone and shopping at the mall."

I had to look up at him then. Just a glance. I wanted to know if he was smiling, and he was. Maybe unique was something he could like in a girl.

I wasn't good at flirting. No guy had ever shown any interest in me, and I wasn't sure if Carter was or if he was just being polite. It was also really hard to be *all that* when holding a dead mermaid tail with both arms. So, in response, all I said was, "Yeah, well, when you're raised by activists it gets in the blood."

I couldn't help but notice the muscles in Carter's arms when he shifted the weight of the mermaid so that he could open the door. They flexed beneath his blue T-shirt and the weight of the mermaid bundle.

"How'd you get a job working for Dr. Schneider?" I asked him.

"School," Carter answered. "They have listings in the Student Center of places that need interns and apprentices. I thought an internship here would look good on my resume when I graduate."

"What year are you?" I found it hard to believe that this guy was close to graduating college. He didn't look much older than me. In fact, he even had a couple bright red pimples on his otherwise perfect nose.

"Oh, I'm just a Freshman," he said. "I've got a long way to go. But who knows what can happen? Maybe this internship will turn into a paying gig before too long." He nodded to the mermaid in his arms, her head tucked against his chest and arms crossed over her torso between his arms. "After a discovery like this, maybe I won't even have to graduate. The National Geographic Society will give us all huge grants and make us all successful. How would that be?"

I didn't say anything. It was a nice thought, being rich and successful, but I knew it wasn't reality. My parents were not about becoming rich. They would find a purpose for this find that would benefit some cause. I didn't know what that would be yet, but my parents would uncover it. I also knew that I really didn't want to skip college. I needed college to get away from my parents, and I needed a degree to do what I wanted with my life. Carter seemed like a pretty motivated guy, so I felt pretty sure he wouldn't quit college either, no matter what happened next.

Without any more small talk, we got both of the bodies inside and spread out on the metal table behind where my father and Dr. Schneider were still animatedly discussing the mermaid in the tank. As soon as we were finished, the men turned their attention away from the tank and onto the corpses.

"Remarkable," Dr. Schneider said. "Astounding."

Dr. Schneider put on some latex gloves and began running his fingers along the deep blue skin of the mermaids, which was drying out quickly. He poked at them and plucked scales off their tails, all the while speaking aloud his thoughts about the skin tissue and biology of the creatures. I knew that I should be paying more attention, like Carter and my dad were. They nodded their heads and said "uh huh" after every sentence Dr. Schneider uttered. But I wasn't following what the scientist was talking about; all the tech talk bored me. While I knew that I'd have to take tests and write essays about this kind of stuff when I went to school, it wasn't the reason I wanted to be a Marine Biologist. It was the actual physical involvement with the animals that intrigued me.

Halfway listening to Dr. Schneider's monotonous scrutinizing, I stepped away from the table to watch the living mermaid. She had stopped thrashing about and appeared to be actively observing the men and the dead bodies with her hands pressed against the glass. She winced every time the scientist prodded at her sisters. Again, her eyes revealed emotions that were anything but happy. They conveyed loss, loneliness, and pain all at once. I was positive she could comprehend that the other mermaids were dead.

"I'm sorry," I said to the mermaid, touching the glass softly. "We weren't fast enough."

The mermaid looked into my eyes. She understood me. Maybe not my words so much, but she recognized the sincerity behind them. Ridiculous as it was, a part of me expected her to talk back to me. If it were a SyFy Channel movie, she'd have a snippy English accent and would tell me important secrets in riddles. In a Disney film, she might even sing. However, she wasn't really partly human with some uncanny ability to talk beautifully in my language even though she'd never heard it before. She was mostly some kind of fish with an upper half that looked vaguely like a woman who lived under water where people don't talk or watch cable TV. So, instead of talking with words, the mermaid simply let out a squeaking noise similar to the sound of a dolphin.

The men heard it and stopped what they were doing to gather around me.

"Did she just make that sound?" Dr. Schneider asked.

"Yes," I said. "I think she was talking to me."

"That's impossible," Dr. Schneider said. "That would mean she was sentient, able to think and communicate."

"Well, why not?" my dad said. "With a human*ish* head, why couldn't she have a brain similar to ours too?"

The mermaid made that squeaking noise again, much more urgently this time. She was definitely trying to tell me something.

I turned to Carter. "We should move the dead mermaids out of her sight," I said. "It's upsetting her to see them like that." My dad and Dr. Schneider stared at me like I was crazy. "Would you be okay to look at the dead bodies of your sisters while people poked at them and talked about them?"

My dad scrunched up his face. "Come on, June. I agree she might be aware of her surroundings and trying to reach out to us, but I don't believe she thinks that clearly."

I stared at him hard. "Imagine standing there and having to watch the autopsy of my dead body. How would you feel?"

My dad blinked and shot a look back at the mermaid. The creature squealed again.

Carter didn't need any more convincing. He responded to that third cry right away by picking up one of the bodies and carrying it down the hall to the examination room. The two grown men were a bit slower to understand that I was serious, so I lifted the other body by myself until Carter came back to help me. When we came back, I could tell the mermaid was still trying to see what was happening by the way she swam back and forth along the glass, but she seemed a bit more relieved.

"Thank you," I said to Carter quietly.

He did the sweetest little half smile. "Not a problem."

The men discussed possibilities of origin and the likelihood of there being more creatures like this in the ocean for another fifteen minutes or so before my dad looked at his watch.

"Oh boy," he said. "We've got to run. If the pictures we took this morning are going to do us any good, we've got to rush them to the papers and television news stations. You'll take care of the, um, creatures, then?"

Dr. Schneider nodded, but I thought I could see his fingers twitching.

"Please don't dissect them," I said. "Not until we have a better understanding of what they are. Please."

Dr. Schneider's eyes went dark. "We can't understand them without dissecting them," he told me.

My father stepped in at that point. "I think June is right on this one," he said. "We should hold off from cutting them open just yet. I'll give you a call later on and we'll discuss a plan of action."

"We don't have long, Peter," Dr. Schneider said. "The smell is only going to get worse, and you know there will be more animals coming as soon as the oil spill is reported."

"I'm aware of that," my dad said. "I just need a couple hours, and I'll be back."

I followed my dad out to the truck.

"Dad," I said. "You won't have time to drive all the way home, do business, and get back here in a couple of hours. It'll take two hours round trip just to drive."

He sighed and put his hand on the hood of the truck. "No. You're right. And I really need to get back to the beach, too." He looked up at the sun well above the horizon. "I left my laptop at home."

"I've got one," came Carter's voice from the door. He had followed us out.

My dad straightened up at the sight of the college intern. "With Internet?"

Carter laughed. "Are you kidding me?"

I had to laugh too. My dad could be so outdated sometimes. I still could hardly believe his stories about going through high school with only an electric typewriter. Half my assignments at school require work done on computers and research from the Internet. I had to do a presentation in PowerPoint just last week for English.

I groaned slightly. School. I kind of forgot it was a school day.

"You okay, June?" Dad asked.

"Yeah," I said. "I just remembered something."

I let my dad and Carter figure out the details of going to Carter's place and using his computer while I walked away from them and called Haley on my cell.

She answered on the first ring.

"Where are you?" Haley said. "I had to leave without you."

Haley had her own car. She usually drove us to school.

"Sorry. I should have called earlier, but I lost track of time. We're doing work for the good of all mankind this morning."

"Oh. Well that's a surprise." With a tone like that, I could imagine the frown on her face. Or was it a scowl?

I tried to ignore her frustration and continued explaining. "So, I'm kind of gross and very far from school. There's no way I can make it to school today."

"Unh-uh," Haley snapped. "Not today. I need you today. We're making our case before Student Council at lunch."

"Oh crap!" I shouted too loudly. Dad and Carter turned their heads my way. I walked further away from them. "Today is not a good day. I'll never make it."

"You have to make it," Haley insisted. "You know they won't reschedule it, because they hate us and want to make our lives miserable. If we don't appear today, our club is not going to happen."

"Okay," I said. "I'll try to be there by lunch. I don't know how right now, but I'll try." I got off the phone and went back to Carter and my dad. "I've got a problem, Dad."

"What is it?"

"I need to get to school by 11:30." I paused, but when my dad didn't act like that was a big deal, I added, "and I can't go looking like this."

He woke up. "Oh!"

Carter, my new hero, stepped up again with his chivalry. "How about you both come over to my house? June can clean up while I get you started on the computer, Mr. Sawfeather. Then I'll drive June to school."

My dad nodded. "Sounds perfect."

"Clothes?" I asked, gesturing to my stained and smelly outfit.

Carter winked. "I'm sure we can come up with something."

It could have been a tease or a flirt. Winking was a deceptive thing. My mind argued that it was just an innocent eye twitch to let me know he had things in control. The hot lava rushing through my veins and my heavy pulse led me to hope that wink was code for something much more romantically devious.

Chapter Five

Can't say how I managed to get into the truck and put my seatbelt on. I don't remember any of that. Next thing I knew I was there, beside my father, with a plan to follow Carter up the road into town. My dad started the engine and backed out of the parking lot. He sported a goofy little smile, his first smile of the day.

"Looks like someone's got a crush."

I tried to be nonchalant about it, but instead I sputtered out a totally fake, "What are you talking about?" As if I didn't know.

"He's going to drive you all the way to Olympia," Dad pointed out. "He doesn't have to do that."

I blushed a little and rolled my eyes. "No. That's not it. He wants to impress *you*, that's all. He knows about you from his professor at school. He thinks you're some kind of idol probably, and he'll get extra credit for knowing you."

My dad shrugged his shoulders. "If you say so."

As much as what I said to my dad made sense, I couldn't help but hope my dad was right about Carter. Maybe his graciousness was a little about me too. Everything about him was turning out to be wonderful.

Dad clicked on the news as we rode along. It was seven-thirty in the morning, and the local stations had now received word of the oil spill. So far the reports weren't anything but headlines, not offering a lot of information. Within an hour that would change. Affron leaked news as much as it did oil, only their version would be skewed to express that no real damage had been done. 'Nothing for the public to worry about,' their report would attest. The news anchors across the country would soon be reporting that the oil spill was just a small one and easily cleaned up. Then it would be forgotten.

No one would mention how many animals, including two apparent mermaids, had died—or would continue to die for the next few years.

That was my father's job. He'd be on the Internet all week, trying to get reporters to acknowledge the seriousness of the situation. With his buddy, Randy, they'd add new statistics and the photographic evidence to his web site and make sure that all of the politicians on the West Coast were aware of crisis. Most of all, he'd be working closely with Mom to make sure Affron was punished for sending out that leaky vessel.

Carter turned into a gated neighborhood of houses with matching red tile roofs and procured a parking pass for us. We followed him down a couple winding streets and ended up in front of a beautiful house that was angled on a hill to have a view of the ocean from the upstairs bedroom windows. Each bedroom had its own balcony. I envisioned myself leaning over one, a glass of cool iced tea in my hand, a wide summer hat on my head and a silk scarf fluttering off my neck in the warm salt-water breeze. Dressed in a white silk button down shirt and slacks, a very tan Carter stepped up behind me and put his hand on my waist…

A honk pulled me out of my reverie. Carter waved us over to the circular driveway where he'd stopped his car. But my dad parked along the curb in the street, regardless. Our ugly, old pickup did not belong anywhere on that lovely property.

We got out of the truck and met Carter at the front door.

"You live here?" I asked. "You don't have your own place?"

"Don't be too disappointed," he said, pretending to pout.

"Oh, I'm not," I said, eager to see what the house looked like on the inside.

"This is my parents' house," Carter explained, unlocking the door. "I have a dorm room at school, but I stay here on weekends and when I don't have early classes. It's too noisy at the dorm, and I have a hard time sleeping without the sound of the waves." Once inside, he typed in a code into the security box on the wall.

"You know," I said. "They have those white noise machines now. You can set them to ocean waves or streams or whatever."

"It's not the same," Carter said.

"Yeah, I guess not. Listening to something like that would probably just make me want to pee all night."

Did I say that? I felt my face heat up.

I walked through the doors into his world of white décor, pivoted and stepped right back outside. My nasty boots weren't allowed to enter this perfect domain, so I slipped them off and left them on the porch. Truth be told, I felt like I should remove every article of my clothing, because I was afraid to bump up against anything.

Carter laughed at me. "My mother thanks you."

My dad had finished getting out of his boots and stepped inside behind me, lugging the camera tote bag over his shoulder. "This is very nice, Carter. Tell your mother she has done a beautiful job with the place."

Carter grinned. "Actually, it's my dad who's the stylist. Mom is an accountant. Go figure."

We all laughed.

"And the shower?" I asked. "I must take one now before I accidentally sit on something."

"Follow me." Carter turned to my dad. "Why don't you go sit in the kitchen down that hall, Mr. Sawfeather. I'll get some coffee going and pull out the computer."

"Sounds great." My dad shuffled down the shiny wood floor in his socks.

Carter grabbed my hand and led me upstairs.

It turned out that there were three bedrooms upstairs, a laundry room, and an entertainment room with a huge flat screen TV and all the gadgets one could wish for. Haley would be in tech-geek heaven if she saw this place. I hoped I'd have a chance to bring her here sometime.

"I can see why the dorm wouldn't compare," I told him.

"You think?" he said.

He opened the door to his own bedroom and led me inside. It was fairly neat, which surprised me a little. I won't say everything was in its perfect place, but nothing was lying where it shouldn't. No underwear on the floor or socks on the pillowcases. I was also surprised to find that he didn't have any posters on his wall of models, sports players, or even rock-and-roll bands. Instead, he had some really interesting abstract splatter color paintings in frames. Like fake Pollock pieces.

"Did your dad decorate your room, too?" I asked.

Carter laughed. "No," he said. "I actually put all this together. The paintings are all by animals. There are two painted by a dolphin down in Florida and one is painted by an elephant."

"You're kidding!" I said.

"Not one bit," he told me, straightening one. "I got them on vacations. I thought they were really cool. I still do, actually. I can't even paint that well, and I have hands." He pointed to a door on the far side of the double bed. "The bathroom's there. It's between the two bedrooms. There are clean towels in the cabinet." I must have looked uncomfortable, because he headed for his dresser drawers and kept talking. "Is your school dress code or wear-anything-you-want?"

"Dress code, actually," I said and winced. "It's not a strict uniform, but we have to wear collared shirts and either tan or navy pants or skirts. I suppose I could just wear a pair of your sweats, and you could swing me by my house on the way…"

"Nah!" Carter said. "I've got what you need. These are a little snug on me." Carter pulled out a collar shirt and a plain navy-colored sweatshirt to go over it. "No need to rush more than we have to." As he handed the clothes to me, he added, "I'm sure my mom's got a skirt or some pants that'll fit you. She's tall like you. Not quite as thin, but she tries. Yoga and Pilates once a week."

"She won't mind?" I asked.

He shook his head. "You're not going to rescue any more mythical creatures covered in oil, are you?"

"No," I said. "I'm afraid I'm just tackling the Student Council at school. A totally different kind of messy situation."

"I know what you're talking about."

Sure he did, I thought. His looks. His house. Carter had probably been president of his school's Student Council.

"Khaki would be best, if she has it," I suggested.

"I'll see what I can find." He led me to the bathroom. "Steam it up real good so I can come in here to drop the clothes off."

I tried to laugh in a relaxed way, but it came out a little choked as he closed the door behind him. The bathroom was as lovely as everything else in the house, and I had to take a minute to touch all the pretty handles before turning on the water faucet in the shower. As the water heated up, I glanced at myself in the mirror. Oh, Heavens! Is that what I'd looked like all morning? Well, that ruled out his wink as being anything other than pity.

I quickly let down my hair and shed my clothes. I balled everything up as tight as I could and placed it on a tile by the toilet where the oil and sand that rubbed off it could be cleaned up easily.

He showered with Axe shampoo and soap, so I'd smell like a boy all day. It didn't bother me too much. I was going to smell like a really hot, exceptionally cool college guy. And that was way better than smelling like fish and oil. The hot water stung the scrape on my leg that I'd all but forgotten about. It took a fair bit of scrubbing to get the oil off my arms and face, too.

At some point he snuck in to put some slacks on the sink counter, but I didn't hear or see him. He must have been very fast. It was possible that he only reached his arm in and didn't come in the bathroom at all. I know it was another act of his amazing chivalry, but I couldn't help feeling slightly bummed out that he didn't try to peek.

Twenty minutes later I was clean, dressed in a combination of his and his mother's clothes, and headed back down the stairs to find Carter and my dad in the kitchen. All the digital pictures had been uploaded, and they had figured out how to upload the video footage too. They put the video in two separate files. One for the regular oil spill information, another for the mermaid discovery. Now Dad was typing up a press release statement.

He was talking to Carter when I walked in. "My only problem now is that all my contacts are on my computer at home. How do I get these sent out?"

Since the mermaid rescue had taken so long, they had precious little time left to get these images e-mailed to every news correspondent they could think of before Affron got its own press releases out debunking everything Dad wanted them to know.

"Let's call Mom," I suggested. "Have her email the contacts. She has them all with her on her laptop."

"Of course, Genius," he said. "I suppose I would have thought of that eventually, but it's nice to have you young, brainy people around to think for me."

He got out his cell phone and dialed my mom. I gestured to the coffee cups on the table. "Any of that left? I'm not a big coffee fan, but I think it might help."

"I'll pour you a cup," Carter said and dashed over to the coffee machine. "Did you enjoy your shower? You look great."

I smiled. I sure felt a whole lot better than I had. I'd like to really clean up for him sometime: put on some make-up and a dress, clips in my hair. However, just letting him know that I don't always stink and look like I've been dragged under a boat was good for the moment.

"Hey, honey, hi!" my dad said into the phone, his voice betraying his energy level.

Carter gestured to the creamer and sugar. I nodded, and he sweetened my coffee up for me.

"You near your computer?" my dad asked my mom while Carter handed me the hot mug. "I need you to email me our press contact list." There was a long pause, and I could hear Mom's voice coming out of the phone. "Look, something happened this morning that slowed us up a bit." Another long pause. "I know it's important to get this out right away, honey," my dad said patiently. "I've been doing this a while too." Pause. "Yes, she's with me." Pause. Dad got up then and moved away from us. I could still hear the sharpness of my mom's voice from across the room. "Let's not get into that right now," Dad said as calmly as he could. "There are other things to discuss."

My dad put the phone on his shoulder and gestured to the laptop. "Hey Carter, can you help June email the video to her mother?"

This only took a moment for us to accomplish on his high-speed computer. It gave me a silly thrill to see it zip off so fast. I'd been begging my dad to let us get high speed, but he insists on dial-up. When I actually need to do stuff online I either go to Haley's house or take my laptop down to a coffee house and work off their WiFi.

Apparently Mom was badgering Dad with a bunch of questions about the oil spill. He was giving her all kinds of non-committal responses as he waited for her to get the video. When she finally got the video a couple minutes later, my dad went silent as he let her watch it.

A couple minutes clicked past.

Then my dad said simply to her, "I know."

All we could hear were excited chirps from my mother's voice as she went through her own version of the shock phase everyone else had experienced. Finally Dad interrupted her to say, "One of them is still alive, down at the rescue center. The other two died."

I couldn't take this one-sided conversation anymore. I had to hear what my mother was saying, so I got up and grabbed the phone. I clicked the speakerphone button and put the phone on the kitchen table. My mom was going on about what an amazing discovery this was and how it could change everything.

"How, Mom? How could it change everything?" I asked.

I heard her take in a sharp breath. It couldn't have been clearer to my ears that Mom didn't want to talk to me right then. Still, she answered. "Because, June, if people know that there are people living in the ocean, they will be more interested in protecting them."

"But they aren't people, Mom," I said. "They're fish that look kind of, remotely, like people. They don't even seem to be mammals. They don't breathe air. They don't talk."

"Do they think?" my mom asked. "Could you tell if they think?"

I hesitated. My mom was so worked up about all this that she might blow everything out of proportion. I thought the mermaid was trying to communicate with me, but I'm not convinced that meant she had clear thoughts like a person does.

My father told her his thoughts on it. "The mermaid seemed to make sounds in response to June's talking to her. Her eyes expressed emotions. I'm not sure she could think any more than a dog or a cat, but she seemed desirous of expressing herself."

"Well, there you go," my mom said. "Sentient life in the ocean that happen to look like beautiful silver women. We've got the key to bringing the world together to save ocean life. Affron won't have a chance against this. Everyone will see them as the inhumane bastards they are. We've got to let the public know."

That's when Carter cleared his throat and said, "No."

"Who's that?" Mom asked.

"That's Carter," I said. "He's letting us use his computer."

"He knows all about this?"

"Mrs. Sawfeather," Carter said, "I work at the marine rescue center with Dr. Schneider. I helped with the rescue this morning."

My mom sounded impatient. "How many people know about this?"

My dad answered. "Just us and Carl."

That seemed to appease my mom, because she didn't say anything else about that. "What were you trying to say, Carter?"

He cleared his throat again. I guess my mom made him nervous. She has a way of doing that. It's part of her magical lawyer powers.

"We don't know enough about the mermaids yet. We might cause more damage to them if we leak information too soon. We've got to wait."

"Wait for what?" my mom asked. "Wait for more of them to wash up on the beaches, dying from oil spills?"

"I agree, Mom. I just don't think it's the right move yet, either."

My dad spoke then. "Actually, Natalie, I think the kids are right. Let's hold off a little on this. Let's wait until Carl can tell us more about them."

Mom let out a long sigh over the phone line. "I don't want to sit on this too long."

"Understood," my dad said.

"I'll be home in a couple days. June? You still there?"

"Yes, Mom."

"You are not off the hook. We will be talking as soon as I get home."

"Yes, Mom."

My eyes shot over to Carter, and he politely glanced away. Thanks to Mom, he probably figured I was in trouble for something. I reached over and clicked off the speakerphone then handed the phone back to Dad. I had nothing left to say to my mother at that point. Why bother? Everything I said from now on was going to go in one ear and out the other. My mom had decided that I was a lost cause. After all the work I'd done that morning, you'd think I'd get some forgiveness. Why did I even bother?

Carter sensed my agitation. "You about ready to go?"

"Yeah," I sighed, sitting down in front of the laptop. "Just let me get these pictures attached to the email, so my dad can send them out while we're gone."

"I've already done it," Carter said. "Get your stuff and let's get rolling. With any luck you could still make third period."

And in a flash, all the wonder and excitement of this morning evaporated into another ordinary day.

Chapter Six

As nice as Carter's house was, his car wasn't much. It was a used clunker with windows that rattled. He kept it pretty neat, but the floor carpets and seats had stains all over them from the spilled sodas of its previous owners. I felt really uneasy sitting on the stains in his mom's nice slacks.

Trying not to sound rude, but burning to know, I said, "I take it Mom and Dad didn't buy you a car for your 16th birthday."

His face reddened like I'd plugged him into the cigarette lighter. His usually confident grin got real lopsided. "Well… actually, they did."

"Was it some kind of harsh lesson?" I asked. "You must have been the only kid in your school with a car that cost less than $15,000."

He nodded slowly. "You're right. This is a posh neighborhood. Most kids get pretty cool cars."

"So what happened?" I pressed. There had to be a reason. My parents wouldn't get me a car because they want to protect the environment from one more vehicle's gas emissions. *As long as you live in our house, we can share a car,* they told me repeatedly. In reality that meant that if I wanted to go anywhere, I needed to ask Haley to drive. I'm not sure why I even got my driver's license.

But Carter's parents clearly had money, and they didn't seem like the kind of people who would share a car with their son for the benefit of the ozone layer. Carter himself appeared to be the perfect son: good-looking, well-spoken, college bound. A parent's dream teen. So, what was the deal with the clunker car?

Carter chewed on his lip for a moment, then gave in. "My folks did buy me a car—a cool Ford Explorer that was only a year old and low mileage. It was 4-wheel drive and V6. I took it off-roading with some friends my second weekend owning it and destroyed it."

"Oh no!" I shouted. "You didn't!"

He grinned sheepishly. "I did. Stupid. My folks informed me in no uncertain terms that if I wanted another car I had to buy it myself." He lifted his right hand and presented his car like a game show host. "Voila! This is what weekends stocking shelves at the grocery store gets you."

We laughed about that and joked about parents in general. He never once asked about why my mom was so pissed at me, and I was grateful for that. We didn't turn on the radio at all because we talked whole ride. I did wind up having to swing by my house after all, because I needed my backpack and I had to change my shoes. I could not face going to school in my nasty boots covered with oil and sand. While home, I quickly changed into my own pants, too, and returned the ones I borrowed to Carter.

"I'm afraid I'll damage them," I told him. Of course, I could have changed out of his shirts and didn't. I know he realized this, too, but he didn't say anything about it and seemed mildly pleased with me that I kept them on. Returning them was an excuse to see him again.

We arrived at school right about 10:30. I'd missed most of third period, but I would catch fourth if I hurried.

"I'll pick you up here at 3:00," he said.

"Really?" I asked. "I can just get a ride home with Haley and wait till Dad gets home later."

"Your dad will still be out at the beach, and I know you want to get back to our friend in the tank."

He was absolutely right. Carter was cute and smart and wonderful. But despite his company and the impending lunchtime of school politics, the thought of that poor creature never left my mind. The mermaid needed help, and I wanted to be there with her. The last place I wanted to be was at school.

"Sounds good," I said. "3:00, right here."

I got out and strolled through the front doors of the school.

Or I would have, except the front doors were locked. So, I had to push the office button, which is apparently attached to some kind of truancy alarm. When the doors opened for me to stroll through, I was intercepted by a pissy office attendant who whisked me off to the Vice Principal's office to explain why I'd ditched school all morning. Because, naturally, with everything going on I had forgotten to have my dad sign an excuse note explaining why I was late for school.

They called him, but they couldn't get through. I knew he was busy on the phone with reporters trying to convince them that the oil damage to the shoreline of Washington was news—important news—and the public needed to be aware of what was going on. That didn't matter to the office staff. They were annoyed by my dad, and I heard them muttering to each other about how my dad was "neglectful", "disrespectful", and "a bad influence."

Like usual, I found myself in that really weird state of mind where I hated my dad for not answering the damn phone and sparing me this humiliation, and being so proud of him for the hard work he does. These women led such small lives. They had no idea what was happening down at the coast and that it might actually ruin their next trip to the beach or the fish they were going to eat for dinner one night this month. They really had no idea that there was this silver sea creature with a woman's torso and giant, sad eyes covered with oil in a tank, only alive because my dad and I found her this morning.

By the time Dad managed to call the school back to verify that, yes, I had been helping him all morning, only five minutes remained until lunchtime.

According to Vice Principal Slater, a heavy-set woman with one of those short porcupine hairdos that has some kind of gel/hairspray product stuck to every individual strand and teeny-tiny eyebrows that had been plucked too much, my dad's reason for my absence was not an excuse. Vice Principal Slater spoke calmly into the phone. "Mr. Sawfeather, it is important that your daughter be at school. She has missed several days this year because of joining you with your *work*." She said "work" like he was having me sort his drug paraphernalia before taking it out on the street to sell from his trunk.

I was so glad Dad didn't see how she rolled her eyes. He'd have come undone. I was pretty close to it myself, but I was afraid she'd shoot poison barbs from her hair at me.

I couldn't hear my dad on the other line, but I got the gist of what he said when Mrs. Slater replied, "Yes, I'm sure your work is very important, to *you*, but school is *more* important for Juniper."

"More important than saving the entire West Coast from being destroyed?" I asked.

She shushed me. Like I was a three-year-old. She put her finger to her mouth and went "Shh!" Into the phone she continued her ridiculousness, "I will allow her to make up the work she missed this morning, but not in the future."

"I wouldn't have missed fourth period if you hadn't made me stay in here."

She pinched up those tiny eyebrows and then turned her back to me. "This is the last time your missions can take priority over her studies."

I know my dad didn't cuss her out on the phone, but I know he wanted to. I wanted to. The restraint I felt was intense. So were the canker sores I was creating by biting the insides of my lips to keep them shut.

However, when the bell rang for lunch and I was still sitting there in the hard chair in her cramped office usually saved for the behavioral bottom feeders of the school, I muttered a small four-letter word.

I was now late meeting Haley and getting to the Student Council presentation. The only reason I showed up at school at all, thank you very much.

The Mistress of Detention spun around, hung up the phone, and glared at me. She was about to condemn me to a lifetime of after school study because of my foul mouth. I saw her hand reaching for that dreaded pad of yellow papers.

Except my phone rang. Haley calling, wondering where the heck I was. And then *that* got confiscated because we're not supposed to have our phones at school. Well, truth be told, everyone has a phone. Everyone. We just aren't supposed to *use* them at school. So, we use them under stealth in the bathrooms between classes and at lunchtime. And that's never really been a problem.

Until now.

After robbing me of my ability to communicate and of my patience, the Office Nazis let me go. I ran through the building to meet Haley, breaking yet another rule: no running through the school. Oddly, I got away with the first actual rule that I broke on purpose.

The Student Council meets in an office near the cafeteria. Haley stood in the hallway outside the room, cell phone in hand, and started shouting at me as soon as she saw me dodging people with trays of bean burritos and cheesy nachos to get to her.

"Where have you been? Why didn't you answer your phone? They're waiting for us!" Then, noting my oversized boy clothes, "And what are you wearing?"

"I know," I said, breathing hard. "I'll explain later. *You* look really cute though."

And she did. Haley had on this really neat combination of pale green and brown. Khaki pants, green turtleneck, with a chocolate brown knit poncho over it. I really liked it, even though I would never have thought of putting those two colors together because I would look like an Andes mint. She even had her hair down and curled, instead of up in her usual ponytail.

She smiled at the compliment, and before the smile could fade, I grabbed her hand, took in one more big breath and opened the door to the tiny classroom usually reserved for tutoring or small group lessons. The four members of Student Council raised their heads to us as we burst into the room. I could see that each of them was about to say something about how it was too late and lunch was nearly over. However, my momentum was way up and my patience way thin, so I didn't even wait for the Council to say anything before I started speaking my piece. Once my mouth opened, I kind of couldn't stop it.

"Hi guys," I said. "Sorry I'm late, I was at the beach all morning rescuing sea animals hurt by an oil spill. It was slightly more important to me than American History and Chemistry, because, you know, these are living, breathing creatures that are dying. A lot of them were dead already, and it took time to walk through all of that and search for the still-living ones. It had to be done because you never know what you're going to find. There could be something really important out there that needs help, something that needs to be discovered and saved. The Founding Fathers are dead and can't help, really. Memorizing what elements make superglue stick is also not going to help."

Everyone looked very puzzled, including Haley. I didn't care. I went on.

"Another thing more important to me than colonists and chemicals is getting to live past forty, which won't happen if the environment collapses on all of us because we aren't taking care of it. Our oil spills kill animals; our trash is killing ourselves. Now, that may not matter to all of you, but it does me, and Haley, and several other people in this school who would like to be in our Recycling Club.

"What is this club about, you ask?" I went on before anyone actually could ask. "We just want to get some trash cans specifically marked for recycling. We want to gather the recyclables once a week and take them to a recycling center. We will keep an eye out for containers littering our campus that could be recycled, and we will put out information to let the students know how to participate in our club and mission.

"What do I need from you?" I went on again, seeing them itchy to interrupt. "Nothing. I mean, it would be nice if you occasionally put your Aquafina bottles or Red Bull cans in the recyclable bin. That would be cool of you. Otherwise, all we really need is for you to give us the big *Okay*. Because, really, our club is nothing that interferes with your other plans around this place and is only going to help you and the school in the long run."

I stopped.

Haley stared at me for a moment in shock. I'm not sure her expression had flipped over to totally upset or angry, although it wasn't exactly "Way to go, June" either. I hadn't done the presentation as we had planned. She had handouts and a Power Point document with bullet points. She was supposed to be the one talking—not me. I had skipped all that. After another beat, I turned my attention to the four seniors in front of us to see what would happen next.

The four of them sat in chairs behind one long table. Marlee Gephalt, our school treasurer, wasn't looking at us. She was busy picking all the raisins out of her salad. Ted Cowley, the group secretary, didn't have a pen out to record any of this. Don't think I saw paper either. He did have a phone in his hand though and seemed to be endlessly texting somebody. Gary Donnelly, the vice president, had his feet up on the desk in front of him and was leaning so far back in his chair he had to be seeing only his size eleven Jordans and not our faces.

Then there was Regina Williams, class president and royal B. Her Blonde Highness leaned way forward and rested her chin in her hands like a little schoolgirl, pretending to be amazed and awed by us. She stayed this way for almost a full minute after I had finished speaking as though she hadn't noticed I stopped.

Finally she asked, "Is that it?"

Haley cleared her throat and answered hesitantly. "No." Regina's eyes cut over to my friend like she was an irritating bug. "I mean that we have some charts and... stuff." Her voice dwindled off as she noticed Regina was no longer looking at her and was focused on me again.

Regina raised her hand like she was addressing a teacher with her question. I nodded uncomfortably, and she asked, "So, do you guys mean that you're going to be digging in the trash to get the cans out?"

Marlee glanced up from her salad. "Ew!" Finally not looking at a raisin, she took in my appearance. "Whose clothes are you wearing? A boy's?" She got up and sauntered over to me in her khaki mini-skirt that tested the school rule of being "fingertip length", peeked at the label of my oversized sweatshirt, and then sniffed really hard. "And are you wearing Axe cologne?"

I sighed. "Yes. I borrowed some clothes and showered after leaving the beach this morning. This was all he had."

"He?" Regina asked. She winked at the others and high-fived Marlee as her friend came back to the table. Ted and Gary started chuckling at some private joke.

I didn't get it at first.

"Yeah, this guy who works at the Marine Rescue Center in Aberdeen," I said. "He let me clean up at his house." They all laughed some more. "I mean it's better than smelling like fish, isn't it? You wouldn't have wanted to see me like I was this morning."

"I don't know," Ted said in this nasty, teasing voice. "Maybe I would have."

Gary laughed so hard he fell out of his seat, his giant shoes taking out his soda can on the way down. Luckily for him it was empty.

Regina smacked Ted hard on the shoulder. "No you wouldn't have." He stopped laughing and rubbed his shoulder. I guess they were a couple? I should have known that, but I didn't follow the popular crowd's comings and goings like most people did.

Haley started edging backwards toward the door. I grabbed her hand and stopped her.

"So, are we getting approval to start the club or not?" I asked firmly.

Ted shrugged. Marlee shook her head. Gary was still laughing. Regina offered a wicked smile she probably perfected in the mirror. "Sure, start your trashy club. It's only fitting." I thought Gary would explode if he laughed any harder. Ted snickered again, trying to hold it in with a hand over his mouth.

"It's a recycling club," Haley said quietly. "Not a trash club."

"Whatever," Regina said.

Gary sputtered, "Does that mean they get used over and over again?" and then started guffawing harder than before. Ted joined in, and Regina cracked a smile.

Okay, I got it.

Did I care? Not really.

Did I care that Haley had her lips shut so tight that they were turning white instead of saying something in my defense? Yeah. A little bit.

I was done with them and their teasing and wanted to say something nasty and walk out. Only I still needed their stupid signatures on our form. Without saying anything, I slapped the paper down on the table. Through their sputtering fits, they each put their scribble on it.

"Are we done then?" I asked, taking back the paper.

"Sure," Ted said. "Thanks for fitting us in and coming to see us."

More laughter.

Haley and I headed for the door.

Regina's voice followed us out. "Now go do your walk of shame where we don't have to see you." She shut the door behind us. The laughter in that room was so loud I could hear it out in the corridor and over the bell ringing to end lunch.

Haley took off toward the cafeteria without saying anything to me. I chased after her.

"Haley, slow down," I shouted. "What's the matter?"

"Are you serious?" she asked. "You just embarrassed me so much."

"They're just being jerks," I said.

"Don't you get it?" Haley said. "They think you're a slut and slept with that guy this morning."

"Oh, they're just joking around. Mean joking, but nothing serious." I reached out an arm and stopped her. "You don't think I skipped school to sleep with some guy do you?"

She started to say something, caught herself and stopped. "No," she mumbled. "Of course not."

She did. She really did think I'd been with some guy all morning and not at the beach rescuing sea animals. How could she think that? I tried hard not to accept that she'd take the insinuations of some preppy social club over what she knew about me. Haley and I had been next-door neighbors for ten years. She'd seen my family rush after every conceivable natural disaster during that time.

"Then what's the problem, really?" I asked. "We got their signatures. Our club is approved. We got what we wanted."

"Sort of," she said. "We'll see."

"Are you mad that I did all the talking?"

"Kind of."

"And that I was late?"

"Yes."

"I couldn't help that," I said. "I'm sorry."

Haley sighed really hard. She glanced around, trying not to look right at me. The cafeteria was nearly empty of students now and we were late for class. "I've got to go. Meet me after school?"

At that moment I was ready to call Carter and tell him not to pick me up after school. I probably needed to be with Haley to reassure her that our friendship was okay. I could go home with her and spend the afternoon eating pizza rolls and bashing the Student Council. I could tell her all about Carter, and she'd be so excited about the possibility of one of us finally hooking up with someone.

Except there was a mermaid dying in a tank in Aberdeen.

And my cell phone with Carter's number on it had been confiscated.

So, I shifted my eyes to the ground and said, "I'm being picked up by Carter, the guy who helped us this morning, to head back to the beach and assist my dad some more."

Haley nodded. "Fine." Then she snatched the club permission form out of my hands. "I'll turn this in." She was out of sight before I noticed the sting of the paper cut on my right forefinger.

I sucked on my finger for a second, adjusted my backpack and turned around to head for class. That's when I noticed Vice Principal Devil-Hair staring at me with her hands on her hips and tapping her toe impatiently.

Chapter Seven

So, after missing another class to sit in the Vice Principal's office again, I only had one period left until the end of the day. It was English and we were reading *Moby Dick*. That's a put-you-straight-to-sleep book if there ever was one, and I knocked right out after two paragraphs. I dreamed about Ahab pouring buckets of boiling whale blubber over the side of his ship and throwing harpoons at all the green mermaid tails flipping up out of the water. Maybe he thought they were tiny whales. I jumped off the ship to swim after the mermaids, because I have that thing about swimming while I sleep. Anyway, the dream was so darn exciting that I slipped right out of my skinny desk and fell on the floor.

"Miss Sawfeather?" Mr. Robles checked, "are you all right?"

"Yes, sir," I said, scrambling back up into my seat to the sound of my classmates stifling their laughter. I thought for a second I'd sprained my ankle on the tray under my seat, but after rotating it a couple times I decided it would be fine.

Mr. Robles raised his eyebrows. "Please believe me, Miss Sawfeather, you are hardly the first student who has drifted off while reading this extraordinary book. It takes a special person to fully appreciate the literary genius of Melville and stay rapt with attention. And it certainly doesn't help that Mr. Garrison's reading style, while riveting to the few students who enjoy monotone delivery devoid of any comprehension as to what punctuation is *for*, does make one feel as though the walls are closing in on us." I saw Bobby Garrison in the back corner sink back into his chair. Apparently it had been his turn to read aloud. Poor guy.

Mr. Robles snapped his hardcover copy of the book shut

dramatically. Very fitting for an English teacher who spends his summers acting with the Washington Shakespeare Festival and liked to remind us of that stunning fact every day. "So, let's take a break, shall we? There's only so much one can handle when it comes to reading about how to extract the blubber from a whale. Yes?" We all closed our used paperback copies. "Read the rest of the chapter tonight at home, and we'll do what would have been your homework right now."

For the rest of the class we were allowed to create our own crossword puzzles with our vocabulary word list from the chapter. Focusing on this was much easier, and I was glad to have one less assignment to have to do that night because I wasn't sure when I'd get home or be able to even think about doing homework.

Finally the bell rang and I dashed to the front parking lot. Carter was there in his beat up old car waiting for me. He had the motor running, and I could see him inside leaning across the passenger seat to unlock the door and roll down the window. No power windows on that old thing. I headed right for him.

But then I saw Haley, too, headed for her car.

"Haley!" I shouted out to her. "Haley, come here! Come meet Carter! He can explain about this morning! Then you'll…"

If she heard me, she didn't show it. She just kept walking across the parking lot and got in her car. I thought about running after her, but I didn't do it. I knew she had to have heard me because several other people walking near her had turned their heads. She was avoiding me on purpose.

I tried not to worry about it. We'd talk later. I'd make a point of it, even if it meant climbing in her bedroom window and forcing her to acknowledge me. I really didn't want her to feel hurt or ignored or whatever she was feeling. I imagine it was probably confusing that I let her down because of an oil spill warning. After griping about not wanting to be part of my parents' craziness anymore, I almost missed our meeting. I could see why that made no sense to her. She just needed to understand that what was going on out at Aberdeen was different than the usual events my dad dragged me to. Once I filled her in on the discovery of the mermaids, she'd get why I was late to school and bungled our presentation.

Sure she would.

I hoped so.

I watched her back her car out of the spot and drive away. Carter tapped his horn.

"You coming?" he asked through the passenger window.

"Yeah," I said distantly, still watching Haley's car as it turned out of the parking lot into the street. I opened the door. As I shifted to toss my backpack in the back seat, I noticed through the back window how many people had gathered on the school's front steps to watch me. Among the looky-loos were Marlee and Regina. My lip-reading skills aren't great, but I'm pretty sure I saw Regina say, "I told you," and several of her friends laughed. One of them gave me a thumbs-up and a wink. Then they all laughed again.

Groaning, I sat back in my seat. I closed the door and put my seatbelt on without saying anything.

Carter flipped off the radio and said, "Well, hi to you too. I'm fine, thanks."

"Oh, sorry," I said distractedly, watching the crowd of popular girls watching *us* pull out of the parking spot. "Hi. How are you? You're fine? That's good."

"Hmmm," was all he replied. Then he put the car in gear and drove out of the lot. Once we were on the highway he spoke again. "Tough day?"

"A little bit." I paused, not sure what I wanted to say about it all. I decided what I really wanted to do was call my dad. I'd let Carter hear just enough and figure the rest out. "Can I use your phone? They took mine away from me and either Mom or Dad has to get it back for me."

"That stinks," he said.

"You don't know the half of it," I told him. I wanted to tell him everything that happened, but since the worst thing of it all was that I was going to get some sort of bad rep for supposedly sleeping with him, I didn't figure he needed to know about it. I mean, we weren't even dating. He hadn't even asked me out. He hadn't even hinted that he might possibly at some time in the future *think* about asking me out. I was probably just some silly high school kid to him. He was in college. He could date college girls. What did he need me for? Nothing. He just wanted to get points for knowing my dad, was all.

What would I say anyway? "Hey, everyone at school thinks you and I got it on all morning. Ha ha. Isn't that a riot?"

How do you sit in the car with a guy for an hour after that?

So I kept silent.

"Did your meeting go well? Did you get your club?" he asked.

"Yeah," I answered. "I think so. They signed the paper at any rate."

"Then it was worth it," he said.

It was my turn to say, "Hmmm."

Carter handed me his phone. I stared at it for a moment trying to remember my dad's phone number. I had it on speed dial on my phone so I never had to actually punch in the numbers. For my life, I couldn't think of the digits.

"I saved it," Carter said softly, as though reading my mind. "Under 'S'".

I scrolled to 'S' and found dad's number. A moment later he answered.

"Carter?" he asked.

"It's me, Dad," I said.

"Why aren't you calling from your own phone?" he asked.

"Dad, I know you've been busy all day, but you *do* remember me being in the school's office all morning, right?"

"Oh, that's right. Sorry, honey." He paused. "They took your phone?"

"Yes," I huffed. "You or Mom have to get it back for me."

"That was very inconsiderate of them. I really need you to be in contact today. What if I have your Mom make a call? Have you left school already?"

I sighed. My mom could not use her persuasive skill for this situation, and I knew it. "Mrs. Slater isn't exactly supportive of our cause, Dad," I told him. "Besides, we're already on the road."

"I'll try to get it back for you tomorrow, okay?" Then he paused for a minute, and it sounded like someone was talking to him. He mumbled a couple "Uh huhs" then said back into the phone to me, "Well, if not tomorrow, I'll get it soon."

Great.

"How are things going over there?" I asked.

He told me that it was very crowded at the beach. The Affron people had effectively shooed off most of the reporters with their fancy double-speak and crisp white eco-uniforms. None of the major network news correspondents had lingered more than an hour. Only a couple nosy journalists from NPR, and some green-friendly websites that Dad had called, stayed. A handful of volunteers from town had shown up along with a few employees of Affron gas stations in the area who had probably been forced to be there. They helped remove the dead carcasses from the beach, and the living creatures had been taken to the Marine Rescue Center. There was still a lot to do, so they would be working until dark.

"Are you and Carter coming here or going to the Center?" he asked.

"I'd like to get back to the Center." I looked over at Carter to see if that's what he had planned as well

Carter nodded. "That's where I'm headed. Dr. Schneider said that the mermaid has been really calm all day, so I was thinking about getting into the tank to help clean her up. I could use your help."

My help? Really? I nearly squeaked with excitement at being asked, but I did my best to sound mature and in control.

"Isn't Dr. Schneider there?" I asked him. It didn't really matter. I wanted to help, desperately.

"He doesn't like to get in the tanks," Carter answered. "He's still studying the cadavers and organizing the traffic for the rescued animals from the beaches. I could call another guy in, but I thought it might be best if we keep the mermaid a secret for a while longer."

I put the phone back to my ear. "Did you get that, Dad?" I checked.

"Sounds like you have a full afternoon," he said back. "I'll meet you over there later on."

My mood picked up after that. The mermaid was still alive. I was going to be able to help her. My dad sounded proud of me. And Carter thought I was worth his time. What had happened at school suddenly became so insignificant, and I put all my worries about it aside to focus my energy on the rest of the day ahead.

An hour later we were both in wet suits and diving gear. My suit was a man's. I'm tall so it fit length-wise, but it was too big in girth and chafed between my legs. I had learned how to scuba dive two summers ago on a whale-watching trip with my parents down in Southern California. We took a crash course so we could swim under water and look for signs of pollution damage.

Yes, that's my parents' idea of a vacation.

I'll confess it was kind of fun. And it was the trip that made me fall in love with California.

"Do you need a quick refresher course?" Carter asked.

"I think I remember the basics," I said.

"Okay," he said. "Just stay calm. I don't know what she'll be like once we get in there, and I don't want you to get hurt."

A large painter's tarp had been draped over the mermaid's tank to hide her. I figured that the isolation had helped to calm her down. She couldn't see the people coming in and out of the building all day. Of course, she couldn't see us either until we had already climbed up the ladder and our heads popped up over the top.

The mermaid's head jerked up at the sight of us, and she backed away, nearly pressing herself against the glass closest to the wall. Her eyes were huge and her body very rigid. She didn't recognize us in the wet suits. I tapped Carter, stopping him from climbing in the tank. "Hold on a second," I said.

I descended the ladder and stood in front of the tank between the tarp and glass. I slipped my mask down around my neck and pulled back the hood of the suit so that my hair showed. Smiling at the mermaid, I said, "It's me. Remember? We met this morning."

I put my hand on the glass and waited. The mermaid cocked her head and stared at me for a moment. Then, very hesitantly, she moved toward me and put up her hand to press against mine. Her eyes softened as she recognized me.

"We're going to come in there with you," I told her. I didn't think she could understand my words, but she seemed soothed by my talking to her. I climbed up the ladder again with my face and head still exposed, talking the whole time. "See what we're doing? We're coming up here and then we're going to get inside. Watch Carter. He's at the top."

Carter put his mouthpiece in, stepped over the top of the tank and slipped into the water up to his chest, holding on to the top of the tank to keep his head above water. The mermaid instantly backed away from him. Her eyes widened in alarm, with her arms out in front of her warning him to keep at a distance.

I leaned way over to the side of the ladder, to make sure she could see me. I kept smiling and talking. "It's okay. That's Carter. You met him this morning, too. Watch me put my mask on." With my left foot on the ladder on the outside of the tank and my right foot on the ladder inside the tank, I balanced and used my hands to put my hood and mask back on. I made sure she was looking at me the whole time, and Carter stayed very still. "See?" I said. "It's still me." I put the mouthpiece in my mouth and finished getting into the tank.

The mermaid continued to shy away from us, waving her arms and tail to keep us from getting too close. Carter and I remained still for a long time, patiently waiting for her to realize we were not there to harm her. I couldn't talk once I got under the water, so I couldn't use my voice anymore to soothe her. I just hoped she understood that we were there as her friends.

Looking right at her, I concentrated all my thoughts toward her. *Shhhh. It's okay. We're your friends. We want to help you get the sticky stuff off.*

After a few minutes, the mermaid stilled. I swear I heard in my mind a voice other than my own. The sound of it was a soothing acceptance of what was going on. It wasn't a word like "okay", but I understood it as though it was a word, and I knew it came from her.

The bubbles coming out of the oxygen tanks caught her attention and her eyes followed them as they drifted upward. Her webbed fingers flickered as though she wanted to touch them. I nodded at her and swiped at some of the bubbles coming out of Carter's tank, making them scatter. This made the mermaid lean in close, and when I nodded again, she swam over to us and did the same thing. Soon she was swimming above us, swishing her hands through the bubbles and trying to catch them. For the first time, I saw the creature smile.

The mermaid had teeth, I noticed, very short and flat teeth. No incisors for biting. No extra-large molars for chomping. She probably didn't eat meat. With teeth like that, she might eat only sea vegetation or maybe even plankton. The smile was pretty. The white teeth sparkled beneath her silver-blue lips. She even had dimples.

While the mermaid was distracted by the bubbles Carter reached out a hand to touch her tailfin. She pulled her body away fiercely and headed back to her safe side of the tank. I looked at Carter and shrugged. How could we get her to let us touch her? He tapped his head, a signal that he had an idea.

Tenderly, he took my hand in his own. A tingle went straight up my arm and made me slightly dizzy. If we hadn't been in a tank of water, I would have thought he might be lifting it for a kiss like in those movies based on Jane Austen books. However, instead of kissing me, he held my hand with one of his and used the other to pull a terrycloth rag out of the pack around his chest. Ever so gently and slowly, he started moving the cloth back and forth across my hand and lower arm. We watched the mermaid's reactions carefully all the while. Gradually, she got closer and closer to us to see what we were doing. I was careful not to act nervous. I even smiled, nodded, and hummed to convey to the mermaid that this cloth felt good on my hand.

Timidly, the mermaid stuck out her hand. The webbing between her fingers was pronounced, but so was the clotting of oil. Carter let go of me and took the mermaid's hand as sweetly as he could manage. He lowered the cloth to her hand and pressed it to her hand so that it wouldn't hurt. The mermaid accepted the sensation and let him continue to dab at her hand.

I knew that Carter would have to rub harder than that to remove the oil, and she might not like that. I thought it would be a problem, but he was very patient and took his time with her. He shifted from dabbing to a soft rubbing with the cloth. I took out a cloth and copied what he did to mermaid's other hand and forearm. The mermaid seemed to like the feeling. She even squirmed and giggled a bit as though it tickled.

Then, as gradually as possible, we both increased the pressure of the cleaning so that the mermaid would accept the touch. It worked. She even waited eagerly when we had to throw the oily cloths over the top of the tank and pull out clean ones from Carter's pack. Although it took nearly an hour, we finally removed a fair amount of the oil from the mermaid's skin. The luster of her silver skin returned, and she shimmered as she moved.

I had to take extra time around her face and jawline, because the oil was thicker there. As I dabbed the cloth around her neck, the strange bumps that circled her neck began to loosen. It frightened me at first, but as the oil wiped away I realized that the bumps weren't part of her. They were shells, strung together as a necklace. Once free, she put up her webbed fingers and rubbed her neck and smiled at me with an expression that made me feel that she was both glad that the necklace wasn't strangling her any longer and pleased that it hadn't broken. I wondered where she had gotten a necklace like that, and how she had managed to put it on.

Time was running out for our oxygen tanks, so we threw our last cloths over the tank and moved to the ladder to climb out. The mermaid followed right behind me and actually held onto the bars of the ladder as if she would climb up behind me. When I got to the top, she let go and popped her head out of the water for a second to watch me straddle the tank and get completely free of the water. Needing to breathe, she dove back under. I joined Carter on the floor, and we removed our masks. As he gathered up the cloths lying on the floor, I took one last look at the mermaid by slipping between the tarp and the glass.

She was right there, waiting for me, fondly touching the glass of the aquarium in front of me. She already seemed to be missing our presence in the tank with her.

"Carter, look," I said.

I moved over and let him slip behind the tarp to stand next to me. The joy in his eyes was unmistakable.

"Amazing," he said.

It was warm and cozy together under that canvas tarp. It reminded me of the forts Haley and I used to build under our kitchen table, except I never felt tingles all over my skin when I got under there with her. Carter's arm pressed against mine. My heart raced.

"Wow," I agreed with him. "That was so incredible. Have you ever felt anything like that before?"

There was this fraction of a second when he turned his face to me, but then he corrected himself to look in the tank again. He shifted his weight to his other foot, and broke the connection between our arms. "I had to get in a tank with a dolphin once. That was really cool, but this tops it by a mile."

I smiled at the mermaid, who smiled back at me. "Do you think we should feed her something? She might be hungry."

Carter nodded. "I was thinking she's probably a vegetarian."

"I thought so too, because of her teeth."

Carter left me under the tarp and headed for some cabinets at the far end of the examining tables. I pulled back the tarp and watched him pull out a plastic bucket. "This might do the trick." He hauled the bucket up the ladder. Reaching into the bucket he pulled out a wad of wet seaweed. "Let's see if she likes this."

He dropped some of it into the tank. The mermaid glanced up at it, seemed to smell it with her flat nose, and swam up toward it. Grabbing a piece with her fingers, she put it to her mouth and sucked on it. She grimaced and shook her head.

"I don't think she likes it," I said.

But she ate it. Carter dropped some more in for her. "She may not like the taste, but she knows it's good for her. I'll talk to Dr. Schneider about it and see if he has some better ideas for her diet." Carter straightened the tarp over the aquarium and then joined me at the stools around the closest table.

"You're good at this stuff," I said. "Are you learning it at school?"

"Some of it," Carter said. "Most of it I learn by doing."

"What's your major?" I asked.

Carter hesitated. "For the moment it's Biology. They don't have a specific Marine Biology major at Washington. I'll probably go somewhere else for my Masters."

"You're going all the way for a Masters?" Ugh. I didn't want to suffer through that much education. I wanted to get it over with and start working.

"They say you have to have a Masters to have a real career anymore. A Bachelor's isn't enough." He smiled and shrugged. "Unless being an assistant is all you want."

Darnit! I guess this means I will have to do that much college. How depressing.

"I might even go for PhD. Then I could be the one to head up a Marine Biology department at Washington. Wouldn't that be great?"

I sneered and shook my head. "Actually, that doesn't sound great to me at all. I have no interest in teaching. What I want is to be in the water with the animals. Helping them. Healing them. I want more experiences like the one we just had with that mermaid. I want to fill my life with successes, not teach about the successes of other people."

Carter raised an eyebrow. "I guess that's a way to look at it." Then he walked away from me and tossed the wet cloths in a basket next to the cabinets. He pulled a couple fresh towels out of the cabinets and handed one to me while using the other to dry his hair.

"Come on," I said, patting my face with the towel. "You can't tell me that what we just did wasn't something you'd like to spend your life doing. You were great with her."

"Thanks," he said. "You too. You really have a knack for it." But apparently that was all he had to say about that, because he completely changed the subject by asking, "You decided where you're going to school next year?"

Nice way to deflect the focus.

"I was thinking about San Diego," I answered.

"Good school," he said. "Far away though."

"That's one of the benefits."

Carter shrugged and turned away from me at that point. "I guess," he said distantly as he popped his towel into the basket and closed the cabinet doors. From all appearances, he was done with this conversation.

Did I say something wrong? Why would he care where I went to school? Did he have a thing against San Diego?

All of a sudden my face began to heat up. Did I just totally blow it with him? Here he had been going on about how great Washington was and how he wanted to stay here forever and teach at the college and all that. And I had to go and blabber about how much I couldn't wait to ditch this place. I knew at that instant Carter would never ask me out. What was the point of starting something up with a girl who was just going to leave once summer arrived?

"Carter, I..." But I didn't know what to say or how to take it back. Carter didn't even look at me when I said his name.

"Hey kids."

The double doors banged open, bringing me out of my misery. Dad

71

entered still wearing his rubber boots with sand plastered to them. The sun had darkened his face, and his stringy hair was pulled back in a tail behind his neck. He looked worn out.

"Things done at the beach, Dad?" I asked.

He groaned. "It's a mess, but the worst of it has been taken care of."

"They didn't bring nearly as many animals here as I expected today," Carter told him.

Dad shook his head. "The initial spill poisoned anything close to it. Just about all of those creatures died. Over the next few days you'll see more that might actually be saved." He brushed my wet hair back over my ears then edged past me and peeled back enough of the tarp to get a peek at the mermaid. "How's she doing? Any better?"

"A lot better," I said. "Carter just fed her."

Carter held up the bucket. "I'm still trying to figure out what she likes. Kelp wasn't a big hit." He put the bucket back into the cabinet. "Can't say I blame her. I only like seaweed when it's wrapped around sushi."

That almost brought a smile to my dad's weary face. Leaning against the glass, Dad took off his boots and rubbed his smelly feet. "Is Dr. Schneider in?"

"He's in his office," Carter said. "He's been studying books and Internet sites all afternoon for some kind of clue to her existence. He wants to link her to some other existing animal. You know, as a product of evolution."

"I don't think he'll find what he's looking for," Dad said, turning his attention back to the mermaid in the tank. "At least not in any science-related site. People have been talking about mermaids for thousands of years. They are scattered throughout all the mythology of the world. Why would they be in so many stories if they never existed until now?"

I shook my head and rolled my eyes. I hated it when he tried passing mythology on like some kind of hidden truth. "Everyone knows that the original conceptions of mermaids were based on sightings of dolphins, porpoises, and manatees. People didn't know what they were. There's even that Irish legend about the woman who is a seal when she's in the water and a human on the sand. People gave human attributes to these sea creatures that behaved in intelligent ways. Over time those attributes added up to be the mermaid legends."

"What was that?" my dad said, laughing. "Your thesis for school?" He nodded at Carter, who smiled politely.

"Come on, Dad," I said. "You know as well as I do that the typical mermaid of legend doesn't look a thing like this. They are Hans Christian Anderson's pretty, blond girls with bright green tales. They have white skin and normal faces and wear sea-shells over their breasts." I blushed after saying *breasts* in front of Carter. If he was embarrassed, he didn't show it.

"I'll admit that's the way they've been described in some fairy tales and that's the way they've been drawn in children's books," Dad said. "You'll find the images of mermaids in folklore from Russia, Africa, China, and pretty much any other culture you can think of that all vary widely in interpretation. There are ocean mermaids and river mermaids. Some are good and others are evil. What I'm saying is that people have believed in mermaids for eons and have depicted them in many different ways. There was just no proof of them before now."

Carter sat down on a stool next to me, all smiles as he listened to my dad and me bicker. "June," he interrupted, "how can you sit there and argue that mermaids are nothing but mixed up perceptions of porpoises and seals when there's one looking at you right now?"

I turned around to see that the mermaid was in fact staring directly at me, over my dad's head, watching my every move. Uneasy, I looked back at Carter. "I just think that Dr. Schneider might have a point with this evolution thing, and that this mermaid and her two sisters are some kind of anomaly. Otherwise, where have they been all this time?"

My dad reached inside his shirt and pulled out the killer whale tooth tied to a leather string that he always wore around his neck. He held it up between his thumb and forefinger for Carter and me to see.

Oh no, I thought. *Here comes one of his tall tales.*

I glanced at Carter, trying to send him a mental message that I was so sorry this was about to happen. Carter didn't seem to mind, though. For the moment, he was taken with my father and his quirky American Indian ways. My dad had a way of casting a spell over people who didn't live with him every day. Those who met him either thought he was cool as a fan or completely off his nut. Most of the time I just thought he was

73

embarrassing. Like right at that moment.

Please don't think my dad is nuts, I thought as hard as I could. *Please don't think I'm like my dad.*

"There are many stories among the Northwest American tribes about the Killer Whale. He is a powerful spirit in this region, and the sight of him on a whaling mission was often the sign that the whalers were doomed to a saltwater death. One of the stories is about the Killer Whale that falls in love with a whaling boat.

"Legend has it that a whaling crew went out on their canoes, ready to tackle the waves and capture a giant beast. Just as they sighted a large whale in the distance that would feed and fuel their village for the entire winter, a Killer Whale jumped out of the waves right at them. The sailors screamed in fear. 'The Killer Whale has doomed us!' the men cried. 'We should turn back before it is too late!'

"The men frantically turned their canoes about, trying to get back to shore before the angry Killer Whale capsized them. Then a strange and magical thing happened. Their boat began to sing. A high, dreamy voice rang up from the bottom of the boat. The men could not figure out how the ship was making such a noise. They could see nothing inside the boat or attached to the sides that could make such a sweet sound.

"More surprising still, the Killer Whale heard the sound as well. It stopped its thrashing about and calmly slid up beside the boat. It nuzzled its large, black head against the ship and made snorting noises to show its affection.

"The men on the ship were too frightened to even row the oars. A few men jumped overboard for fear that the Killer Whale was toying with them. The others stood perfectly still, waiting to see what would happen next.

"Slowly, the boat and the Killer Whale beside it drifted quietly toward the shore. When finally they were close enough for the men to step out of the boat and wade to the beach, the singing stopped.

"The Killer Whale came out of his trance and seemed very confused about where he was. Angry that he was so close to shore, he flipped the boat over, but no man was injured for they had already made their way to safety.

"As the Killer Whale made his way back out to sea, the men

gathered around the toppled boat, believing the boat had saved their lives with its ability to sing. They carried the boat back to their village and posted it on stilts, where it was used as the roof of a religious house for the Shaman."

My father stopped talking then. He stood up and walked to the aquarium. Touching the glass just in front of the mermaid's hand, he sighed. "All this time my people thought it was the boat that came alive and saved them. All this time."

Carter lowered his head into his palms as if he needed to hold the information in so it wouldn't disappear. "You think that a mermaid saved them?"

"It had to be," my father said. "One attached herself to the bottom of the boat. She made the noise that attracted the Killer Whale. It's the only thing that makes sense."

This time I spoke. "It makes sense in a way, Dad, but it's still just a legend. There's no proof that any of this ever happened. Plus, why would she save your people? They were going to kill a whale."

He didn't even bother to look at me. "The legends of our people do not require proof, June. You need to learn that. They require only faith and understanding. That is the whole purpose behind them. The point is that this legend has been around for hundreds of years and only now do I realize where the singing came from."

"What about the killing of the whale?" I argued. I hated to be lectured about my father's people. I felt as much part American Indian as I did part elephant. "Maybe she wasn't rescuing the people at all. She was saving the whale that they would have slaughtered."

"In those days," my dad explained, "our people were careful about nature. We only used what we needed. Even the story suggests that the one whale would have fed the village for the entire season. There would have been no waste. The mermaid would have understood that."

I flashed a look at Carter. "All this from a vegetarian." Carter laughed.

"It's a good story," Carter said. "It would be worth studying."

"That's all I'm saying," my father said, turning back around to face us. "That's all I'm saying."

At the far end of the room, the double doors opened. Two men in white uniforms with Affron logos on the sleeves stepped inside. One held a clipboard, while the other carried an animal carrier with a squawking seagull inside it. Both were surprisingly bulky for scientists.

"Could you direct us?" the one with the clipboard asked. "We've got some wildlife from the oil spill down at the beach that could use some emergency attention."

My dad tensed. I tried really hard not to glance at the tarp, but I know I did, because I remember thinking there was a gap and a smidge of tank could be seen through it. Carter, however, acted very naturally. Nonchalant. As though he'd been expecting these gentlemen to show up and had it all planned out. He strode right over to the men, took the clipboard right out of the one man's hands before the man realized what was happening and then continued on to the office, urging the men to follow him. "Let me get Dr. Schneider for you."

The eyes of the scientists stayed on Carter the whole time, because Carter didn't stop talking once. He asked them all kinds of official-sounding questions about what kind of animals they had, how bad off they were, where they were found, in what manner they were brought here, and so on. They followed him to Schneider's door and struggled to come up with answers as fast as Carter was asking the questions. Well, the man who had come in with the clipboard did anyway, the whole time holding his hand out for the return of his clipboard. The other goon-looking one with the carrier didn't say anything at all. He actually looked baffled, like a kid who hadn't studied for the quiz.

Carter knocked on the door. "A couple men from Affron, Sir," he announced through the door. He focused on the men. "What were your names again?"

Clipboard Man cleared his throat then pointed to himself and his partner. "Waller and Boyles,"

"A Mr. Waller and Mr. Boyles," Carter repeated clearly through the door.

Waller pointed at the clipboard. "May I have that back now?"

"Oh," Carter said as if he'd forgotten he was holding it. "Of course."

While they faced the other direction, I quickly closed the gap on the tarp to make sure it completely hid the mermaid's tank. Dad made himself look busy at the smaller tanks, as if he were checking on the fish.

"What are we going to do?" I whispered.

All Dad could offer was, "Simple. We have to keep them away from her tank."

Chapter Eight

Dr. Schneider opened his office door and nervously whisked the Affron men inside, peering past them at my dad and the tank the whole time. Wow, he was about as obvious as a tour guide holding up a microphone and announcing, "And in the back corner we have hidden a mermaid in a tank. Why don't you take a look?" But Carter was on top of it and shut the door in Schneider's face.

As soon as the men were out of sight, Carter dashed back to us.

"Come on. Help me make this thing look like crap."

"Do you think they suspect something?" I asked. "I mean, how could they?"

"I don't know why those men are here," he said, "but it has nothing to do with rescued wildlife. There isn't anything written on that clipboard. It's just empty forms that at a glance look like Affron job applications."

My dad gawked, "What?"

"If they were on the level, I'd have expected a list of the animals they have with them. That's not what I saw."

"Maybe they're here to offer Schneider a job."

Dad laughed, but Carter didn't.

"No time!" Carter said, throwing some nasty, mildewed tarps and wet towels at my dad and me. We quickly readjusted the tarp one more time so that not a bit of the glass underneath was showing. Then we threw those tarps and towels along the top for good measure. Now it really looked junked up, and it smelled like a swamp.

We'd only just tossed the last one up when the door to Schneider's office opened. He followed the two men out. They immediately took in the sight of us in front of the giant tank. Waller squinted. "Something wrong with that one?"

Carter ran a hand through his hair. "I've been messing with it all day, but I can't get it to regulate at an even temperature. It's got something wrong with it. So, I'm draining it and have to figure out how to fix it before we can use it."

Schneider put on a big, fake grin and said, "Carter's my man for all that kind of stuff. Don't know what I'd do without him."

"Hmmm," Waller said.

Boyles held up the animal carrier and kind of grunted.

"Where should he put that?" Waller asked for him.

"I'll take it," Carter said. "June, why don't you and your dad help these men bring in their rescues?"

My dad and I went outside with Boyle while Carter stayed inside to ready what was left of the empty cages and aquariums. Apparently Clipboard Dude didn't feel like he needed to do anything but stand around and observe. Outside, Dad tried engaging Boyle in conversation as we headed toward his white van. I was kind of curious to hear the guy talk and was beginning to wonder if he could.

"Which beach did you pick these up from?"

The man didn't answer.

"Are any in critical shape?"

Nothing.

The man opened the back of the van, and we saw that he had some more carriers with seabirds and one with an otter. There were a few fish swimming around in dirty water in gallon-sized zip-close plastic bags. Not a lot of critters, I thought. Not as many as I expected.

"Is this all that survived?" Dad asked.

Boyle handed me one of the plastic bags and didn't say anything, but his eyes looked rounder, as if alarmed by Dad's question. My theory was that Boyle was told not to say anything. Maybe it was because he was just a grunt and didn't really know much about the science or protocol. Maybe, like Carter suggested, it was because this mission wasn't on the up and up, and he was too stupid to come up with intelligent-sounding responses. Whatever it was, he clearly didn't know how to handle all these questions.

"Mr. Boyle?" I asked carefully, as he reached into the van to pull out the carrier with the otter for Dad. "Are there other vans coming, or is this it?"

His eyes flicked from my dad to me, searching our faces for some kind of help. "Doesn't this seem like enough?" he asked. From his buddy this might have sounded belligerent, but from him it sounded like a little boy asking if he'd eaten enough dinner even though there was a whole serving of veggies still on his plate.

"Actually, no," my dad said, clearly irritated. "I expected at least three times this much."

"This is all we found," the man answered dully. "The spill wasn't that bad."

"Are you kidding me?" I nearly shouted.

My dad shot a look to me behind the guy's back and shook his head. I set my jaw to keep from saying something I probably shouldn't.

It took a couple trips to get it all inside, and during that time the man refused to talk any more. He didn't even offer up a "thank you" to us for helping him carry stuff or an "excuse me" when he stepped on my foot. We put everything on the big tables for Carter and Schneider to analyze. They had several buckets of water and bottles of dish soap ready for the cleaning of the critters. Carter reached in to help the otter first, holding the nervous creature carefully with gloved hands and looking over its furry body for any oil that had to be removed from it.

"Otters are so furry," he said, clearly fascinated by the animal. "There is more hair per square inch on a sea otter than the entire coat of a Golden Retriever."

I stepped up beside him. "It's so cute."

"And all that hair makes it hard to clean. Oil is very dangerous to otters." He darted his eyes at Waller, hoping the man got his point.

"How does it look?" I asked, wanting to know how I could help.

"Oddly, not bad," Carter said. "This little fellow looks like he barely has anything on him." Carter carried the scared otter like a baby over to a larger tank that already had another otter in it, and let the animal slip out of his arms into the water. An oil sheen came off its fur and sparkled in the water. "It won't take much to get that guy back to normal."

He moved on to one of the birds in a carrier. Schneider asked me to take one of the plastic bags of fish from him and dump it into an aquarium behind me. None of them looked bad to me either. They could breathe with a fair amount of ease, from what I could tell, and they swam around to check out their new home without any visible difficulty. What was going on?

I sneaked a peak at Waller, who stood at the end of the tables shaking his head as if very dissatisfied with what we were doing. Suddenly, he brushed past me and headed for the large tank. I elbowed Carter hard in his back, and he jumped, dropping the poor seagull on the table. The bird squawked, and that got Schneider's attention.

"Carter, careful!"

But Carter wasn't listening. He dashed to Waller's side. "Is there anything else you need?"

"Yes, actually," he said. "I need to see this tank and find out what's wrong with it."

"I told you. It's broken."

Schneider came over to the two of them. "What is your concern, Mr. Waller?"

"Your small tanks are too crowded," Waller said. "The animals are going to fight. They're going to go crazy with this little space." Boyle, the silent cohort, nodded, although I felt pretty sure that guy had no idea if the animals might fight or not. I didn't get a sense that guy knew much at all except how to drive the van. And judging by his parking job out front, he probably wasn't too good at that either.

"There's nothing we can do about that right at this moment," Carter said. "As soon as we get that tank cleaned and repaired, we'll transfer some of the larger animals over. Until then, we're just out of luck."

Dr. Schneider added, "It was just bad timing for us, huh?"

"Yeah," I said. "I mean, who would have expected Affron to send out a ship that leaks oil into the ocean?"

"June," Dad warned.

I rolled my eyes at him. For an activist he was being mighty low-key all of a sudden.

"This isn't the time, and these aren't the people who matter," he whispered in my ear as if he knew what I was thinking.

Waller reached for the tarp, "Let me look at the tank. Maybe it's not as bad off as you think. Some adjustments? I can do that for you."

I chewed on the insides of my cheeks to keep from squealing.

Schneider waved his hands as he said, "No! No thanks. We have it under control."

My dad tried a distraction, letting go of the seagull he'd caught and been holding and then chasing it ineffectively around the table. It caught the attention of the Affron men, but neither moved to help him.

Carter, as always, the only one to keep his cool, leaned against the tarp with his arms crossed. "I appreciate the fact that you might have some insight, sir," he said. "I'm sure your help would be invaluable, but I really do know how to fix this. I won't be able to get to it until I get these animals accounted for and put up safely. There's a protocol we have to follow."

"I'd still like…" the man started, way too insistently

"We know," Dr. Schneider said. "We'd all like it to work out better." He placed a hand on the man's back and gestured toward the double doors. "Tomorrow. It should all be fixed by tomorrow."

Carter grinned and did a melodramatic sigh. "Even if I have to stay all night."

Ah, clever. Not only did the guy get the clue that he wasn't going to get to see the tank, but he couldn't come back in a couple hours and try again. Waller grunted some kind of compliance. I'm pretty sure he didn't like being told by a nineteen-year-old what he could and couldn't do.

Dad finally wrangled the seagull now that the drama was over, and he plopped it into the hands of Boyle, who juggled the poor bird like he didn't have a clue how to handle it. I dashed over to him and gently took the poor creature and put it into the cage my dad had opened for it. Boyle looked visibly relieved, though he was kind of frantically looking around for a sink to wash off the bird crap all over his hands. It was a huge effort not to laugh at him.

Carter nodded at me and crooked a finger for me to come over to him. "Let's get started on this." He made a big show of flipping pages in a folder for me to look at, and I nodded my head a whole bunch and added some "mmm hmmms" for good measure. While we did this, Dad got busy finding a mop and cleaning up the floor.

Dr. Schneider led Waller to the double doors. "I imagine you have more work to do down at the beach."

"Not really. The spill was very minor. I doubt we'll have anything else to bring over."

"Well, that's good news," Dr. Schneider said. "That's very good."

Boyle joined them at the double doors, wiping his wet hands on his pants. "Need a shower," he moaned.

"Yes," Dr. Schneider said, patting the man on the back. "Well, you go have a pleasant evening."

"We'll do that," Waller said. He took one more glimpse over at us. I waved at him, but I knew he was looking over my head at the tarps hanging over the big tank.

Dr. Schneider opened a door and held it open. "Mr. Waller," he said, and then waited for both men to walk through before following them out.

The second they men were gone, Carter dropped to the floor like he'd deflated. "Wow." Dad and I laughed, and then he joined in too.

"It takes a lot to be that cool," my dad said. "I'm thoroughly impressed."

"Thanks, Mr. Sawfeather," Carter said. "Coming from you, that's huge."

"No, I'm serious. We were all ridiculous, and you were the only one with his wits about him."

I picked up two bottles of dish soap. "We didn't even use these."

"Yeah, I noticed that," Carter said, pulling himself back up to his feet. "Interesting huh?"

Dad watched the otters getting to know each other in their too-small tank. "Yeah. This guy should have probably been near death. We should *still* be cleaning him. I've seen animals today so coated with oil we couldn't do anything about them. And there will be more tomorrow as the oil continues to spread."

"I heard on the news that they've already put dispersants in the ocean," Carter said.

"They have," Dad said. "And that'll help the top layer, but a lot of that oil is going to sink. This spill is not as bad as that one back at the Gulf, but it's still going to cause some serious long term damage."

"So, why wasn't this van-load more affected?" I asked.

"You know what I think?" Carter said. "I think they just smeared some oil on these animals to make it look like they were part of the spill to give them access here. I think they were after something else."

"Not the mermaid!" I said. "They couldn't possibly know about that."

Carter shook his head. "No, it's not that. That's way too far-fetched. I mean, how could anyone possibly suspect…?"

"It's not the mermaid," Dad said. "Those men clearly weren't scientists. Just Affron spies. I've run into those types before. They're trying to see how bad the spill really was, so they know how much they have to cover up."

"Well, they couldn't have been more obvious," said Carter.

Dr. Schneider came back in the room and nodded for my dad to follow him to his office.

All of a sudden Carter laughed. "What would that guy have done if I said, 'Sure go ahead and try to fix the tank'? Would he have had the slightest clue?"

"I seriously doubt it," I said, handing Carter the dish soap. At the slightest brush of our hands against each other, I felt my face turn instantly hot. Praying the blush wasn't visible, I slid past him and pulled back the edge of the tarp to look at the mermaid instead of him. The mermaid wriggled toward me, a feeling of relief flooded through me, and I wasn't sure if it was me feeling relieved to see she was still okay or her feeling relieved that I was okay. "Should we leave these tarps on here? Will it be too dark?"

"I think we should leave them on for now," Carter said. "You never know who's going to pop in here. I don't think this was the last we'll see of those Affron men." He came up behind me and put a hand against the glass over my head, his body awfully close behind mine. "I'll be here a while tonight taking care of things around here, and I'll be sure to leave some lights on. She's used to living in the deep ocean, so darkness shouldn't scare her. I wouldn't think, anyway."

"This is a different kind of darkness," I said, "and a very different kind of environment."

He was silent a moment before he finally said in a very serious tone, "I know." He turned me around to look right in his face. "I'll take care of her. I promise."

It was suddenly really hard to breathe, but somehow I managed to whisper, "I could stay here too. And help some more."

"Don't you have homework?"

From across the room I heard the click of Dr. Schneider's door and my father tease, "Yes, June. Don't you have some homework? Some *high school* homework?"

My breath came back. I sighed and rolled my eyes and moved away from Carter enough to be dad-approved. "Ugh."

"Ah, there's that American Indian in you, Miss Sawfeather," Carter laughed.

I smacked him. "That is so inappropriate. I take away your coolness points."

"Sorry," he said, but he was still snickering.

"Don't you have homework too, college boy?" I flung back at him.

"I do, but it's not as interesting as all this. I'll get it done between classes tomorrow."

"I wish I could do that. I just felt a massive wave of tiredness wash over me." Now that the adrenaline rush of cleaning the mermaid and distracting the Affron dudes was over, I suddenly felt like I was going to drop. It occurred to me that I'd been awake since three in the morning and it was now eight p.m. Well, if you didn't count falling asleep in English class this afternoon, but that was hardly a satisfying snooze.

Carter smiled at me and put a hand on my shoulder. It wasn't that charming smile he faked the Affron men with, but a sweet, genuine one that made his green eyes twinkle. How did he keep smiling throughout all this work and stress? "You should go home. We'll catch up tomorrow."

"Are you sure?" I asked.

"I'll pick you up after school again," he said. Then he added, snidely, "That is if it's convenient for you."

"What's that supposed to mean?"

"Oh nothing, Miss San Diego State."

I stuck my tongue out at him, which was probably unladylike, and I kind of regretted it ten minutes later because it was the last thing he saw me do before grabbing my dad and pulling him out the door. "Come on, Dad," I said. "You need sleep as much as I do."

Dad tried to veer me back inside before we got past the tide-pool aquarium up front, but I kept my grip firm on his arm.

"I mean it, Dad. It's pizza, a shower, and night-night."

"Oh, fine, *Mom*," he said, laughing. "Speaking of which, I need to get home and call your mom. I'm way overdue for a check in, and she's probably ready to throttle me."

During the drive home, I forced him to listen to a classic rock station instead of the news, any talk shows, or NPR. It was tough for him, but when we got into singing some Queen at full volume, it helped keep us both awake enough to make it home without crashing or running off the road.

We gobbled up the cheese pizza as soon as we got home, and I listened to relentless advice about how to handle a nineteen-year-old boyfriend even though I kept explaining to him that Carter was not my boyfriend and probably never would be. All the tension from the night before was gone, and I was glad that he didn't bring up any of it. At least for the moment I could enjoy being with my dad, even if he did tell ridiculous stories about mermaids singing to killer whales.

After dinner, I showered for the second time that day and put on some sweats. Then I went up to my room to plow through my homework. I decided to save reading the *Moby Dick* chapters for bedtime, since I was sure it would knock me out for the night. I called Haley a few times from our home line, but she didn't answer. Her parents didn't have a home line, just cell phones, and I felt kind of weird about calling her mom's number, even though I had it. I saw the light on in her room, but her shades were closed. I wasn't sure if she was in there or not. I leaned out my window and yelled across the divide between our houses. That didn't work either.

I got on my computer and I.M.'d her. Nothing. I emailed her and waited for a response. Nothing.

I knew she was mad at me, but I really didn't think she was mad enough to be ignoring me like this. Maybe she was into a really great episode of *100 Most Shocking Videos*. There was nothing else to do except the old fashioned thing. I slipped into some shoes, headed downstairs and out the door, and walked over to knock at her front door. Her mom answered, a little confused to have me at her front door at ten p.m.

"June? Is everything okay?" she asked.

"Is Haley here? She's not answering her phone or emails, and I wanted to talk to her."

"She's here," Haley's mom said. "I think she might be in bed already."

"She's not," I told her. "Her light's still on."

"Oh." But her mom didn't offer to go get her.

"Mrs. Dunlap? Could I see her?"

Her mom scrunched up her face as though really confused. Was it really that weird for me to show up like this? I mean, just because neither of us had ever done it before? "Of course. I'll go get her."

She left me standing at the front door while she disappeared into the depths of her house, calling for Haley. A couple minutes later she came back. "June, she can't come to the door right now. She told me she's taking a bath."

"A bath? Really?" That was a new one. I love Haley, but honestly the usual dingy cast to her hair suggested only occasional showers at best. Plus, her twitchy thumbs were always a little too eager to be holding a game, cell phone or remote control to allow her to sit still in a tub of water for long.

"That's what she said."

I offered Haley's mom a polite smile. "Okay. Well, tell her to call me when she gets out."

I walked back to my house. My dad was standing in the living room when I came back in. "Where have you been?"

"Next door," I said. "Trying to see my best friend, who doesn't want to see *me*."

"You went to her house?" he asked. Apparently this was strange to him too.

"I don't have a cell phone, remember?"

"Oh, that's right."

I went back upstairs and kicked off my shoes. Guess I had a lot of making up to do with Haley. I didn't realize I'd upset her as much as I did. I wasn't even really sure why I'd upset her. Honestly, it was me the kids were making fun of, not her. If anything, she should be upset for me and by my side defending me. But she was acting like I'd just embarrassed her and ruined her life by wearing Carter's sweatshirt.

Haley was a great girl. She wouldn't be my best friend if she weren't. She was really deep and cared about the environment and always rooted for the underdog. She cried at movies and sometimes when reading books. A real softie. If she knew everything that was going on with me today, what I'd been through with my parents and what had happened at the beach. If she knew about the mermaid...

That was it. I'd fill her in on all of it. She might not be responding to my emails, but that didn't mean she wasn't reading them. I got on the computer and wrote for half an hour telling her everything about my dad, including finding the mermaids and how Carter and I cleaned her up. When I was done, I uploaded the video to my computer and attached it to the email and zipped the whole thing off to her.

The video made it a huge file, and it took forever to send and would probably take just as long to open on her end. Odds were that Haley might not even see it until morning, so I got into bed with *Moby Dick* and promptly fell asleep, certain I'd be riding to school with my best friend, Carter would be caring for the mermaid and everything would be fine.

Yeah, well, a few hours of blissful ignorance was about all I got.

Chapter Nine

For a fleeting moment I hoped Haley would be taking me to school. We'd cut up about how awful I looked in the video, and then she'd get serious and ask what was really going on. The story would make her a little teary-eyed. We'd bond again and all would be well with the world. But, like I said, it was a fleeting moment, because as soon as I got out of bed I checked my computer and there was no response from her. Her shades were drawn in her room so we couldn't compare outfits through the windows like we normally did to make sure we didn't overtly match or clash with each other. Clearly, she was still avoiding me.

I dressed and headed downstairs to choke down a bowl of the awful granola my parents always have on hand as cereal. It tastes okay, but some Trix or Cocoa Puffs wouldn't hurt once in a while. The newspaper was on the table, but the oil spill didn't make the first page. I was curious to know how far back the editors ranked that news item, but I was too lazy to deal with flipping those large pages. Dad stumbled into the room, and caught me with the folded up paper in my hand.

"It's on page ten," he said. "No pictures or anything."

I shook my head slowly but kept my eyes on the headline, which was something about a congressman—in another state, mind you— caught cheating on his wife. Yeah, I could see how that was more important than an oil spill on our very own coastline. Affron had some power, that was for sure.

"When is Mom coming home?" I asked. I didn't like the idea that she was still up there in Alaska dealing with them.

"Soon, I hope. There's not much else she can do up there now." He grabbed his coffee tumbler and shoved his wallet in his back pocket.

"You going to school today?" he asked.

I cocked my head and squinted at him. "Don't I sort of have to?"

"I don't know. Do you?"

I think he was hinting that I could go with him and do some more work. It was really tempting. However, I figured there were some things I needed to hammer out with Haley at school, and I didn't want Vice Principal Slater giving me crap again. Oh, and speaking of her, I needed to get my freakin' phone back.

"Yeah, and I need you to drive me, so you can help me reclaim my phone from the clutches of the evil warden."

He grinned at me. "I guess that would come in handy, wouldn't it?"

"A little."

He was in a good mood. Mom must not have ticked him off on the phone, and I imagine he slept as hard as I did after that long day. His eyes were bright, and most of all he seemed to have completely forgotten that he was royally finished with me twenty-four hours ago. Dad drove me to school and argued with Slater in the front office for a good twenty minutes before Spike-head finally gave over the phone. Part of me was surprised it still existed. I envisioned her eating things like that for dinner. Or maybe she threw all the gadgets she confiscated from kids in a big pile out in the back parking lot and drove back and forth over them with her car while screeching our alma mater like it was a punk rock song.

"If I see her using it on campus, it will be taken from her until school is out for the summer," she warned as her claw grip on the thing loosened enough for Dad to wrangle it from her.

"I'm sure Juniper understands the rules," my dad replied as calmly as he could, flipping the phone to me.

"Hmmm," was all Slater said before slinking back into her office and shutting the door in our faces.

Dad patted me on the back. "Don't get caught."

"Gotcha."

Then we walked out of the office, and in the grand hallway of my school were about two hundred teenagers. I think it's safe to say that every single one of them either had a cell phone in their hand or to their ear. My dad and I started laughing so hard tears filled our eyes.

"Well, okay then," he said with a snort. "Have a great day. Uh, call me on your *illegal* phone, and let me know what your plans are this afternoon. I'll be at the beach."

He headed out to the parking lot still chuckling to himself over the absurdity. I turned my phone on, but there weren't any messages on it. With only a couple minutes to spare, I jammed the phone in my back pocket and dashed for my first period class. I'd only gotten a couple steps when I heard someone shout at me. It caught me off guard, and I tripped and fell to my knee. When I looked up Regina and Marlee were standing over me.

"Why are you running, June?" Regina said with that nasty teasing voice that popular girls perfect. "Did you get dropped off late by your boyfriend again?"

"Yeah," Marlee joined in. "Was that him?" She pointed toward the front doors.

"That was my dad."

Regina gave her the "duh" look, but Marlee just shrugged. "You said he was older."

"Not like gross older." Regina turned back on me again. "Did you have another all-nighter this time? Did Daddy come to find you in the middle of the night and threaten to shoot the guy with his bow and arrow?"

They both snickered. I can't think of another word for it. It wasn't a laugh, and it was kind of similar to the sound snakes would make if they could laugh.

I looked from one to the other as I stood up, trying to put together what they could possibly be saying to me because none of it made any sense. There were so many insults twined together, and they were all ridiculous.

"I'm going to be late," I finally said, and I walked away from them.

"We're talking to you, Juniper!" Regina shouted, aghast that someone would dare to walk away from her.

Was I supposed to stay and argue? Defend myself? Cry because the popular girl was insulting me? I didn't feel like doing any of those things. I saved a mermaid's life the day before. I was a hero in my own mind. Regina should have been in awe of me. Maybe someday it would all come out, and she would know. Someday when she was thirty or so, when she got tired of hocking beauty products at a department store counter at the mall and realized that I was making a living doing things like helping Killer Whales give birth, she'd think of this day and wonder why she ever thought she was better than me.

Other kids stared at me as I continued down the hallway away from Regina and Marlee's calls. A couple of them gestured that I should turn around. A lot of them laughed when they saw me, and I heard some whispered, "That's the one I told you about" type comments. I ignored them all, turned a corner where I couldn't hear the girls anymore. I actually couldn't believe they hollered after me that long. How embarrassing. For them.

I was just about to slip into my homeroom, when I saw Haley across the hall. She had her cell phone out and was watching something on it. Probably a music video or that internet joke site. I couldn't tell, but she was really focused on it

"Haley!" I shouted. "Did you get my email?"

She looked up at me and said simply, "Yeah," like it was no big deal. Like I had sent her a message as simple as, "I'm going to school tomorrow, see you there." Then her attention went right back to her phone. She walked on, disappearing into her own homeroom a couple doors down the hall.

I stood dazed for a second, unsure about what had just happened. Maybe my message got messed up somehow and the whole thing didn't go through. Maybe the attached video didn't open. Something must have gone wrong, because her response didn't match the gravity of the email I'd sent. I thought about grabbing her out of class and making her talk to me, but as I took a step that direction I heard Mrs. Leapfer, my homeroom teacher, call my name. I knew I couldn't be late again, so I ducked into my room like a good little girl and tried to think of how I could get Haley to talk to me at lunch.

The first three periods went so slow. I didn't see Haley at all as I passed from one class to the other, which was weird, because we usually saw each other all the time. I knew where all her classes were, and for the first time I realized how much she used to walk out of her way just to bump into me in the hall. What could I do to get her to stop being so mad at me?

Advanced Photography was my fourth period. It was my only elective this semester. The rest of my schedule was jammed with college prep classes so I could get ahead. Smart, said my parents. Stupid, said I. However, I love photography, and I usually enjoy the class. But that day we had a sub, and all she was having us do was look at a PowerPoint slideshow of famous photos projected on a screen. Boring. All around the room I heard the familiar dying cow moo of vibrating cell phones. It seemed like every kid in the class had at least three messages or more come in within five minutes' time. Kids were checking texts by holding their phones inside their open backpacks under their desks, like the sub really cared or would do anything about it.

My phone didn't moo. Mine was the only one that remained silent. It was just as well, because I couldn't have checked it anyway. I promised to have good cell phone behavior—at least for a day.

Whatever was happening in the cellular world was apparently very exciting. Fingers frantically tapped messages. People started leaning over desks to whisper in other kids' ears. This had to be about more than where they were meeting up for lunch. At first I guessed there was a fight being held somewhere on campus. That usually got a buzz going. But then I began to notice that after each exchange whisper or rapid fire of texting fingers, glances shot my way. Oh, they tried to be subtle at first, but they quickly became super obvious. I got it. Regina was spreading more rumors about me.

The thing I didn't get was why anyone cared. I wasn't popular. No one really knew me well. And it wasn't like kids getting it on was a new thing around the high school. It happened all the time, so they say—I didn't really know this for sure. But it happened enough to know that every girl who had sex with a boy did not became an instant headline. Lord knew Regina wasn't a virgin. So what was the big deal?

And what really sucked about it all was that I hadn't done what I was getting a rep about. I wasn't sure if Carter even liked me.

I sat there, getting madder and madder about the whole thing as the clock ticked as slowly as it could toward twelve o'clock. All I wanted at that moment was to go sock Regina in the face and call her a hypocrite. I began to cringe at the sound of each cell phone moo and was about ready to pop out of my seat and say a thing or two to this class of people I'd been teaming up with for projects for the past three years. If anybody knew me, it was this group. They were mostly nerdy, yearbook staff types. Not your typical top of the list kids. How dare they look down on me? Shoot, if I had really made it with a college boy, they should all worship me. Like, they *wish*!

The phone of Nathan Price, the guy right next to me, a pimple-faced kid I'd known since sixth grade, buzzed. Who did he know that made him three phone calls more popular than me? I'd had it.

"What?" I shouted at him. "What are they telling you?"

Nathan snapped his head toward me like I'd just scared the crap out of him. "Jeez, June. Calm down."

"No, I will not calm down. What is everyone freaking out about? What did I do that was such a big deal?"

Nathan's eyes were real big, and I wasn't sure how to read it. They didn't look accusing, that was for sure, but it was some kind of mix of fear and awe. Weird. Then he asked, "Is it true?"

I sighed. "Why do you care?"

"Because it seems kind of unbelievable."

"What?" I nearly shouted. Why was it so unbelievable? It's not like I'm hideous or something.

"I mean, I can't figure out how it happened?"

Um, duh, boy meets girl. Remember that class in junior high? "Look, Nathan…"

I didn't know what I was going to say exactly, just that it was going to be pretty mean, but he interrupted me to add, "If you faked it, you did a good job."

"Faked it?" Faked what? Did he think I was *trying* to get everyone in the school to think I was a slut? "I didn't fake anything. I mean…"

"Because the pictures look real to me."

Now he had me. "Pictures? What are you talking about?"

"It's all over the Internet. Look." He started to hand me his cell phone but then stopped himself. "Wait a second." Nathan got up and went to the substitute teacher. I didn't hear everything he said, but I think I heard something like "…by someone in our class." She nodded like she really didn't care, and next thing I knew he was typing in a YouTube link onto the class computer. The PowerPoint slideshow came to an abrupt stop, replaced by a loading video. A moment later a picture of me was frozen on the screen. Nathan hit play.

There I was on the beach, frazzled and dirty, trying to hold up one of the dying mermaids so my dad could get a better angle with the camera. I heard his voice droning on about the discovery, but the words were nonsense in my ears. All I could think was *How? How? HOW DID THIS HAPPEN?*

Dad's voice continued as the camera zoomed in to get a good shot of the gills on the mermaid's neck. "The mermaids have mere moments to live unless we can get them to a tank of water and get the oil cleared away from their gills."

Then my own voice from the video cut through the loud noise of my brain protesting the reality of all this: "Dad. Stop taping. We don't have time. They're dying." And a second later, a much more urgent, "Dad!" Then the video stopped.

Everyone in class was staring at me, even the substitute who had now pulled out her own cell phone probably so she could type the link for all her friends to see too. No one spoke.

"Is it real?" Nathan asked.

"How did this get on the Internet?" I asked.

"It was on Regina's wall this morning. Haley sent it to her. I thought you knew." When I didn't answer right away, stunned to silence by what he'd just told me, Nathan asked, "Is it real or a hoax?"

"I've got to go." I grabbed my backpack to the sound of my classmates calling out to me to answer Nathan's question. Just as I was about to walk out the door, I turned and looked at them all. These were people I liked to think of as friends, and I was kind of glad that it wasn't the subject of my virginity that had them all hyper-texting each other. Having no idea what to say to them, I raised an eyebrow and acted really mysterious as I threw out, "Does it look real?" Then I took off before I had to answer any other questions.

I was halfway to Haley's classroom when the bell rang for lunch. A wave of kids came toward me from every door. As soon as people saw me, they rushed at me with their questions about the video being real, if the mermaids talked, did they survive, where were they now, and so on. I couldn't move any further down the hall, blocked completely by curious teenagers who had never before uttered a word to me.

"Please let me through," I cried, trying to squeeze sideways between a small gap created by two skinny Freshmen. I broke through the immediate cluster and began to run. Coming toward me from the other direction were all four members of the Student Council walking side by side so that they filled the width of the hallway and no one could pass them. People had to slam their bodies flat against the lockers to make room for the wall of popularity passing. Right behind them Haley's head popped up and down between their heads like she was trying to figure out where she should be in the line, but while they weren't telling her to go away, they weren't exactly letting her in either.

I skidded to a stop in front of them.

"Wow, Juniper," Regina said. "Looks like you're in a hurry. More mermaids on the beach?"

"Haley," I said, gasping for breath. "What did you do?"

"I thought the video was cool, and I forwarded it," she said. "Everyone loves it. You're, like, super popular now. Of course, I have to keep telling everyone that it's real, because I know you don't know how to even do basic Photoshop, let alone edit a video like that. You're pretty lame with the tech stuff."

"Can we go see them?" Marlee asked. "Are they pretty? You can't really tell from the video."

"What? No! You can't see them."

"That's because they aren't real," Gary said.

"They are real," Regina snapped at him. Then she turned super sweetly to me and said, "Right, Junie?"

I didn't answer. "I didn't give you permission to forward that video, Haley. I just wanted you to know why I was late yesterday, 'cause you wouldn't talk to me."

Regina nodded, "Saving mermaids is a very valid reason, we think. Haley has completely forgiven you. Us too. In fact, we're 100% behind your little Recycling Club now."

Ted scratched his head, "We are?"

"Yes, we are," Regina said. "And we're all going to join. Can't have trash going out in that ocean with beautiful mermaids swimming around, can we?" Regina put a hand on my shoulder. "Of course, you have to take us to see them. That's how it works. We get to be first."

"What is going on here?" I asked.

Haley almost exploded with joy, "We're popular, June, that's what!"

My phone buzzed in my pocket. I pulled it out and saw that it was Carter. Trying to move away from them as much as they would allow, I answered.

"Get out here, now," Carter's voice insisted. "I'm in the parking lot and need you to come with me. Hurry."

"Did you see...?"

"Yes, and no time. Come now."

I slipped the phone back in my pocket and shot a hard look at Haley. If she thought she was mad at me yesterday, she had no idea how I felt about her today. "I've got to go."

"More mermaids?" Marlee squeaked. "Can we go?"

"No and no," I answered, pushing past her and heading for the front hallway.

Haley started to follow me. "Can I come?"

I pivoted back to her for just a second and said, "You've done enough damage, thanks."

I walked as fast as I could through the throngs of teenagers who mercifully were a little more interested in getting to the cafeteria before the burritos ran out than stopping to talk to me. As I pushed the front door open Mrs. Slater stepped out of the school office and hollered, "Juniper Sawfeather, come back this instant!"

Knowing full well that a suspension would probably be in my future, I continued on my way. At the bottom of the front steps Carter waited for me in his car, motor running. He had his hand firmly on the horn to make sure I noticed him. I waved my hands frantically to let him know he could stop any time he wanted and sooner would be better than later. I got in and flung my backpack into the back seat.

Before I even said hello, Carter told me, "I tried to get you out of school earlier, but the administration people said no way." He hit the gas before I even had my seatbelt on.

"Is everything all right?" I asked, thinking something was wrong with the mermaid and forgetting my personal trouble for a second.

"No," Carter said coolly. "Nothing's right at all."

He sped off, ignoring just about every traffic law that I remembered from my driving test last summer. His charming smile was absent, replaced by a clenched jaw and muscles popping intensely out of his neck. For the first time he looked more like the adult he claimed he to be. The high school was shrinking in the rearview mirror when it dawned on me what was happening.

"You've seen the video."

"It's gone viral," he said. "We need to get to the center—fast!"

My phone buzzed again. I looked at the screen and saw DAD CELL. I was in so much trouble.

Chapter Ten

I thought about not answering and telling Dad later that Mrs. Slater took the phone from me again. But the tension in the car made me positive that Carter would not back me up. I hit the answer button on my phone and said a very weak "Hey, Dad."

"What the Hell is going on?" he yelled. "Did I tell you to put any of the footage on the Internet? I don't recall giving you permission to do that. Your mom is about to lose her mind. What on Earth were you thinking? Haven't we taught you anything? This is the most irresponsible thing I have ever seen you do. Do you know how this has hurt our mission? What impact your actions have had on our work? Do you have any idea what this is going to do?"

His rant was even longer than that, actually, but it was hard to catch every insult and guilt trip he blared at me. After a few minutes he paused for a breath. I hardly knew what to say. All I could do was whisper, "I didn't know this would happen."

And then it started all over again, with Carter in the seat next to me joining in.

"You didn't know this would happen?"

"What did you think when you stuck it on the Internet?"

"That people were going to ignore it?"

"That evidence of real-life mermaids wasn't going to be a big hit?"

"You aren't stupid, June. How did this happen?"

"What were you smoking?"

I went ahead and put Dad on speaker, so they could hear each other rip me apart.

I explained what I had meant to do, but that didn't help. They just

99

started all over again with a new round of angry questions.

"Why did she need to know that?"

"Did you think of asking me first?"

"You put your friendship with this girl over the safety of the mermaids?"

"What about the oil spill and the sea life?"

"Did you think about anything besides yourself?" they asked in unison, as if rehearsed.

There was a pause, as they registered what just happened. And then they both laughed.

"Yeah, you guys are really funny," I said. I noticed how tight my muscles were, my arms crossed, my body pressed up against the passenger door as if trying to get away from Carter and the cell phone, which I had stuck in the drink holder.

Carter raised his left hand and literally wiped the smile off his face. He looked at me, his eyebrows raised in the middle in some kind of mock sincerity. "I'm sorry, June. You're right. It wasn't funny."

"Nothing about this is funny," Dad agreed. "But we do need to lighten up. You made a mistake –"

"Boy did she," Carter said, followed by a corny whistle like were suddenly in a *Little Rascals* skit.

"And now we have to fix it."

Carter steered onto the highway headed west. "We're going to the Center now. Will you meet us there?"

"I can't," Dad said. "There are already looky-loos showing up out here. We've had a dozen or more people come with cameras just in the last hour. I don't understand how this happens. How do people find out about Internet videos anyway? I don't think I've ever even watched one."

"I don't understand it either," I mumbled.

"Well, Carter, let me know what's going on over there with the mermaid and Dr. Schneider. I'm going to try to keep these idiots out of the water."

"Yes, sir," Carter said.

"And June?" Dad said. "Do not do anything else unless I say okay. Do you understand?"

"Yes, Dad."

He hung up. Carter was silent. I felt like I wanted to throw up.

I thought Carter might launch into a new string of complaints or at the very least tell me what his plans were for the rest of the day. I knew he probably hated me right now. Any hope I'd had of anything happening between us was dashed. He thought I was a dumb, high school kid who deemed her popularity more important than major scientific finds or ecological issues. I had no hope of convincing him otherwise. I didn't know why he even bothered to pick me up and take me with him, except maybe to keep me from causing any more damage.

Carter didn't talk at all as he drove toward the ocean, even though I badgered him with questions about the mermaid and the Center. I wanted to know if he'd been there yet and knew what was happening. It seemed he wanted to save the impact of the bad news for when we got there. He also needed to keep some concentration on his radical driving so we wouldn't be killed.

I subtly adjusted myself in the seat so I could hang on tightly to the armrest on the door. I knew it annoyed guys if they saw people clutching to car parts for life when they drove. My dad always complained about it, but I had to hang on because Dad liked to drive as close to the car in front of him as possible and then switch lanes really fast. He also had a thing about driving so close to the side of the road he'd go up on the curb. Still, as much as I hated to insult Carter's driving when he was already pissed at me, I also feared a sudden lurch through the passenger window every time he careened around a corner.

Remarkably, we made it to the Rescue Center in one piece. Carter pulled into a spot, got out of the car, and slammed the door shut behind him. I saw him grab the door handle and yank on it. The door didn't budge. Locked.

"What the..." He pounded on the door. "Dr. Schneider? Dr. Schneider!"

Nervously, I stepped up behind him. "Maybe he locked it so he could go to lunch?"

"That's not like him," Carter said, rifling through his key ring and finding the one that matched the front door. "He hasn't been answering the phone either. Not the one here or his cell."

"Do you think he's okay?"

"I don't know."

Carter got the door open and held it for me to step inside. All the lights were off in the front room except for the glow coming from the aquariums and the tide pool. I slipped on a pile of mail on the floor that had been put through the slot in the door. I bent over and picked it all up so Carter wouldn't slip on it too. The double doors to the lab were closed. Nothing seemed out of place to me, but it was pretty dark and I wasn't so familiar with the place that I would know what might have been moved.

After entering behind me, Carter locked the front door again. "Just in case," he whispered as he passed me and headed for the double doors. Those weren't locked, but all the lights were off in there too. Windows high up in the walls allowed a touch of sunlight to leak in around the closed blinds, and there was more of that glow from the racks of aquariums. Schneider's office door was open and a bit of light came from there, like a desk lamp had been left on.

"Could he have fallen asleep in there?" I asked.

Carter shrugged. I guessed that wasn't out of the realm of possibility. Of course that didn't explain him not answering the phone. The ringing would've woken him up. "Dr. Schneider?" Carter said in a voice a touch louder than a whisper as he approached the office. "You here?"

We stepped around his door and found his small office empty. The glow was a combination of a small desk lamp and the screen saver on his computer, a series of slides featuring ocean mammals. I bet that was a Christmas present someone gave him one year, thinking it was the 'perfect thing' for that old nerdy uncle that didn't quite fit in at the family gathering.

"Where could he be?" Carter asked, not really intending for me to answer.

I offered some suggestions anyway. "The library? The university? Some kind of lab? Home? Lunch?"

I guess I had lunch on the brain, since I was whisked away at lunch break before I had a chance to eat. A grumble from my stomach punctuated that thought.

Carter poked around Dr. Schneider's desk as if looking for a note. "No. He would've answered his cell phone. Something's happened." He lifted his eyes to me sharply and then out the office door to the tanks. "You don't think…"

Pushing past me, he practically ran toward the mermaid's tank.

"What is it, Carter?" I asked, chasing after him. "You think something's happened to the mermaid? The place doesn't look like anyone broke in. It looks just like we left it."

"No it doesn't."

Carter was right. The large tank was farthest from the bleak light of the windows, and in a pretty dark corner, but now that I was paying attention I could clearly see that the moldy blankets had been removed. The tank was inky dark, and I didn't detect any motion from inside as we got closer. Dread ripped through me. I slowed down, not really wanting to see if the mermaid was floating lifeless at the top.

"June," Carter said over his shoulder. "Catch that light switch over on the wall next to the cabinet, will you? I can't see enough."

I brushed the light switch on the wall and set the room awash in florescent light and winced at the brightness.

Carter cussed and banged the glass. Not quite the reaction I'd expect if the mermaid had died. I dared to look. The mermaid wasn't floating at the top or sunk at the bottom. She was simply gone. The tank was empty.

"Where is she?" I asked.

"How the Hell would I know where she is?"

"Maybe she's dead," I said. "Maybe Dr. Schneider put her with the other mermaid bodies."

"Yeah, maybe," Carter said. He moved to the back examination room, a walled-off room in the far back corner of the facility. I hadn't dared to go into that room yesterday because I really didn't want to see the dead bodies or how they were being kept. But now I followed Carter because I had to know. Every step I took felt so heavy. My heart hurt, and my body felt really tired all of a sudden. The grief that overwhelmed me made me want to cry so badly, but I fought it off with a good solid bite on my lower lip.

We stepped into the room and Carter let out another couple expletives. I understood why. There, along the wall was a large empty tank about six feet long and four feet high. It was empty save for a lot of ice water.

"Is that where they were being kept?" I asked, gagging at the rotten fish smell coming off of the dirty salt water.

Carter nodded and started pacing the floor. "There's no water on the floor, so it had to have dried up. The ice is mostly melted. They were taken out of here hours ago. Nothing's really been moved out of place, and the locks weren't damaged. It doesn't look like anyone broke in here. Dr. Schneider must've just let them in."

"Let who in? Carter, do you think someone stole the mermaids?"

He shot me a look that froze my blood. "This is all your fault."

"My fault? Because of the video?"

"Someone found out they were here. Someone came and took them."

"My video didn't say anything about where we took the mermaids."

"No," he answered, "but this is the closest facility to Grayland Beach, which was mentioned. You don't have to be a genius to figure it out. I'm kind of surprised there isn't a crowd out front banging the doors down for a peek."

"Oh come on, Carter," I said. "You're being a little ridiculous. It's just a stupid video that no one is going to take seriously. Maybe Dr. Schneider just moved them somewhere else. Maybe he decided to dissect them after all."

"Where?" Carter shouted. "This is his lab. Where else would he have taken them?"

"Well, where is he now?" I asked. "Surely, if someone stole the mermaids out of here he'd still be here. He'd have called you. The police would be here."

"Maybe whoever took the mermaids took him as well," Carter suggested. "Maybe they..." He stopped himself and shook his head.

"What? Maybe they killed him? Is that what you think?" I grabbed his shoulder. "Who would have done that? That's kind of crazy."

But a part of me knew it wasn't. I thought of the fear I felt when Mom's call from Alaska came early the morning before. Hadn't I been afraid that Affron thugs would have done the very same thing to her for nosing into their business? It didn't happen, though. She was fine. So, my worries weren't founded. Surely Affron didn't really have thugs. That was just TV stuff.

Carter shrugged me off and ran his hands through his blond hair and clenched it with his fists, his eyes closed tightly. "Think. Think. Where could they be?"

"The computer," I said, the thought popping out of my mouth the moment I had it. "It's still on. The lights are out, the door was locked, but the computer was still on. He left, planning to come back."

"That doesn't mean anything. They could've come so early this morning he hadn't even opened up the place yet and turned the lights on. I'll bet you ten to one that Dr. S. slept here last night in that office. He has before."

I threw up my hands in defeat, and that's when I realized my right hand was still clutching all the mail I'd picked up on my way in. I hadn't taken a moment to put it down yet.

"What's that?" Carter said, pointing at the mail.

"Nothing. Mail for the Center, I guess."

"No, that one, right there." He grabbed one of the envelopes out of my hand. "From Affron."

"What?" I grabbed it right back. Sure enough, the envelope had the Affron logo on the return address corner. "What's this about?" Carter plucked it from my hands once more and opened it. "Are you going to get in trouble for that?"

"I work here, right?"

"I guess so." I really wasn't sure if being an intern gave him the right to open Dr. Schneider's mail, but I also really wanted to know what was inside.

He pulled out a two page, three-fold application. "It's for a grant. Some kind of research grant." He showed it to me. At the top of the form was the Affron logo and their feel-good motto: *We Make the World Better*.

"Why would he have a grant application from Affron of all places?" I asked, thinking maybe I needed to call my dad. This was his area of expertise.

Carter gestured to all the equipment around us. "This place is run on grants. It couldn't operate without donations and grants. The government puts a tiny amount into it, and there is some funding from the University, but otherwise it's all grant money. Dr. S. does a lot of the grant writing himself, and he was going to teach me how to do it too."

"But Affron? That's kind of contradictory, don't you think?"

After giving the application another quick look over, Carter strode out of the examination room and back to Dr. Schneider's office. I really wanted to bolt to the back door just for a whiff of fresh air. My head was getting pretty dizzy from the odor in this place, but I stuck close. Once in Dr. Schneider's office, I grabbed a tissue from a box on the shelf behind his desk and put it to my face to help me breathe something that wasn't so foul. Carter moved the mouse around until the desktop showed up. He started opening folders and poking around.

"What are you looking for?" I asked.

He didn't answer. Instead he told me to look through the office drawers and files to see if I found anything else that was from Affron.

"But why?"

Carter looked at me right then like I was an idiot. "It's kind of weird timing, isn't it?" he asked. "A research grant application from Affron? The day after we find mermaids on the beach? The morning after a couple fake rescue team workers from Affron show up at our door with animals that clearly weren't in the oil spill? Do you see the coincidence?"

"But this came in the mail, Carter," I said. "Snail mail. Take-a-couple-days-to-get-here-mail."

"Not if it was mailed from nearby and, say, yesterday morning." He went back to opening files.

"Does Affron have an office in Washington?" I asked. I opened the top drawer of a metal filing cabinet in the corner.

"Oh, probably something in Seattle," he said. "That would make sense. I know they have some kind of outfit up in Vancouver. That's not exactly far from here. Just a couple hours." He clicked the mouse. "Here's something! Oh. Never mind."

I flipped through file folders with tabs that held no meaning for me but apparently meant a lot to Dr. Schneider because each folder held a lot of paper. It was hard to get to the back ones. "So, you think that Dr. Schneider called Affron yesterday morning after we dropped off the mermaids and asked for a grant to research them?"

"Yeah," Carter said. "Something like that. I think those guys that came last night knew about the mermaids and would have taken them then if we hadn't been there. So, they came back after we were gone."

"Dr. Schneider doesn't seem like he would do that," I said.

"Yeah, that's what I thought too," Carter replied. "I've always respected him. Until today."

I opened the second drawer down and found what I was looking for: a tab marked "Grants and Donations". I pulled it out and found copies of applications, letters, and check stubs from various grants. They weren't in any particular order, and as I went through them I found ones dated as far back as five years and some as recent as a few months ago. Every time I saw the Affron logo I pulled it aside. By the time I was done I had at least fifteen check stubs from Affron. A quick estimation in my head had them donating close to $250,000 to this institution over the past several years. I handed the stack to Carter who was in the middle of trying different possible passwords to open Dr. Schneider's email.

"Looks like Affron is our main benefactor," he said.

"Looks that way," I agreed. "Dad's gonna be pissed when he hears about this."

"You think?"

"He would have never used this facility if he'd known."

"He didn't have a choice."

"I should call him."

"Please don't." That voice came from Dr. Schneider's office door. We both looked up to see the skinny old man standing there. Neither of us had heard him enter the building. He was still in yesterday's clothes. His glasses exaggerated the deep purple bags under his eyes. And I think he was shaking a little, like he had Palsy. "Juniper, please don't call your father. I've had enough humiliation for one day. I know what you two must think of me."

"We're not sure what to think, sir," I said. "We've gone back and forth from wondering if you were kidnapped or killed to being the thief who organized it all."

"Oh, I was hardly any of that," he said, weakly moving into the office and lowering himself into the cushioned reading chair by the bookshelf. "I am far too unimportant for any of that."

"So what *did* happen here?" Carter asked. "You haven't been answering your phone. I had to come down to see for myself."

"Is that what you're doing on my computer?" Dr. Schneider asked, pointing at the screen.

Carter didn't bother to apologize for their invasion of the scientist's office. He only spoke in icy tones that betrayed his distrust of the man. "Just trying to understand a few things." With a click from his right finger, he closed the web service.

I moved my left arm slightly to cover the Affron grant pay stubs. He didn't need to know that I'd been snooping though his file cabinets just yet.

"You won't find anything there," Dr. Schneider said. "It was all by phone."

We stared at him until he went on. "You want to know about the mermaids? Well, go ahead. Ask me." He crossed his arms and readied himself for our attack.

Ask him? I didn't get it. Why was he being so cavalier? Was he proud of himself that the mermaids were in Affron's oily hands? At least he wasn't smiling. I'd have slugged him in the jaw.

Carter continued to do the talking, which was fine with me. I had nothing productive to say to the man. "So, what happened?" His tone left no room for sympathy. He expected to be told the truth by Dr. Schneider, and he didn't expect to like it.

Neither did I.

Dr. Schneider let out a long sigh. "Everything that has happened here is my fault."

I shot a look to Carter that related only one thought: *Duh*!

"I called the president of the Board of Directors for the Sea Mammal Rescue Center yesterday morning. These seven people make all the decisions regarding how funds are to be used and which projects are going to take priority. Very little of what happens around here is up to me." He fidgeted with the pen in his lab coat pocket. "I had to call them regardless to let them know about how the oil spill affected us and that we were full up with rehabilitation cases."

"You didn't have to tell them about the mermaids," Carter said.

"Not yet. Not until we'd learned more about them."

Dr. Schneider grimaced. "I didn't. Not exactly. I told them we had an extraordinary find that would require more research. I suggested that if they could arrange the funding, I could triple my efforts to learn about our discovery." He paused, then added, "I could have been the one to declare what these creatures were with definitive testing results. I could have…" He raised his hands to his face and pushed his fingers under his glasses to rub his eyes. "I could have been a pioneer."

"Those men last night?" Carter urged him on.

"They *were* from Affron," Dr. Schneider said. "They weren't who they said they were. I could tell that as well as you. I thought they were sent to find out what my discovery was, but I didn't think they knew exactly what they were looking for. I assumed they were just making sure I wasn't trying to fraud Affron into grant money I didn't need. And we had nothing 'unusual' here last night that they could see, did we? It was all very awkward for me."

"Did you call them back after we left?" Carter asked. The accusation in his tone was clear. "Is that what happened?"

"I don't know what happened, Carter. Honestly. I was here all night studying and I fell asleep on my desk. I woke up to banging on the door. It was those same men. I let them in and they went straight to our mermaid's tank and ripped down the tarps. Within moments they hauled her and the mermaid cadavers out of here without saying one word to me."

I couldn't take this any longer. "Why aren't you with them, then? Why aren't you wherever they took the mermaids and testing them and becoming famous like you wanted?"

"I don't know where they are," he said, burying his head in his hands. "I chased after them, but I lost them about forty miles up the highway." He clenched his jaw and looked almost like he would snarl. "I don't have anything. I didn't get a chance to take pictures of her. I don't have any lab results. I don't have a single thing that suggests that she ever existed." He shook his head. "I swear that I never mentioned to anyone that we had discovered mermaids. I don't know how they figured it out."

"I do," Carter said, the ice from his gaze cutting through me. "And there is evidence, thanks to June and her father doing some taping at the beach when they found the mermaids."

I could sense the relief flowing back into Dr. Schneider as he realized that this fiasco wasn't completely his fault. The guilt transferred to me. I didn't want to deal with it, so I nearly shouted, "So, how do we find them?"

"They work for Affron," Carter said. "We figured out that much."

"But why would they want the mermaids? Where would they take them?"

Dr. Schneider stood up and nudged me aside so he could reach the computer mouse. "It could be any number of places. Affron gives funding to every marine facility from Monterey, California to Valdez, Alaska. Their way of 'giving back to the community' as they put it." He opened the Internet and went to a site all about Affron's philanthropic deeds. Their motto 'We Make the World Better' scrolled across the page accompanied by some pretty classical music.

"Guilt money," I griped. "They ruin our oceans and then put money into the rehab centers to make it look like they care. With promotion like this, Affron lets all the people know that they are the good guys who work very hard to take care of the environment. They back up their slogan by putting money into aquariums like this one. This way, no one can say they're lying. That's why they're always the first to show up at major oil spills, too. Oh, my parents are going to have a field day with this."

Dr. Schneider went to a link on the site that had a map of all the marine centers supported by Affron money. Along the Atlantic shore of the United States there were only a couple. Only one in Hawaii. However, from Northern California to Alaska there were about twenty-five.

Carter pulled out his cell phone and opened up the video link he'd saved there and played back my mermaid video. I glanced back and forth from the video to the dots on the map on Dr. Schneider's computer screen. "Or there could be another reason Affron always shows up first."

A chill ran through me. They knew.

Affron knew about the mermaids all along.

Chapter Eleven

"I have to go," I told Carter and Dr. Schneider. Before they could open their mouths to argue, I was up and heading for the door. "Carter, can you give me a ride home?"

"We're kind of in the middle of a discussion here, June," he said, gesturing to the computer.

"There's nothing else to discuss here," I said, heading out the office door.

Carter pushed back from the desk and followed me. "I think there is."

I stopped and looked him dead in the eye. "Affron knows about the mermaids. I'm sure of it. I'll bet they discovered them long before we did." I turned to Dr. Schneider who was standing in his office doorway wringing his hands. "Those men last night weren't here to check you out for grant fraud. They were looking for the mermaid. They knew exactly what we had and where we had her. My video only made them move faster so they could snatch up the mermaids before anyone else had a chance to see them. I'll bet the next move is to prove that you never saw them, Dr. Schneider. You said yourself you had no evidence. And then they'll figure out how to prove my video is a fake."

I started toward the double doors again. Carter reached out and grabbed my arm. "But why? Why would they do all that?"

"Because my mom is right. If people, ordinary people, knew that there were real mermaids swimming around in the Pacific Ocean, they wouldn't allow Affron to continue leaking oil in the ocean. People will finally stand up against them."

"Why do you think it would make a difference?" Carter said. "Polar bears, whales, sea otters... I could go on. The slow extinction of those beautiful creatures hasn't stirred that kind of reaction."

"They don't look like people," Dr. Schneider said. "The mermaids are very humanesque in their upper torsos and face. Human looking enough to stir the mind into thinking they are like us. They are also mythological, and the human race will go to extremes to discover and protect a find such as that. And what if we can prove that the mermaids can communicate? People will want to know how many mermaids exist. Are there male as well as female mermaids? Where do they live? Are there cities under the oceans? Are the mermaids immortal? Could they have existed since the age of the Ancient Greeks? If so, does that mean that the Greek gods are also in existence—or that other mythological creatures exist? What impact could that have on the religions of the world and our existence on this planet?"

"You've thought a lot about this," Carter said to the scientist.

"Up all night."

Okay, that was taking it a bit further than my brain could handle at the moment. But it sounded right. I only nodded and said, "So, are you going to drive me or not?"

"Where are we going?"

"My house. We're going to let the secret out and make Affron scramble."

"I don't understand," Carter said. "Don't you want to help find them?"

"Yes," I answered. "I'm going to make that *his* job." I pointed at Dr. Schneider. The way his neck stiffened I could tell he didn't like being told what to do by a seventeen-year-old girl, or by anyone for that matter. "Dr. Schneider, you need to figure out where Affron might have taken the mermaids."

"I don't know how," he almost whined. "I used up my cell phone battery trying to get through to someone at Affron to find out who those men were and what department they were with. No one over there could help me. No one seems to know anything."

Carter took his keys out of his pocket and tossed them up and down in his right hand. "Which direction did they go this morning?"

Dr. Schneider shrugged. "North. I lost them."

"Yeah," Carter said slowly. "After forty miles you said. That would have taken about half an hour. What have you been doing since then?"

A good question. I hadn't thought about that. I took a step back toward Carter.

"I followed them to the freeway, but once they got on the 5 I couldn't keep up," the scientist said. "Then I kept driving for a while, hoping I'd see them at a gas station or something. I drove quite a ways. Finally, I realized I was being ridiculous and pulled over and got on the phone. I was on the phone for a while, being put on hold over and over again. When my phone died I started back."

I bought it, but I wasn't sure Carter did. His lips were pressed tightly together, like he was trying not to say anything. I spoke for him. "So, you know they went north. That's a starting place. The mermaid can't survive long without being in a good-size tank, so unless they wanted her to die, they had to have taken her someplace not too far away."

"I'll look into our options," Dr. Schneider said.

Carter raised his cell phone out of his pocket and waved it. "Charge your phone and please answer it when I call." With a dismissive nod and a wave, Dr. Schneider pulled out his own phone and wiggled it in response before turning his back on us and sitting down at his desk. Satisfied, Carter tapped my shoulder and led me out the door.

After a quick stop at the drive-thru, we were on our way back to Olympia. Carter practically devoured his burger in one bite, wiped his mouth and then said, "So what's your big plan?" I was a bit preoccupied with texting a message to Haley and took a moment to answer him.

"Hello."

"Sorry," I said, putting down my phone and grabbing a couple fries. "I'm trying to get Haley to meet me at my house."

"Not Haley again," he moaned. "Hasn't she caused enough damage? You need to get rid of her sorry butt."

"No, you don't understand," I said.

"I understand that she's not cool. That's all there is to it."

"She's my best friend."

He shrugged as if to say that made no difference to him at all, but he didn't say anything. He kept his eyes on the traffic, his right hand on the wheel while his left arm rested on the door.

"She made a mistake, okay?" I said. "She didn't get what was going on here. But she's a good person. Plus, she's the one who can help me do what I want to do."

"What is that exactly?"

"I'm going to improve the video and get even more attention to it."

Carter swerved into another lane to avoid running up the bumper of the car in front of us. My drink tipped a bit into my lap, but I saved it in time. "Why?"

While I dabbed at my jeans with a couple napkins, I reminded Carter about the phone conversation I'd had with my mom at his house the morning before and what my mom had suggested about releasing the video so people could know about the mermaids.

"You heard all that, right?" He nodded at me, so I went on while I freed my French fries from the bag so I could shove the soggy napkins in there instead. "I thought she was wrong, jumping the gun, but now I think she was right on the money. I've got to make a splash with what we know. National. International. People have got to know what we know."

Carter reached over and grabbed the paper bag out of my hand and tossed it over his shoulder into the back seat, uncaring of where it landed. Then he took my hand and lowered it to my knee gently and held it there. His hands were remarkably warm compared to mine, and the touch was soothing to my tense nerves. "Breathe, June," he said. "Calm down a second."

I did as he suggested, allowing air to pull in through my nose and fill my lungs. I took three long breaths before taking my free right hand and placing it over his, making a hand sandwich.

He waited a moment for me to collect myself before speaking again. "You need to think this stuff through. You're being impulsive."

"I really don't have time to think this through," I told him. "I've got to act now while there's still oil on the beach. If I wait, the oil will be cleaned up and no one out there will relate this discovery with the problem. We need to get Affron in the spotlight."

Carter laughed then. It wasn't an outright guffaw like he was making fun of me, but it had a teasing tone to it. "Little Miss Activist. You really are the product of your parents, aren't you?"

"No, I'm not!" I barked back too quickly.

"Wow," he said, pulling his hand back to the wheel. "Touched a sore spot, did I?"

Heat flushed my face. Anger? Embarrassment. I didn't want to talk about the fact that despite everything going on at the moment, I still had this nasty gut reaction at the mention of my parents' work. You'd think I could be a little more mature, especially as I was up to my eyeballs in activism at the moment. But no. At the slightest comment that I might be anything like my parents, who were nearly psychotic with their activist movements, I turned right back into one of those brainless teenage girls Carter had said didn't interest him.

Whatever tender moment had been building a moment ago between us was now lost. After a minute of silence, Carter turned on the radio, and we listened to classic rock the rest of the way.

He didn't cut the engine when he pulled into my driveway. As I opened my door to get out, Carter sighed and asked, "Do you want any help?"

I didn't. Not really. I had Haley for that. However, my impulse was to say yes. Even if there was nothing for him to do, I would have liked him stay with me.

"Thanks. No," I answered instead. "I'll call you later and tell you how things are going."

"I guess that'll have to do," Carter said. He turned up the radio volume and didn't even say goodbye. I closed the car door and stood on the front path and watched him drive away.

I was blowing it right and left with him. How many more things could I say and do wrong? If I waved my arms at him and signaled for him to come back, I might have been able to fix this. I could tell him I was sorry. I'd say I was just in a 'mood' or really focused on what I had to do and not thinking. Maybe he'd understand and hold my hand again.

But I didn't wave him back. I just watched his car disappear around the corner, not knowing when or if I'd see him again.

Disappointed with myself, I went inside and dropped my backpack on the kitchen floor. I was glad my dad wasn't home, so he wouldn't get in my way as I worked. Knowing him, he'd want to take over and do it all himself. He was definitely not the "helpful hint" kind of dad. He was more like the "I'll take care of it, you can watch if you want" kind of dad.

Frankly, he'd really screw this one up since he knew nothing at all about computers, editing videos, or uploading them to the Internet. Thanks to him and Mom I knew next to nothing. They didn't put me in front of a computer much as a kid. Books, books, books, they preached all the time. God bless Haley and a couple good computer teachers in 7th and 8th grade. Without them, I'd still be living in the 1980's world my parents are stuck in.

My phone jingled, and my heart jumped. Was Carter texting to say he was coming back? I flipped the phone open, but the message wasn't from him. Haley wanted to know if I was home yet. I typed that she needed to come over already. I only had time to pop open a soda before she was at the door.

With Regina and Marlee in tow.

I put an arm around Haley and ushered her inside, closing the door on the other two. "I didn't tell you to bring them."

"They wanted to come."

"Haley!"

"Do you want me to tell them to leave?"

"Yes!" I said, but as I did Regina took it upon herself to open my front door and step inside. I should have locked it.

"That wasn't very hospitable," she said to me.

"So rude," Marlee agree, stepping in behind her best friend. She took a quick glance around my living room and sneered.

Right, I thought. *I'm the rude one.*

"Just go away," I said to Haley. "I'll do this without you."

Haley raised an eyebrow. "Really? Your text said you needed help editing the mermaid video. Do you have any idea how to do that?"

"No. But I'll figure it out."

Regina put out her hand for me to shake. I didn't take it. "Look, June," she said in a very even, non-chiding voice. It was the kind of voice that I guessed won her over with teachers and parents and made her so damn successful at school. "We really don't want to be a problem. I think the mermaids are very interesting. Truly. Finding them like you did really impresses me, and I want to help somehow. I mean this, I really do."

I studied her brown eyes and perfect eye shadow that she had to have redone recently because it was very fresh. Her gaze didn't waver. No sneer formed on her glossy lips. She actually seemed sincere. So, I took her hand and shook it.

"I'm in charge," I said. "What I say goes."

The other three nodded and then followed me up to my room where I promptly turned on my computer and opened the file with the mermaid video. I continued to buy their sincerity because there wasn't one single comment about the authentic American Indian quilts hung all over the walls. My grandmother and her sister made them, and my parents insisted I keep them up to remind me of my heritage. I imagined Regina and Marlee's rooms were covered with posters of celebrities. Or large mirrors. Regina and Marlee both probably had make-up tables and walk-in closets. They probably had pink desks with satin comforters on their beds, their own HD flat screen TVs and shelves of old Barbies they used to play with as girls but now just sat on display in fancy get-ups they wished they could wear. But instead of comparing or insulting, the two popular girls simply sat on the floor, leaning against my bed patiently until I was ready. Regina kept her eyes on Haley and me at the desk while Marlee grabbed a book from the bottom row of my bookshelf and read the back cover.

The size of the video on my screen was only about two inches square. Between that and the dark quality, it really was hard to tell for sure that these were pictures of mermaids and not just large fish. I told Haley that I wanted the picture brighter, with the mermaids enhanced so you could see them very well. I looked like Hell, but that part of the video couldn't be changed, unfortunately. She dickered with it for a moment and then raised her face to squint at me.

"Your computer sucks. You know that, right?"

I cocked my head. "Does that mean you can't do it?"

"Oh, I can do it," Haley said. "But not with this. Hold on."

She put up a finger signaling me to wait and then dashed out of the room. I glanced at Regina who just shrugged. "I'm not good with computers either," she said. "Do you have a pillow I could use?"

I handed her one off my bed and she plumped it and put it behind her. Other than that she didn't say anything else or move, choosing to inspect her nail polish. Marlee opened the book and flipped to the front page with a strange caution that made it look like she was afraid something might jump out at her. She squinted as she began to read and then her body visibly relaxed as she realized the book wasn't going to harm her. I plopped into my desk chair and tried to come up with something to say to break the awkward silence, but I couldn't think of anything nice. I figured Regina was pretty much in the same boat, so we just sat there with the uneasy tension between us until I heard my front door open again and Haley pounding up the stairs.

"Thank goodness," I heard Regina whisper a second before Haley reappeared at my bedroom doorway with her laptop in her arms.

"Ah ha!" Haley cheered. "Now we are armed and ready!"

I moved my own laptop out of the way and let her set up. It only took moments for her to pull up the video I had sent her last night and get to work. On her computer the picture was nearly full screen but for the tools on the side from the editing program she was using—an editing program I didn't have on my computer. Better than I hoped, she used her genius to brighten the color a touch and added a bit of contrast. Now, I could clearly see the bodies and tails of the creatures. I warned Haley that I didn't want to adjust the picture too much. Then people might think the pictures were fakes. "They have to look genuine," I said.

"Yeah, naturally," Haley said with a nod, keeping at it until it looked just right.

As soon as the images looked clear enough, I tackled my dad's voice-over narration. The waves from the ocean and the shakiness of his voice made it really difficult to hear him. I wrote down what he said on a pad of paper, changed it ever so slightly for impact, and then re-recorded the narration myself into the video camera's microphone.

Regina raised her hand as soon as I was done, which I thought was pretty funny. Imagine, her asking permission to speak. I nodded for her to say whatever it was she had on her mind.

"I don't think it makes sense to hear your voice as the voice-over, when you are clearly the one on screen. That makes it look fake."

I hadn't thought about that. She was right. "What should we do, then?"

She cleared her throat. "Well, I am the captain of the debate team at school. I'm pretty good at speaking. Let me do it."

Haley shook her head, and Regina gave her a sharp "don't mess with me" look. Haley stopped and nodded instead. "Yeah, good idea."

I understood Haley's hesitation, though. "Yours is still a girl's voice. No one will know the difference if it's you or me talking. Plus, a lot of people have already heard my dad's voice on it."

Marlee looked up from the novel. "What about more of a narrator. You know how in books there's, like, a guy that tells everything in between what the characters are saying? What if Regina kind of says stuff in between your dad's voice-over, to, I don't know, make it clear what he's talking about?"

"We know how narration works, Marlee," Regina said to her friend. She offered a weak smile to me and said, "She's more of a magazine kind of girl."

Still, as convoluted as Marlee's suggestion was, it made sense to all of us. We worked out a few new statements and recorded Regina's voice. It pained me to admit it, but her speaking voice was way better than mine. Haley edited the new voice-over onto the video and then played the whole thing back for us.

It was perfect.

Piggy-backing on the WiFi from her house, Haley logged onto the Internet and in the time it would take me to type my name, she had it whizzing through cyberspace. Regina immediately popped up and opened her personal page and typed the new hyperlink on her wall with a note: "Updated and so much easier to see and understand. Everyone check it out and pass it on. Mermaids are real! Isn't that the coolest thing ever? ☺"

Okay, that was cheesy, but she had like eight hundred "friends", so right there we had a head start on our video going viral for the second time.

"All done," Regina said, logging off to be sure I couldn't hack her page.

I addressed Haley. "So, if I want to send that to someone specific, all I have to do is give them the link, right?"

"That's it," Haley said with a big grin.

"Awesome."

I thanked them all for coming and told Marlee she could borrow the book. It was nice to see her reading. It was kind of like watching a kid discover popcorn for the first time the way she flipped the pages with such enthusiasm. They wanted to stay and talk, but I told them I still had a lot more work to do.

"We can help," Regina said.

I smiled at her as politely as I could. "I'll call you if I think of anything for you to do."

"Okay," she said. Then she grabbed me up into a hug. In the bubbliest voice I've ever heard, she said, "Love you!"

"Uh, yeah," I said, pulling back away from her. "You too."

Haley gave me a more uncomfortable wave as she stepped outside, while Marlee tripped a little over the landing, refusing to look up from the book while she walked. Regina followed them out and I closed the door before they said or did anything else. I felt sure I'd hear from Haley again and that things were mended between us. I just wasn't sure we were best friends anymore. That, I suspected, was changed.

I went straight to my parents' office and turned on their computer. Next, I opened up the e-mail list of news correspondents. I wrote a quick press release with the link to the video and then CC'd all those addresses. All I had left to do was press "send".

I held off, though. I wanted to talk to my mother first.

My mom was still a little on edge with me at first; we still hadn't had time to talk things out. But when I told her what I was going to do, her enthusiasm jumped through the phone. "Push the button, June," she cried. "Do it right now. No hesitation."

"Mom," I said, my finger hovering over the "enter" key on the keyboard. "Are you sure this is the right thing? Could anything go wrong, do you think?"

"I don't see what could possibly go wrong," Mom answered. "Expose these Affron hypocrites and let the world know there are people who live in the ocean. This is your finest moment, June. I am so proud of you."

My mother was proud of me. I couldn't remember that last time my mom had said that. It always seemed like the other way around: I was rooting for my mom. "Go Mom, save the whales!" "That's it, Mom, rescue the owls!" "Right on, Mom, you saved that Redwood tree! You're so amazing!" What did I ever do that could make parents like mine proud?

Up until now—nothing.

I pressed send.

Chapter Twelve

The mermaid images zipped through cyberspace and opened on the desktops of over two thousand news editors across the United States. They went to the magazines, newspapers, major news, and some minor web sources, and all the television news channels. For good measure, I sent a couple more releases to places my parents wouldn't think of, like MTV, VH-1, TMZ, and Comedy Central. By the following morning you couldn't open your eyes without seeing some image from the video.

I'd already heard an earful from my dad when he got home from the beach all the way up until I went to bed (which I did early just to be done with him). He was ticked at my mom and me for making this decision and was "astounded" that we would be so "damn stupid". Well, this was a change: to have Mom's approval instead of Dad's. The world must have been tipped on its axis.

After a brief and unfulfilling text-only conversation with Haley, where she told me the video already had like 300,000 hits or something like that, I called my mom to say goodnight. She assured me one more time that I had done the right thing while I cried in her ear. "I'll be coming home tomorrow," she told me. "Be strong."

Dad never came back in to say he was sorry, but I heard him say as much into the phone when Mom called him right after I hung up. He hollered at her some more, loud enough for me to hear through both his and my closed bedroom doors. Eventually, though, he got quiet, and I drifted off to sleep.

He was up and gone when I woke up for school in the morning. He'd left the newspaper spread out on the kitchen table, the leading headline reading: LOCAL ACTIVISTS CLAIM TO HAVE

DISCOVERED REAL MERMAIDS. I read enough of the article to get that it was suggesting that we were trying to make a bigger deal out of the so-called oil spill by inventing a story to garner attention. It said something to the effect of, "Well known activist, Peter Sawfeather, has been known to stretch the truth on occasion to further his causes, and now he appears to be teaching his daughter to do the same." In another paragraph it let the reader know that photographic experts would be studying the video for any fakery. Basically, they thought it was all a hoax and we were nothing more than the weirdos that chase after Big Foot and the Loch Ness Monster. The article belittled all the work my dad really did as though it were nothing more than bellyaching.

I thought about calling Dad to see if he was okay, but Haley honked her horn from the street and I had to run.

When I got to school I was mobbed by students wanting me to sign their newspapers or printed web pages. All of them had questions about the mermaids and wanted to know which beach they should visit to see more of them. The biggest question of all, over and over again: "Where are they now?" Each time someone asked it, my stomach flipped. I didn't know, and I didn't know how to find out. My mermaid was probably dead.

Suddenly, Regina was at my side. She grabbed my hand. "Leave my friend alone," she said firmly to the crowd. "We will answer all your questions later. Right now, we have to get to class." Like Moses parting the Red Sea, I saw a corridor full of teenagers split down the center so Regina could lead me through and drop me at my Homeroom classroom door. "I'll come back in twenty to help you to 1st period, if you want." Haley was practically jumping up and down behind her with glee.

"Sure, thanks," I mumbled before slinking into my classroom and going straight to my desk to sit down. I put my forehead down on the cool, flat desk and closed my eyes for a second. The buzz of all those people talking at once calmed down, and I began to single out individual voices again. My teacher calling role up at the front of the room. The kid in the front row saying "here."

"Juniper Sawfeather."

Had my ears been that messed up? I swear my teacher suddenly sounded like she was right in front of me.

"Here," I said, lifting my head.

It hadn't been my teacher. Mrs. Slater stood to the side of me, a rolled up newspaper in one hand, smacking it against the other like she was deciding whether or not to hit me with it. "You missed the second half of school yesterday, Miss Sawfeather. Do you have an excuse?"

"No, Ma'am. At least not one you'd probably accept."

"Then come with me."

As I stood up and slung my backpack over my shoulder, I was careful to push my cell phone as far down to the bottom of the pack as my arm would reach. Let her work for it, I thought. A few stragglers paused to gawk at us in the hall. Mrs. Slater clapped her hands and hissed at them to get on to class. Each of them skittered into a room followed immediately by half a dozen heads popping back out to watch us head toward the front office.

As we rounded the corner into the front hall where the offices were located, Regina came practically skidding toward us from the other direction. "Mrs. Slater," she called. "Where are you taking June?"

"It's not your business, Regina," Mrs. Slater said, passing the school favorite right by without so much as a glance. "You'd do better to associate with other students. Not liars like this one."

"But Mrs. Slater," Regina said, keeping pace with us as we walked. "I need June to come with me. The Student Council and the Recycling Club are going from classroom to classroom to make presentations about the new rewards program we're starting on Monday."

"I don't know anything about that," Mrs. Slater said. "It's not on the calendar."

"We just planned it at our meeting two days ago, and we were so excited we wanted to get started right away."

Mrs. Slater stopped then and turned so abruptly on Regina I actually saw the girl lose her cool for a second and stumble backward. "Juniper Sawfeather is going to be doing an in-school suspension today and possibly all next week. Your presentations will have to wait."

"But Mrs. Slater, it's such a good cause…"

"Another week of soda cans in the trash won't bring about the end of the world any sooner, Regina. Go to class. Now."

Regina flashed the sorriest look at me that I've ever seen. I gave her a weak smile to thank her for trying. Mrs. Slater put a firm hand on my back and led me toward the office. She sat me down at a skinny, rickety old school desk that was stowed by the file cabinet behind the reception area and informed me that my classwork would be gathered and brought to me.

"If I so much as see you touch your cell phone, you'll never see it again. Is that clear?" she asked. I nodded, glad I'd put the thing on silent because I could feel it buzzing through the canvas of my backpack against my leg. I hoped it was just Haley trying to find out what was going on and not Carter or my dad trying to reach me for something vital.

I'd seen so many kids stuck at this very desk over the past three years. They were always the kind you'd expect, I guess. Troubled kids with stringy hair, tough bullies who barely fit, trampy girls who had their bra straps showing, and occasionally a skinny Freshman just choosing to hide out for a bit. Never did I look at one of those kids and wonder what it would be like to be them. The times when I'd popped into the office because I was late for school or turning in the attendance for a teacher, or something like that, I would see those kids and figure they deserved to be there for whatever stupid thing they had done. It had never occurred to me that some of them might not have done anything wrong and were being forced to sit there for no other reason than being on the nerves of that crazy woman. And I never, not once, thought that I would be sitting in this chair.

It was going to look so bad on my college transcripts.

I slunk as deep in that uncomfortable wooden seat as I could and sulked. I didn't try very hard to get my class work done with any hurry or accuracy. Mostly, I just doodled in the margins and tapped a pencil on my books, which were full of blurry paragraphs. I couldn't help it. My attention was seriously being tested because the phones in the front office rang off the hook. Mrs. Campbell, the school secretary, and the Mom-volunteer-of-the-day receptionist could barely catch their breath for answering them. From what I could tell, a handful of the calls were regular school business: a kid getting called out for an appointment, someone had the flu, the paper order was running late, blah blah blah. The rest of the time, though, the calls were all about me.

At first all I noticed was how their eyes kept shifting to me as they talked on the phone. Then I started to really listen to what they were saying.

"She's in class right now, ma'am."

"No sir, we can't get her out of class for an interview."

"She's going to be busy until 3:00."

"We have no information for you about that. You'll have to talk to her parents."

"No, you absolutely may not come here and find her."

"A press badge does not give you the right to interrupt her education."

And on it went until right before lunch when one reporter was tired of getting the brush off and barged through the front door with a cameraman right behind him. I recognized him from the Channel 4 News but couldn't think of his name. He was pretty decent as reporters go. My dad often sent him releases, and this guy actually reported it once in a while.

"I am Juarez Peña, correspondent for Channel 4 News, and I am looking for Juniper Sawfeather." That was it, the guy with two last names. I used to laugh at that when he came on the news, and my parents would bark at me for making too much noise when they were trying to watch.

I smiled at him, but Mrs. Campbell rushed at him, waving her arms like a maniac at the camera, so he didn't notice me.

"Out! Out!" she screeched. "The news camera needs to be off the school property. I told you on the phone that Juniper Sawfeather is in class."

"I know what you told me," he said, "but I need to talk to her now before anyone else gets to her. And don't try sending someone else. There's already a blonde girl out on the front steps giving interviews to everyone like she knows something, but she's not the girl who found the mermaid. I need Miss Sawfeather."

I stood up. "What blonde kid? Regina?"

Peña waved me off, "Yeah, I think that was her name. Says she's the voice you hear on the video. Who cares about that? I want the face."

"She can't do that!" I said, digging through my backpack to find my phone. "She has no business talking to reporters."

"That's what I say," Peña agreed. Then he turned back to Mrs. Campbell, "So, what's it going to be? Call her out of class, or my team is going from room to room looking for her." He pointed at the door, and the camera guy swiveled as though he were going to take off running.

"Hold it! Hang on!" Mrs. Campbell was frantic. "Wait!"

That was finally enough noise to pull Mrs. Slater out of her office. Naturally, her beady eyes went straight to me and not to the actual problem. And, of course, right at that moment I had freed my phone and had it square in front of my nose.

"Juniper Sawfeather, I said no cell phone! Hand it over!" She put out her hand.

Juarez Peña's head snapped so fast I'm surprised he didn't get a crick in his neck. He leapt over the receptionist's desk and got to Mrs. Slater's side before she had a chance to put together what was going on. "Did you say Juniper Sawfeather? Is THIS Juniper Sawfeather?" Then he took in my long, black hair and dark complexion. "Of course you are. Who else would you be?" He leaned in to me and handed me a business card. "You are the spitting image of your father. He's a friend of mine."

Sort of, I amended in my head.

"Yeah, I'm Juniper…" I tried to get out before Mrs. Slater's hand popped on top of my lips to stop any further noise.

"That is none of your concern, and may I add that you are trespassing."

Peña snapped at the cameraman, who had to maneuver around the furniture rather than leap like a gazelle. His camera was on his shoulder, the red light on.

"Miss Sawfeather, the video suggests that you found the mermaids at Grayland Beach, is that correct? If so, where are the mermaids now?"

Mrs. Slater stepped between Peña and the cameraman, so the back of her spiky hairdo filled the shot. "There is no point in interviewing her, Mr. Peña. She is a liar. This mermaid story of hers is just a trick and a lie and nothing you need to report. She is suspended for truancy, and you will have to go find another ridiculous tale to chase somewhere else."

Peña nodded at the imposing woman, but he didn't budge. He simply asked me, in a quieter voice that gave me the impression that he as a person, not a reporter, really wanted to know, "Are they real? Is this a lie?"

"Mr. Peña!" Mrs. Slater bellowed. "You will leave now or I will call the police! Mrs. Campbell, get the police on the phone. I want all the reporters off the school property now."

He started to back up, but he kept his face toward me as he moved. A huge smile crossed his face. Although I didn't answer him, something about my expression must have convinced him, because he looked so excited his eyes were slightly teary. "I knew it. I just knew it." Mrs. Slater pushed him toward the door, but he poked his head in one last time to say, "When you get out of school, call me at Channel 4 News. We'll give you and your parents an exclusive!" Mrs. Slater slammed the door so fast it nearly cut off Peña's fingers.

Mrs. Campbell held the receiver up toward Mrs. Slater. "I've got the police on the phone. What do you want me to tell them?"

"To get their butts over here and get these reporters off our front steps." She turned to the poor volunteer mom, who actually flinched as though the Vice Principal might strike her. "And would you get Regina in here. I am about done with her. I don't care how popular she thinks she is, she does not get to break school rules just for a chance to be on TV." The poor little woman hustled out of the front office without a word.

"The policeman says that they can move the reporters off the steps, but all they'll do is stand in the street out front, which is public property, and obstruct traffic. He says the best thing to do is to just let Juniper go out there and talk to them and get it over with."

"Give me that phone," Mrs. Slater said, grabbing it from the meek lady's hand. She immediately began yelling at the poor dispatch person. I used that moment to sit back in my tiny desk and pop off a text to my dad about what was going on and added the warning that I might lose my phone at any minute.

A burst of noise exploded in the hallway of the school so loud it penetrated the glass walls of the office as the doors opened. In walked the volunteer, Regina, and Principal Mains. The principal patted the air in front of them for the reporters to calm down and then closed the door behind him. A moment later he stepped into the front office.

"What is going on out there?"

Mrs. Slater hung up the phone. "I have the police coming."

He noticed me in the back corner and then said to Mrs. Campbell, ignoring the Vice Principal, "Would you call the parents of these girls please? They need to come and escort their daughters out of here and decide what they are going to do about all this press outside."

I stood up and cleared my throat. "My mom's probably on a plane, and my dad's probably in the middle of his own mess at the beach. Could someone else pick me up and take me to him?"

Mr. Mains's forehead creased as he considered that.

"I've got my own car," Regina said.

"You two will never get to it," he said. He paused for a moment as he considered the problem. "Let's get one of your friends who has a car here to go get it and meet you both at the cafeteria entrance. I'll escort you there, and you should be able to get out without too much attention. Call me when you are clear of the building, so I can do something about these vultures outside."

"But Mr. Mains..." Mrs. Slater said. "I've got Miss Sawfeather under suspension."

His eyes grew wide with anger. "You what? For what?"

"Truancy."

He sighed and ran a hand through his thick brown hair. Mr. Mains was young for a high school principal, probably ten years younger than Mrs. Slater, at least. As fake as she was with her spiky dyed hair, he was all natural. He had a touch of gray around his sideburns and in his eyebrows, and wore tweed blazers with Dockers instead of suits. Everyone liked him because he used to be a school therapist before going into administration and he was known to be really fair. Like right now.

"You do know *why* Juniper has been out of school, right?" he asked. "It's been in the news."

"You don't believe any of that hogwash, do you?" she asked, her hands on her plump hips, talking up to the tall man like a fourth grader with attitude.

He raised an eyebrow at her. "It doesn't matter if I believe in mermaids or not. I do believe there was an oil spill, however, and if her family needs her to help with the ramifications of that I see no reason to prevent her from doing her part. Both of these ladies are Honors students. I'm not exactly worried about them falling behind." He leaned over to put his face right in front of hers and said in a very low voice, "And if you haven't noticed, all of those reporters out there believe at least something about her story. Our students can't safely exit this building until those folks are gone."

"Yes sir," she responded, her eyes nearly slits. I imagined she'd be throwing darts at a picture of him after hours as she drank gin and tonics and wondered for the thousandth time why he got promoted over her.

He took Mrs. Slater into his office where their argument continued for a few minutes. Only her voice carried through the door, though, because his was so calm and collected compared to hers. While they went round and round about school policy, we had Mrs. Campbell page Haley to come to the school cafeteria. She would be able to get to her car without drawing any attention from the press. Mrs. Campbell ran down there to meet her and tell her the plan.

Mr. Mains emerged from his office and wiped his hands together as if washing off something nasty. Behind him, Mrs. Slater was so red in the face I thought she might explode. The phone rang, and the poor little volunteer mom picked it up.

"Hello? Um, no. She's in class at the moment. We aren't allowing any reporters…" Mrs. Slater grabbed the receiver and slammed it down on the base. Mr. Mains shot her a warning look, and she stared right back at him with some serious contempt.

I felt kind of bad about being responsible for the drama happening between them and hoped that it would boil over soon, but I had a feeling this rift was about more than just me. It kind of looked like this wouldn't end until one of them was fired or dead.

Mr. Mains guided Regina and I out of the front office away from the staring reporters at the windows and down the hall toward the cafeteria. Five minutes later we were driving down the road in Haley's car and laughing so hard we could barely breathe. Haley had to pull over into the mini-mall parking lot until we calmed down.

"So what do we do now?" Haley asked, through her subsiding giggles. She turned her head to me for an answer. Regina leaned forward between the seats and expected an answer from me too. Suddenly it wasn't all that funny anymore. My heart thumped in my chest like I'd forgotten my lines in a play. I really didn't know what to do next.

Chapter Thirteen

We all got out our cell phones and got busy. Haley called the school to let them know we were safely away from campus. Regina texted Marlee, Gary, and Ted and told them to ditch school at lunchtime and meet at her house. "Well, you can't go to your house," she explained to me when I asked what she was doing. "The press will be waiting for you there."

I ignored her for the moment and called my dad. He said the same thing as Regina about going home. He didn't want me there without him and mom. "Are you coming home then?" I asked him.

"I can't," he said. "The beach is packed with people. I have to try to keep them away from the water and the damage from the oil. I don't have enough help here at all."

"Do you want me to come there?" I asked.

"No. It looks like a storm is brewing, and I'm hoping that'll chase some of them indoors." He paused. "Can you get hold of Carter?"

"I don't think he's speaking to me right now."

"Oh, well, that's unfortunate. I could use him out here."

"I'll text him and see if he can join you." Regina and Haley were done with their calls, and the motor was still running on the car. I needed a plan. "Dad, we have to talk to the reporters at some point."

"I know," he grunted. "Your mom will be at the airport soon. Why don't you go to her office and meet her there?"

Regina didn't take the news that I wanted to be dropped off at my mom's office downtown very well. "Why can't we stay with you? I thought we were a team?"

"Look Regina, you've done enough already," I told her. "I don't know what you were saying to the reporters in front of the school, but you shouldn't have been out there at all. This really isn't your business."

"Oh, it's not, is it?" She got out of the car and slammed the door. Then she opened Haley's door and said, "Come on!"

Haley switched off the ignition and pulled her keys as Regina tugged her arm to get her out of the car. Before Regina slammed that door too, she said, "Get there on your own!" And they left me sitting in the passenger seat of Haley's car as they walked into the Espresso Café.

I sat for a moment, wondering if I should follow them inside, tell them I'd changed my mind, and invite them to be part of whatever was going to happen with my mom this afternoon. My mom's pretty imposing. They wouldn't get away with much in her presence. They'd probably be sorry they tagged along as they sat in the corner bored to death.

Only Mom was still on the edge with me, and I'd only just earned back a fraction of respect from her. I didn't want to test her patience. I didn't want to blow it again with her so soon. It would be better to come without the teenage sidekicks.

Plus, didn't Regina just set up for her whole entourage to meet her at home? I really didn't want Marlee, Gary, and Ted along as well. That would be popular kid overload, and my brain could explode from the weirdness of it all.

So, I got out of the car, slipped on my backpack and closed the door behind me. A beep of the car doors locking assured me that Haley was just on the other side of the darkened windows of the shop watching me. I walked away from the café toward the grocery store, not quite sure what to do now. I texted Carter my dad's request for assistance at the beach but didn't dare ask him to pick me up. I considered leaving a message for my mom to come get me after she landed, but that would be a long time from now, and the inconvenience would irritate her. In the store I grabbed a soda and a candy bar and walked up to the counter. When I reached into my pocket for some cash, I pulled out a business card.

Problem solved.

Ten minutes later I was seated in the Channel 4 News van beside Juarez Peña and his cameraman, one of those beefy bald guys with a goatee named Chuck Emory, who squatted behind our seats and kept his balance by holding both of our headrests. I think he refused to sit back in case he needed to grab his camera for a quick shot. Both of them grinned like they'd won some big prize, and Peña clobbered me with questions.

"I can't answer anything until my mom gets here," I told them several times. "I promise you that you will get the story first, but you'll have to wait."

At last it clicked that they weren't going to squeeze anything out of me, so Peña relaxed and just drove out of the parking lot. I saw Haley and Regina run out of the coffee house waving their cell phones to get my attention. I ignored them and turned my phone to silent.

Chuck finally settled back in his seat. I didn't hear a seatbelt click, though.

"I've wanted to meet your parents in person for a while," Peña said. "I'm very impressed by their work. Do you think your dad will join us?"

"He's pretty busy working."

"With the mermaids? And where would that be again?"

"Nice try."

Both of the men laughed, and then Peña gave a little sigh. "I give up," he said. "You want some lunch?"

We got some fast food, since we had time to spare, and he was very good about not asking me anything else about the mermaids or oil spill. Instead, he commented on my name. "Which tribe is Sawfeather?"

"Chinook," I answered. "A coastal tribe of the American Northwest. We are famous for our canoes and totem poles."

"Why canoes?" Chuck asked through a mouthful of hamburger. "What's interesting about that?"

Before I could answer, Peña spoke up. "Most of the American Indian tribes in this region were whalers. They made canoes out of cedar wood and rowed them into the ocean to kill orcas."

I nodded. "That's right. How did you know that?"

Peña smiled. "I'm part American Indian too. The Lummi of the San Juan Islands."

"Really?" I couldn't believe it. "Your name is Spanish though. Double Spanish actually, since you have two last names."

He laughed. "I know. I still haven't forgiven my mother for that. She

134

insisted that her maiden name be my first name. But yeah, my Spanish ancestors invaded Washington, and it was common for many of the men to take American Indian wives because they were the only women in the region. So, way down deep, I still have some of that heritage, and I've made it a point to learn about it."

"Interesting," I commented before taking a long drink from my soda. Wow, I really didn't want to get this guy and my dad together in a room. It would be blah, blah, blah city.

Chuck waved his right hand as if to erase all of the family history stuff away and get back to what was more interesting to him. "Are you saying they tried to kill killer whales from canoes? Were they crazy?"

"No," both Peña and I said almost too defensively.

"It was dangerous, to be sure," Peña said, "but they had no choice. They needed the meat and blubber."

I tried to suppress the thought as it came to me, but it blurted out anyway: "My dad tells this old story about killer whales and a mermaid."

"Oh!" Peña cried out. "Is it the legend of the American Indian fisherman who was thrown overboard and instead of drowning was magically transformed into a killer whale? I love that story!" He leaned across the little yellow table toward Chuck. "They say that's why there are so many orcas in the straits of Georgia and Juan de Fuca around the islands. One of the islands is even named Orcas, and there are sightings all the time."

"Sounds like a day trip is in my future," Chuck said. "If I ever get a day off."

Peña waved a French fry at him like a teacher with a pointer. "The best time to go is in August for the Potlatch."

"Pot Luck?" He grinned madly. "I'm in for that!" He ate his second hamburger.

"No, the *Potlatch*." Peña corrected. "It was an old tradition when all the tribes of that region would get together to celebrate the peace between them by making offerings to the sea. They went out in canoes and dropped handmade items like necklaces, headbands, shawls, and things like that into the water as gifts to the sea spirits that kept them alive. Just a couple years ago a few of the American Indians from the islands got together and decided to start up the tradition again. It's become a huge festival week, and tourists come from all over."

He lost me somewhere around "old tradition", and I only half listened. When he finished, I said, "Sounds like something my parents would like."

As if in response to that, my phone buzzed with a message from my mom. Her plane landed. I let the men know, and we loaded back into the van and continued to her office.

* * * *

Mom was all business. She had her statements prepared and gave Peña a full account on camera of what happened in Alaska with the Affron negotiations and the initial results of the oil spill. After all the preliminary information was given, she went on to talk about the impact of the possibility of mermaids being in the Pacific Ocean. She mentioned that she believed the mermaids were real and she said she wanted to know if there were more of them, if they communicated, or if they had emotions like us. She wanted to know how human they were.

"But where are the mermaids now?" Peña asked when it seemed like she was coming to the end of her spiel. "Can we go see them?"

I took a sharp intake of breath, but my mom didn't hesitate a bit. She had that answer planned. "I can't share that information with the press yet because we strongly believe that there is an organization that would try to eradicate all proof of these mermaids if they could find them. A company that will not benefit from the public knowing that there are creatures with human attributes and perhaps even human minds. That company is Affron Oil."

Mom refused to let me say anything on camera to Juarez Peña, but she did allow for the cameraman to shift away from her and get me in the picture now and again. Peña thanked my mom for the exclusive, although he was frustrated that he couldn't get *me* talking and that we still didn't name the location where we were hiding the mermaids we'd found. That's what he had really wanted. As I walked him to the door, I promised him that if we learned anything else, he'd be the first reporter we called.

After he left, my mom patted me on the head. "He was a good choice, June. I'm glad you picked him." She ran her fingers through my long hair to get out some of the tangles, something she'd always done to me when I was little. I always screamed at her back then, but now her touch felt good. I turned to her with hours' worth of things I wanted to tell her ready to burst from my lips. First, I wanted to apologize about the College Night fiasco and say I'd reconsider some of her choices if she really wanted me to. Then I wanted to tell her about Carter and ask her what to do to get him to like me again. She needed to know about my experience with the mermaid, and I wanted her to make me feel better about having lost her. I wanted so much from my mom. Her fingers through my hair made me feel like all of this would happen. She'd forgive me, and our relationship would be better than it ever had been.

Her glasses hung around her neck, and as she cupped my chin sweetly with her right hand, she used her other to put her glasses back on her nose. Those deep brown eyes of hers were magnified behind the frames as she looked me straight in the eyes and raised her eyebrows with expectation. I took a breath to speak, but she was faster.

"Let's get to work."

Just like that her touch was gone, and she moved across the office to her desk.

She gestured for me to sit in the seat across from her and wait. With a quick intercom message to her office assistant Lisa that she was ready, the phone began to ring. For the rest of the day she fielded calls from reporters. Mostly I just sat there and watched her. I've seen her do this kind of work before, but she was truly marvelous that day. I've never seen her so on her game. Her responses were fast, well spoken, and to the point. If any of it flustered her, she didn't show it. That perfect bob hairstyle of hers never drooped; her forehead never creased; her make-up stayed fresh. It's almost like the effort exhilarated her instead of exhausting her. I, on the other hand, started fading just watching.

The only thing that would occasionally break her coolness was the insisting request from a reporter that they talk to me directly. It was my face in the video, after all. Oh, she tried every trick she could think of to distract them, and sometimes it worked. Several times she failed to divert their intention, and she'd have to give in. Begrudgingly, Mom then handed the phone over to me, clearly not liking the loss of control and hovering until she could snatch the phone back into her safe hands.

Lisa covered the e-mails from her desk. Each time she needed a quote or piece of information, my mom jumped in to give it to Lisa before I could even open my mouth.

By the end of the day, Natalie Sawfeather, the nation's best environmental lawyer and spokesperson, managed to triple the number of editors that had the story. Now the mermaids would be seen in papers worldwide. *Newsweek* was going to meet us for a cover story. Dateline and 20/20 were bidding for the exclusive television rights. The story was hot. Real-life mermaids had washed up on the beach after the latest Affron oil spill. People wanted to know more.

At six o'clock we wrapped up and headed home. Mom turned on the radio, and we listened to a talk show completely focused on the issue of the mermaids. The main debate was whether the mermaids were real or not. Could they talk? Could they think? If they could communicate, what country were they citizens of: Canada or the United States? Would they be Republicans or Democrats and could they register to vote? Yes, it was that ridiculous, and the show host propagated most of it.

Most of all, people wanted to know where the mermaids were found and how they could see more of them. A few callers shared that all the hotels, motels, and RV campgrounds were filling up quickly. A manager of one of the hotels said he was offering a free night's stay to anyone who got a clear picture of a mermaid. One caller, who called himself "Jim", said that he'd seen Peter Sawfeather at Grayland Beach in Aberdeen.

"That's not good," Mom said with a shake of her head and switched off the radio. She immediately called Dad and told him to quit for the day and get home before he got mobbed.

During dinner, Dad confirmed that all the beaches in the area were packed with people who had flocked to the shores with binoculars and cameras, hoping for a glimpse of something large and silver with a tail and breasts. Boats had been chartered, and the waterways were so jammed with mermaid-seekers that it looked like a game of bumper boats off the horizon.

"It's completely ridiculous out there," he said as he stirred his soup around in the bowl not eating any of it. "We can't get the oil cleaned up with all these tourists. They're stomping all around with their trash and cigarettes, making more of a mess than there was to begin with. All of those boats are spreading the oil around more." He slammed his spoon on the table. "This shouldn't be allowed. Where is the Coast Guard? Where are the police?" He lifted his eyes and gave a pretty flat-out mean look at my mom and me. "Everyone's so concerned with the mermaids, no one's helping with the real problem. There is a lot of oil in the water killing sea life and vegetation."

"Honey, the fervor will calm down when no one finds any more mermaids," Mom said. "In the meantime, a lot of attention is being brought to Affron and what they've done."

"Really?" Dad asked angrily. "I don't see anything at all being directed at Affron. I don't see any information about the oil spill hitting the prime-time news. It's just about the mermaids. That's it. No one cares about Affron or the oil spill at all!"

"They will, Peter," Mom insisted. "I'll make sure of it."

"It's too late." Dad got up and opened the blinds to the front windows and revealed the army of news vans out in the street and the cameras set up on our front lawn. Then he snapped it shut again. "This is all screwed up now." Dad stormed out the room, and I heard him a moment later banging glasses around in his office as he made himself a drink

Like my dad, I also got up from the table and went to the window where I pulled the blinds toward me so I could take a peek. Immediately, lights flashed in my eyes. I flipped around and leaned with my back against the wall. "He's right, Mom."

My mom cleared the dishes. "No. He's just frustrated that things aren't happening the way he wants them to. We made the right choice, and it'll all come out right in the end."

"But what about the mermaids?" I asked. "What if they get hurt?"

My mom actually laughed. "Oh, June. Really? Do you really think any more of them are going to be found? No one has ever seen one before. Ever. Odds of seeing one again are so rare."

"We found three at once, Mom," I said. "And people are looking now."

"Who knows if they're even looking in the right places?" My mom waved a hand like she was erasing me. "You're worrying about nothing."

"Am I?" I stomped up to my room with my mom calling after me to come back and help with the dishes. I ignored her. I shut my door behind me and flopped on my bed, burying my face in my pillow.

Yesterday I thought I could create an emotional crisis in the people of this country that would make them help in my cause to defeat Affron. I hoped the unwelcome attention to their company might make them give up my mermaid in the short term and in the long term stop them from sending out leaky vessels. That's not what happened. All I did was create chaos. Every whacko in the world was knocking at our door and dialing our phone number. The rest of the world seemed to be spilling off of planes and out of cars in droves to see the freak-show that was reported to be in the waters nearby. So far nobody had spotted a mermaid out there, but that didn't mean anyone was going away. It just meant that these people would start challenging me more. "You told us they were here, so where are they?" would be the next round of interviews. It would go on until somebody found one.

I hoped, prayed, that the mermaids were far away. That they were deep underwater where no scuba divers could find them. If they did exist out there in the Pacific Ocean somewhere, I knew that this mermaid obsession could harm them. What would people do if they saw a mermaid? Catch her? Trap her? Kill her? Stuff her and mount her on a wall like a prize swordfish? "Look, Earl! I caught me a mermaid *this* big!"

And if the mermaids were harmed it would all be my fault.

Not to mention the fact that in all this time dealing with reporters and talk show hosts, no one had been doing a single thing to find the one mermaid we knew existed and was alive the last time I saw her. Dr. Schneider hadn't called once. I hadn't heard from Carter all day, and Dad said he never showed up at the beach. When I telephoned the Sea Mammal Rescue Center, no one answered.

We'd all been way too busy creating this "mermaids are real" buzz, that we'd completely forgotten about the one that needed us. For all I knew, our mermaid, the one who loved bubbles and liked having her arms rubbed, was dead.

From outside my door I could hear her parents talking about me as they climbed the stairs.

"I think it's too much for her," Mom said. "She didn't expect all this. I don't think any of us did. I should go talk to her. Give her a little pep talk."

Oh no, I thought. *That's the last thing I need.*

Dad seemed to get that pairing mom and daughter together for a heart-to-heart wasn't the solution. "I'll talk to her," he offered as a better option.

I really didn't feel like having a talk-to at the moment. If there was anyone I wanted to talk to it was Carter, but he must've been really sore at me for the way I behaved in the car. I wondered how he was taking all this mermaid craziness. Did he agree with Mom that it was a great political ploy to use the press? Was he with dad that the issue of the oil spill was getting ignored? Or was he worried to death that our silver friend was still missing? How could I get him to know that was my main concern, too? What could I do to make things better between us again?

Knowing my dad was about to enter my room to chat whether I wanted it or not, I sat up. I propped myself up with pillows and picked up a magazine, trying to make it seem like I wasn't fretting at all before he opened the door.

"Not buying it," Dad said as he entered and shut the door behind him.

Trying my best to sound nonchalant, I replied, "What?"

He didn't answer. Instead, he sat down cross-legged on the braided carpet in the middle of the floor. "You want to tell me?" he asked.

I looked at him (sitting "Indian style" of all things) on my floor, his shoulders slumped from a long day and his long hair still drying from his shower. All of a sudden I did want to talk to him. I wanted to tell him how terrible I felt. Dropping my magazine, I stumbled out of my bed, and collapsed in front of him, burying my face into his shoulder as I sobbed. Dad patted my back softly. He didn't say a word.

When I felt like the last shudder had gone through me, I sat up and leaned back against the bed. Dad reached over and grabbed the tissue box from my dresser top and handed it to me.

"Sorry," I said, wiping my face.

"Not a problem," he answered. "That's been building up for some time. I'm surprised you didn't break before now."

"I kind of wish I had," I said. "Then maybe I wouldn't have wasted so much time."

"That's all perspective," Dad said. "There is a legend about the great Chinook war hero…"

"Dad," I stopped him. "You're not going to tell me another crazy Chinook story, are you?"

"Just for motivation."

I shook my head. "I don't need motivation. I feel like I've lost control."

"Yeah, I feel like that too," he said. "I think we've all lost sight of what's important."

I knew he was talking about the oil. I knew he was blaming me—again. I stifled my defensiveness and sat up on my knees.

"Dad, listen to me. Hear me. I'm going to tell *you* a story. It goes like this. Our people have lived on this land for thousands of years, right? We lived in harmony with the cedar tree, the whale, the elk, and raven. Less than three hundred years ago white men came here and took our land from us. They killed us when they couldn't understand us, and they put us to work for them when they could. They chopped down our cedar trees, massacred our whales, shot our elk, and captured our ravens. Now we're just ghosts walking in a desolate world. Do you recognize that story, Dad?"

Dad nodded. "Of course. I taught you that."

"Yes," I said. "Over and over again."

"What's your point?" Dad asked. It surprised me that he didn't see the connection.

"My point is," I said slowly, "just because people have learned about the tragedy that befell the American Indians doesn't mean they'll remember it when confronted with mermaids." I leaned forward. "Protecting the rights of our people has been your most important cause. Are the mermaids any different? Do they deserve this exploitation? If we don't stop this madness, all that will be left of the mermaids are just their echoing cries from the sea."

Dad stood up and walked to the window. He angled himself so he could see a bit of the street between Haley's house and ours, observing the number of news vans and reporters milling about outside. "You're right," he said at last. "We have started the very kind of insanity that I would normally stand against."

I stood up and joined him at the window. "Well, I started it," I confessed.

"Maybe. But your mother and I propagated it." He turned away from the window and put his hand on my shoulder. "I'll talk to your mother and try to convince her to hold off on any more comments about the mermaids. We'll contact a couple reporters who might do a piece on how we need the water traffic to stop until the oil is cleared up. That might give the mermaids some room to hide, if they're out there at all. I don't know what else we can do." He kissed me on the forehead and left the room.

I figured I wouldn't see either of them for a while. He would have to get Mom away from the phones, and then it would be a long discussion before she would be convinced to give up project "Mermaid News Release".

But I don't think Dad got out much more than one sentence before I heard my mom shout, "Absolutely not!" Two seconds later she banged my bedroom door open so hard I jumped to my feet.

"I don't think either of you understand the gravity of what is happening here," she started as Dad stepped in behind her. "Yes, we want the oil cleaned. Yes, we want the mermaids protected. But none of that will make a difference if Affron spills oil again and kills more mermaids, will it? We need to milk this attention for every ounce that we can get, because we will never get an opportunity like this again. All eyes and ears are on us now. We will use this platform to our advantage. I don't want to hear another word about it. Tomorrow you can help me or you can stay home and do nothing. Got it?"

I swallowed hard. "How do you want me to help?"

"Get some sleep. We're going with your father to Grayland Beach in the morning. You will need to be made-up, so you look good on camera. I'm going to get you on TV showing the damage from the oil, where the mermaids were found, and you're going to make it clear who the culprit is. You want responsibility? You got it."

Mom turned on her heel and left the room. I heard her muttering to herself down the hall as she walked to her room as if she couldn't stop the ranting machine she'd turned on. Dad had this pained expression on his face, and I'm not sure if it was because his wife disagreed with him or because he'd failed me. Maybe it was a combination of both. If I were younger, I think I'd have rushed over and hugged him. He kind of looked like he needed one. I didn't do that, though. Instead I just pulled my pajamas out of my dresser to let him know I was ready to be alone.

"I'll see you in the morning. Set your alarm for 5:30," he said before he left, closing the door behind him.

I dressed for bed and then went to the window. The lights were on in Haley's room. For a moment I thought about calling her, but then I decided against it. She wasn't my friend anymore. I couldn't call Carter, because he clearly didn't like me anymore either. My parents were impossible to talk to. I had no one.

Or did I?

I sat at my desk and got on the Internet. After searching my own name, I found thousands of entries. Late into the night I read posts from people who thought the mermaids talked and lived in magical lands under the sea. I saw drawings that people had made based on my video that turned the mermaids into something much more glamorous than what was real. I laughed out loud a couple times at blogs that suggested I could communicate with the mermaids and knew where they lived. A few times I got really interested in the comparisons of the features of my mermaids to ones from ancient legends. People were so strange, from the bizarre fanatics to the ultra-scientific. Even the naysayers caught my attention as they worked so hard to debunk my video as a fake by explaining all kinds of photography techniques I'd never even heard of that could be used to alter the images.

All of it was interesting, and most of it seemed pretty harmless. My mind reeled that so many people were stirred by my video. That something I'd done could cause so much commotion. However, not one of the thousand links had it right. None of them captured the uniqueness of my silver mermaid, her shiny skin, bald head, and straight flat teeth. None of them had a clue that she wore a mysterious shell necklace or that she had had a dimple in her cheek when she smiled. Most of all, they were missing all the emotion in those large midnight blue eyes of hers. How I longed to see them again.

5:30 came before I'd even bothered to get into bed. I'd been up all night. I heard my parents stirring in their room, and I switched off the computer to get ready. I didn't know what was in store for the day, but I was determined to get a few things straightened out. I wanted Haley on my side again. I wanted Carter to speak to me again. Most of all, I wanted people to know my mermaid was missing and needed to be found.

Chapter Fourteen

There are a lot of places where you could go to a beach in October and have a glorious time. Hawaii stands out in my mind. Jamaica probably. The Florida and Gulf Shore beaches were supposed to still be great for Fall Break. I've even heard that the Southern California beaches could be a destination because it wasn't too cold yet. But the beaches in Washington State on a Friday morning, at dawn, in the rain, weren't usually vacation hot spots. Dismally cold, moist and a little foggy, I couldn't think of many less pleasant places to spend my time. However, thanks to my video, Grayland Beach was packed with people like it was a hot summer day, and the sun hadn't even fully risen yet. The campground around the beach was filled with trailers and tents. People stood around in the sticky sand in their rain gear, holding umbrellas over friends with cameras.

What were they hoping to see in the dark, cold rainy morning? I couldn't imagine being so fascinated with the idea of something that I would purposely drag myself out on a morning like this. I was only here because my parents insisted. My warm bed at home beckoned me, "Come back home, you silly, stupid girl. You can't do anything there, but you can come here and sleep."

I drank more coffee and tried to shut that thought out.

It didn't take long for people to recognize the three of us. We were who they had been waiting for, after all. My dad and I had a pretty distinctive look with our long, black hair and dark skin. Not too many American Indian dads and daughters in the news on a regular basis. I made a point of not wearing a hat, but I'd pulled my hair into a long ponytail to keep it out of my face. I wore a good sweater and jeans without holes in case the rain ever stopped long enough for me to take off my slicker and pose for a few pictures. Dad had work clothes on, not planning to be on camera at all. Mom, though, she was dressed as well as she could manage despite the weather. Her brown hair was pinned back neatly in a French twist so it wouldn't frizz in the rain, and she wore a dress suit under her fitted raincoat. Her high-heeled leather boots sank in the sand, but they prevented her from ruining her nylons. All around us people looked like the rain falling on them was the closest thing they'd had to a bath in a couple days, and my mom looked like a super model. God bless her.

"We'll be right with all of you," my mom insisted, as we pushed through the crowd. "We just need to survey the situation here first and make sure the animals are safe. That is our first priority."

Surprisingly, the people backed off and let us do our job. Right at the shoreline, we found a few more dead fish and birds, but nothing like the devastation of three days ago. I could still feel the slick oil in the water when I dipped my hand in it, and balls of it were scattered all over the sand in the tide line, mixed with the algae and shells. I gathered up the dead creatures in trash bags, and dad put what was living in some buckets full of ocean water.

Mom, naturally, did not touch anything that would make her dirty. She sought out a great little spot near the rocks at the far end of the beach. She spread out a blanket and set up a couple director chairs on them. A couple male reporters helped her assemble a gazebo tent over it to keep the rain off of her (and their cameras). This would be her station for the day, where she would conduct her business. By the time she was done with her set-up, she had made the interview spot look like a small movie set.

Mom settled into one of the chairs and crooked a finger at me to come join her. After a quick wash of my hands with some sanitizer, I sat next to her. From where Dad stood, a foot deep in the ocean, I saw him shake his head in disgust. I'm pretty sure that head shake was about my mom and I, not what he was seeing in the foamy waves. Mom tugged the ponytail holder out and spread my hair around my shoulders. Then she gave me a smile and sang, "Here we go."

The local news teams closed in first to get some shots for those people who mostly watch the news in the morning to see if they needed to grab their umbrellas before heading out to work. These reporters weren't looking for a lot of detail and they didn't ask many questions. Mostly I heard things like, "It's a cold, rainy morning here at Grayland Beach with Internet sensation Juniper Sawfeather. It might not be the best day to go mermaid watching, because the clouds are not going to clear up at all today. What do you think, Trudy?" And then they'd shoot it right back to the weather girl and the traffic guy at the station.

Once the sun came up, the local news teams took off and made room for the more invested journalists who took turns talking to us about what we had found, what Dad was still doing out there in the water, and what we were planning to do next. I wanted to tell them that my next plan was to get off this beach and go in search of my lost mermaid, but Mom wouldn't let me say that the mermaid was missing. Instead, she took over and made up a whole story that none of us discussed ahead of time.

"Naturally we are hoping to find more mermaids from whom we can study and learn. We'd like to know more about the way they think and feel. If they are organized into family structures or communities. We'd like to know how they communicate. When we have that information, we will then know if they are to be considered animals or people. Dr. Carl Schneider at the Marine Animal Rescue Center right here in Aberdeen has already begun research on the three mermaids found the other morning and I'm sure is making all kinds of amazing discoveries that could change the world."

"Like what?" asked one reporter after another.

Each time my mom would look at me first before saying more, a small warning that I should not interrupt.

"I'm told that while being cleaned of oil, the mermaids were able to communicate pleasure at the touch of the cloth on their skin through smiling and expressing some kind of relief and gratitude. Clearly, they are not just oversized fish if they are able to express those kinds of emotions. These are creatures with hearts and minds, creatures that should have rights and be protected from environmental hazards, like Affron's leaky oil vessels."

The first time it flabbergasted me that she was giving all the credit to Dr. Schneider. When she kept repeating it over and over again, the lie burned right through me. Did she really hate me so much that she had to steer all the attention away from me and give it to that whiny scientist? He didn't do anything with the mermaid except lose her. What was so wrong about admitting to the press that I was the one who discovered the mermaid had feelings and had tried to communicate with her? I sat beside Mom with my arms crossed and fumed. I didn't care if the reporters noticed.

They *did* try to get me to talk. I was the story after all, not my mother. "Juniper Sawfeather, is this true about Dr. Carl Schneider's work? Were you witness to this phenomenon after rescuing the mermaids from the oil spill?"

I didn't want to lie to them, but my mom, ever the role model, nodded her head enthusiastically to insist that I agree with everything she said. So, I'd pull my lips tight into a fake grin and say, "I'm not the scientist. Dr. Schneider is, as my mother clearly explained to you. I'm just a teenage girl who did nothing but help get the mermaids to safety with my dad." When pushed, I added, "I do think the mermaids have the ability to express emotion, though, because they looked genuinely stressed when I found them and not just in an animal panic way. They looked like they knew they were dying."

It worked like Mom wanted. The reporters got all excited about what we were saying and stumbled off to put together their pieces with our juicy quotes about thinking, feeling mermaids living in the Pacific Ocean. After we went through our half-true story with a sixth reporter, I stole a moment to grab Mom's arm before she could signal the next guy over.

"What are you doing?" I asked her, still holding her arm as I got up from my seat and crouched in front of her to keep the reporters from seeing my face as I talked. "Dr. Schneider doesn't know anything about the mermaids. He didn't clean the one and the other ones are dead. In fact, he told Carter and me he hadn't managed to even take any pictures of them yet. He's been less than useless."

"That doesn't matter," my mom said, waving me off like an irritating fly. "It sounds better than it being your opinion."

"Why? Because I'm just a kid? Because you don't think my opinion's worth anything?"

"Don't take this personally," my mom sighed agitatedly at me. "This isn't about you."

"It isn't?"

"Don't be ridiculous, June. You don't have any degree, and we need something more authoritative than a high school student's perspective to hold weight with the bigger presses. I'm sure Carl will back up all the statements we are making. It makes him look good."

"No, it kind of doesn't, Mom. Being that the mermaids aren't there anymore, I don't think that looks good at all. What if the reporters go over there?"

"Oh hush," she said, looking right over my head. She waved over the next waiting reporter. "It'll all be fine. You'll see." With a flick of her wrist, she gestured for me to return to my seat while she stood and shook hands with the guy from the *Seattle Times*.

"What can we do for you?" my mom asked him.

He turned to focus on me. "You can tell me something exclusive, that you haven't shared with any other reporter today."

"The only way I could do that would be to start making crap up," I told him. I reached over and patted my mom on the shoulder pad of her raincoat. "I'm sure my mom can spin up something for you. It's her specialty." Then I lurched out of my seat and right out of our little interview station. I could hear my mom calling after me, trying to come across as the cool, calm mother she wishes she was and not have that crazy shrill she gets when we're at home and I haven't cleaned my room. I imagined her waving her hands around like she does and saying through a laugh, "June just needs a little break. She's been at this all morning and that's a lot for a girl her age. Why don't you have a seat?"

She's so together, even when she's not. It made me want to puke.

As I strode across the sand, I vaguely noticed the people pointing at me and beginning to follow me. I think some of them were calling my name, but I didn't respond to them at all. Out in the water, my dad looked up and frowned. I thought he might come to me, but he didn't. I didn't go to him either. I just wanted to get away for a minute, so I headed straight for the ramp that led up to where we parked the truck, my eyes on the ground so I wouldn't slip like I had the other morning.

I was halfway up the ramp when five sets of shoes blocked my path.

Two of the pairs were high heels, and I didn't need to see who was attached to the skinny legs to know who was stupid enough to wear heels to a beach in the rain. With my eyes closed, I lifted my head and inhaled deeply before taking in the sight of Regina, Marlee, Ted, Gary, and Haley standing before me.

"Aren't you supposed to be at school?" I asked with as little emotion as I could project.

Regina grinned madly. "Actually, Mrs. Slater sent us here to fetch you and bring you back. She said," Regina imitated the Vice Principal's voice "being interviewed for the news is not an excuse to be out of school." All her friends laughed. Haley laughed too much and came across slightly mental. I shot her look that was supposed to get her to shut up, but she wasn't paying attention to my cues anymore.

It was a good impersonation, actually. I had to give Regina that. It just didn't strike my funny bone at the moment. "She sent all of you?"

"Mmmmm, no," Regina hummed. "I kind of arranged for their release by getting Mrs. Clefton to agree to us doing a piece on you for the yearbook."

"So, you're all journalists now?" I pointed down at the flock around my mom. "Join the fun. I'm leaving." I took a step up the hill, but five sets of hands reached out to stop me. "Let me go."

Ted had a tight grip on my shoulder. "I just drove all the way out here. You aren't leaving yet."

"Besides you don't have your own car," Haley pointed out, prompting a snide chuckle from the Student Council rich kids. My old best friend wouldn't have embarrassed me like that.

"We just want to take some pictures," Regina said, gently leading me back down the hill to the sand. "And maybe be in a couple with you."

I sighed. "If this whole thing is just so you can get on TV, it's not going to work. They aren't interested in you."

"They would be if we found a mermaid," Marlee said with a little giggle.

Okay, she's too stupid to have come up with that thought. I studied their faces and tried to figure out what horrible plan they had hatched in the car on the way here. I noticed they had some duffel bags with them. Nothing weird about that. The bags could have towels and changes of clothes in them. That made sense. It's what sensible people did when they went to the beach.

Except Marlee was turning her pumps over to get out the sand and whining about how dirty she was getting, and Gary kept running his fingers through his hair to try to keep his hair up despite the fact that the drizzle had already washed away most of his gel. These were not sensible people. Plus, Haley was suddenly avoiding my eyes, and all of them were looking around at the people on the beach and not out at the water, which would have been more natural if they were really there to watch for mermaids.

"There aren't any bathrooms here," Ted said. "What kind of beach is this?"

"A small one," I answered. "There's a restroom up at the campground."

Gary nudged Regina, "That won't work."

I reached out and snagged the bag off Haley's shoulder, and before she could get her hands on it, I had it unzipped with the contents spilling out onto the sand. Costume make-up, a bald cap, some silver material...

"Oh, you've got to be kidding!" I shouted. "Really? You were going to dress up like a mermaid? Did you really think you could pull that off?"

Haley dropped to her knees and frantically shoved everything back in the bag, her eyes darting around hoping none of the reporters were looking. "It wasn't supposed to look real," she muttered. "It was supposed to look like a hoax."

Gary grinned his Student Council V.P. winning grin at me. "Come on. It would've been fun to get everyone all riled up out here."

"It would make everything that my parents and I are doing look stupid," I said. "You guys need to leave."

Regina put up her hands. "Okay, okay, June. We won't do the mermaid costume thing. It was kind of a lame idea anyway." She shot a look at Gary to make sure he got credit for thinking of it instead of her. He shrugged like he didn't care. "Just let us hang around for a while. Okay?"

"Do whatever you want," I said, moving back toward the ramp. "I'm done here."

"June," Regina called after me.

At the same exact moment Marlee screamed, "Mermaid!!!!"

I spun around fast. "Regina, tell her to shut up. You aren't doing the trick. Obviously, she didn't get what we were all just saying."

"But there's *really* a mermaid!" Marlee shouted, pointing straight out at the ocean. "Look!!! Mermaid!!!!"

Her shouting caught the attention of all the people nearby. The crowd pushed toward the water's edge, shouting and pointing.

"Marlee!" I yelled through gritted teeth. "Cut it out! Look what you're doing!"

"No, June," Haley said, yanking my arm and pulling me to the water's edge. "She's right. Look."

Haley pointed out toward the buoys. Sure enough, I saw a silver tail flipping around in the water like the creature was stuck. Enough of the long, slender body was out of the water to reveal the absence of a dorsal fin so it couldn't have been a dolphin, and it was too large to be a fish.

Regina stepped up and patted me on the back. "How's that for timing, huh?"

I brushed her hand away and grumbled, "Fantastic."

Chapter Fifteen

I immediately tore my arm from Haley's grasp and propelled myself forward, ankle-deep into the water. Regina and Gary grabbed me by my shoulders and prevented me from diving into the waves while people dashed forward around me.

"What are you doing? Let me go!" I shouted at them.

"What? Are you going to swim all the way out there?" Regina asked. "You need to stay dry for when you're on camera in a few minutes. Let your dad go get the mermaid and bring her to you."

I screamed, "Dad!" My dad was just standing there, gawking at all the people splashing toward him and tripping into the water. He didn't hear me. I screamed again, "Peter Sawfeather!" My so-called friends joined in. "Peter Sawfeather!" Finally, we caught his attention. I pointed at the flapping tail. His face became instantly alarmed.

"Call Carter!" he shouted back. "And get these people out of the water!" He dove under the water and began swimming toward the buoy nearest the flailing creature.

I dug my phone out of my pocket and dialed Carter's number. To my surprise he answered right away.

"Hey, we're having an emergency. It looks like a mermaid has been spotted. Dad needs you at the beach."

"I'm almost there already," he said and then hung up.

I flipped around and addressed Gary and Ted. "Help me."

"Do what?" Ted asked.

"Keep these people back."

"Seriously?" Ted stared at me, completely useless. "It's a mob. What do you expect me to do?"

"You and Gary need to help push them back."

He didn't move, and the crowd kept going farther and farther into the water.

"Look," I said. "Your girlfriend is going to be pissed if her mermaid gets damaged by all these crazy people, and she won't be able to get the best view. Do you want to deal with that all afternoon?"

Ted sneered at me, but he knew I was right. He grabbed Gary by the arm, said something in his ear, and they both took off chest deep into the water, hollering at people to get back to land. We had to push people a couple times, and Gary helped one man who'd fallen face first into the waves by grabbing the back of his shirt and pointing him back toward the sand.

"My dad is taking care of it. Wait on the sand, please!" I said over and over to the masses. "You're making it harder for him by trying to come out here."

Eventually we got all of them out of the water, but they still formed a wall at the water's edge, snapping pictures to capture every moment of the rescue. Out in the water, the flapping of the tail got weaker by the moment, losing its struggle against the oil. I was completely drenched from the waist down in saltwater, and the rain had done a number on the top half of my body. I certainly wasn't going to be taking any better pictures at this mermaid recovery than the last one. I stood in the water with Gary and Ted to make sure no one went past us. Over at the interviewing station my mom was up out of her director's seat, standing behind the row of journalists trying to figure out how to break through and become the center of attention again. At the other end of the beach Regina, Marlee, and Haley were all fixing their lipstick and hair as best they could, using matching compact mirrors.

My dad rested on the buoy for a moment to catch his breath. I saw him dodge the frantic tail and a couple of times he put out a hand to block his face from getting smacked. He couldn't pull in the mermaid by himself. I remembered the mermaids being pretty heavy. Two men from the crowd were swimming out there, but they stopped halfway to tread water and catch their breath too. One of them raised a finger to my dad as if to say, "Just a minute. We're coming." He was too out of breath to talk. Equally, my dad, whose shoulders heaved with his breathing,

155

seemed too tired to answer them back.

Carter's voice pierced through the crowd. "June!" He dashed down the ramp and passed the girls right by without a glance. I know he was only a year older than Gary and Ted, but that year made a big difference. His body was much more sculpted and manly than theirs. He was a young man, and they were still boys. My heart raced at the sight of him in his t-shirt and jeans as he hurtled through the small waves to get to me. "Where's your dad?"

"Out there!" I shouted back, pointing to the buoy. "He needs help."

"I'm on it." Without hesitation he dove into the water and began to swim. He passed the old farts in a minute and didn't need to stop once before he got to my dad. By now the tail only flapped a couple weak times a minute. This meant the creature was probably dying, but it also meant that Carter and my dad would have a better chance of being able to capture it. They both lunged toward the creature and dove underwater.

The silver tail flapped. It flapped again much weaker than before. And then it was still. Nothing moved out there but the buoy bobbing along the surface. For a moment it was strangely silent on the beach, and then a small murmuring began in the crowd as they began to conjure up bleak ideas of what was happening out there.

I tried to tune the voices out. I didn't want to hear them say the mermaid was dead, and worse, that it had dragged my dad and Carter down with it. I searched the shore for my mom. She had broken through and was in the front of the crowd. She stood there with her hands over her gaping mouth, staring toward the spot where my dad should have been rising up for a breath any moment. I watched her instead of the water. I couldn't bear to watch the water, and I knew her face would tell me what I needed to know. Her eyes grew wide. Her fingers stretched up past her nose and cheeks as though they wanted to cover her eyes but she wouldn't let them. Mom's head shook slowly, denying what she was seeing.

My brain began to count. 3, 4… 7, 8… They should be up by now. I dared to peek.

The two older guys finally got to the buoy. They dove into the water like they saw something and thought they could help. I hoped they weren't too late. I looked back at my mom. A million wrinkles crossed her brow.

Then the crowd uttered a collective, "Oh!!!"

My mom's hands had moved to the sides of her head, fingers destroying her perfect hair. She was crying, but I could detect a smile under it. That was all I needed. I spun around to see the heads of all four men above the water. Two were on one side of the creature and two on the other.

And then I gulped for my own breath, suddenly aware that I'd been holding it probably as long as they had.

Together, the men swam back to shore. As they got closer we began to see the outline of what they were carrying.

"That's not a mermaid!" some lady shrieked from the crowd.

"What is it?" people cried out, desperate to know.

I plodded a little deeper into the water to get a better look. From what I could see, it was a creature about four feet long and relatively thin. Its head had a high, round forehead, and two flippers stuck out on both sides of the upper torso. I bit my lip to keep from laughing and called back to the onlookers, "It's a finless porpoise." The missing dorsal fin on this breed of porpoise made its body long and slender, easily mistaken for a mermaid tale at a distance.

The chorus of groans and jeers behind me was terrifically loud. You'd think I just told them they'd lost the lottery. They yelled things about how we'd played a trick on them and were just a bunch of fakes and liars.

I shrugged at all of them and said only loud enough for Gary and Ted to hear, "I haven't lied about anything. A finless porpoise along our shore is almost as rare a sighting as a mermaid. If they knew that they'd still be snapping pictures." The boys, with soaking wet clothes and ruined hair, both gave me a look like I was nuts and they waded back to the girls.

"You are so not worth this," Ted said as he passed me.

A few people from the mob stayed at the water's edge to see the porpoise—to make sure it wasn't going to turn out to be a mermaid after all, I guess. Most of them went back to their towels and chairs to wait for another sighting. A handful grabbed their stuff to leave, probably figuring that the whole thing was a big waste of time.

Regina snapped her compact shut as I walked out of the water. "Well, that didn't turn out the way I hoped," she said, staying a few feet away from me so she wouldn't get any seawater on me as I shook my legs to loosen my wet jeans.

"Yeah," Marlee agreed. "I really wanted to see a mermaid."

"So did everybody here, Marlee," Ted said. Then he turned to Regina. "Can we got get something to eat now? I saw a doughnut shop when we drove through town."

"No, silly," Regina said, reshaping his hair again as lovingly as she could. She worked her eyelashes and pouty lips on him. He grinned wide. Did he really like that crap? "We're not done here yet. There's more fun in store. Right, Junie?"

I winced.

Gary plopped down in the sand and put his arms over his knees. "I still think this whole thing's a fake. You guys haven't proven anything to me."

Regina smacked him on the top of his head. "You're getting all sandy and are not going to be riding in my car that way."

"I'll ride with Ted."

I wandered away from them to wait for Dad and Carter at the spot where it looked like they would be coming ashore. Haley stepped up beside me.

"I'm glad your dad's all right," she said quietly. "It got scary there for a minute."

There she was—my old friend. I knew it was only going to last for a moment, but it was nice to see her again. I put my arm around her waist and dropped my head to her shoulder. She wrapped her left arm around my shoulders and we stood like that for the next couple minutes, until the men got close enough for me to get to them and help tug the porpoise to shore.

It was a baby—very slender, only about four feet long, with a deep blue-gray sheen to its skin that sparkled a bit against the overcast sky. All four men dropped to their knees as soon as they were out of the water. The two older volunteers flopped to their backs.

"What can I do?" I asked. "Do you want me to try to clean the oil out of its blowhole?"

"It's too late," Dad said. "He already suffocated." Dad caught Mom's attention and beckoned her over. "There's nothing we can do for him now."

Carter stood up and walked away from us, his hands on his hips, his head back. I followed him.

"If I had just gotten here a couple minutes sooner," he grumbled. "Just a couple minutes, and we could've saved him."

"Carter, you didn't know…"

He spun around. "I knew you were here," he said. "You were on the news this morning. The second I saw your face I jumped in my car and headed over. But then on the radio one of the reporters said that you told them Dr. Schneider was doing experiments on the mermaids at his lab, so I thought I should go there first. If I hadn't, I would have been here sooner."

"I didn't tell them all that stuff about Dr. Schneider. My mom did."

I pointed at my mother who appeared to be getting instructions from my father about how to share the facts about the dead porpoise with the reporters behind her. I imagined he was filling her in on what a rarity this particular animal was and how the oil spill may very well have wiped out all the finless porpoises on our coast. My dad is nothing if not very focused on his goals. If Carter weren't here, I'd probably be helping by pulling up some extra details from Google on my phone that we could throw at the press for extra sympathy. My dad knew deep down that the press wouldn't care about this porpoise, but he would convince Mom to make this moment about the oil spill and not the mermaid.

Carter shook his head at the two of them and then gave me a half grin. I guess I hadn't done anything to earn one of his genuine golden grins yet. I longed for it, though. "Okay," he said. "I'll blame your mom then." He nodded at the porpoise. "Want to help me get this up to the truck and back to the Center?"

He wanted my help! I almost chirped with happiness, but I kept it under control. "Yes. Anything. I'd love to help you… I mean, I really want to get out of here." Well, I kind of kept it under control, if you consider babbling like an idiot some form of control.

I crouched down and wrapped my arms around the tail. He lifted the head. The porpoise was heavier than it looked, but nothing the two of us

159

couldn't handle. As we started away, the two swimming volunteers got to their feet and asked if we needed them anymore. We thanked them for everything they did.

"Check with my dad," I told them. "I'm sure he could use some help with what he's doing, if you're still interested."

They checked with each other through a glance, and the older of the two rubbed the back of his neck. "Uh, we really just went out there because we thought that thing was a mermaid."

Carter tugged me toward the ramp that led to the parking lot to keep from saying something he shouldn't. I said thanks to the volunteers one more time and left it at that.

Haley chased after us. "June! Aren't you going to say good-bye or anything?"

Oh my gosh! I totally forgot she existed the moment Carter showed up. Here, I'd been griping about what a lousy friend she was, but I wasn't any better.

"I'm so sorry, Haley," I said. I gestured with my shoulder because my hands were full of porpoise tail. "This is Carter."

Haley smiled and gave him an approving once-over. "I thought you might be," she said. She pointed at the porpoise. "Where are you going? Don't you need to be here for the interviews and stuff?"

"We're taking the porpoise back to the rescue center," I told her.

Haley's eyes brightened and she hopped up and down in the sand. "Really? Where the mermaids are being kept? Can I go? Can I see them?"

Regina, Ted, and Marlee stepped up behind her. "You're going to see the mermaids? We're totally going to be a part of that." Regina hit Ted to make him go fetch Gary from where he still sat in the sand.

Carter began taking quite wide strides up the ramp, and I had no choice but to try to keep up. It didn't take long before we were out of earshot of Regina's crew. For a second he craned his head back to look at me before focusing on where he was going again. His forehead was so creased he could have passed for 35. "Don't they know?"

I felt a little sick to my stomach over the way he said it, like I was some kind of jerk. "I haven't really talked to Haley much over the last couple days. And Regina's kind of the last person I'd tell anything to."

"All of these interviews and the video on the Internet, and you don't bother to mention once that the mermaids are missing? That's kind of important," he said. "Instead of having people help us look for them, we've got a crowd of people filling the parking lot at the Center, desperate to get inside and see something that's not there."

"It's that bad?" I asked. "I mean, I knew it would get bad the moment my mom said that stuff about Dr. Schneider, but it's that bad already?"

"It's only going to get worse," Carter said. "I didn't even bother parking because I didn't want all those people bugging me and trying to push inside. I'm guessing Dr. S. has the door locked so no one can get in there." We got to the top of the hill and Carter stopped and stared at the parking lot. "Great."

"What?"

"How are we going to get this thing to the Center? Drape it across my back seat? Shove it in the trunk?"

I bit my lip before saying gently, "Well, it is dead, Carter."

He raised his eyebrows. "The smell will be in there forever." I stifled a laugh.

"What about my dad's truck?" Carter nodded and we took the porpoise over and dropped it in the bed. "I'll get the keys from Dad."

As I dashed over to the ramp to head back down to the beach, Regina and her club of popular dorks came over the top.

"Oh! Were you coming back for us?" Regina asked, her eyebrow cocked high enough to let me know she was fully aware that I was not. "How sweet of you." She put out her arm and stopped me. Haley and her friends blocked my way.

"I need to get to my dad," I told them. "I need his keys to the truck."

"Ted's got a truck," Regina said. She elbowed Ted in the ribs, and he nodded.

"Uh, yeah. It's over there." He pointed at his Dodge pickup in the lot. Then he looked at Carter with his arms wrapped around the torso of the slick porpoise and the tail dragging on the ground. "You want me to help you with that thing?"

Carter glanced at me, shook his head slightly in defeat and then waved Ted over. The two of them hauled the porpoise into the bed of

Ted's truck.

"Damn, that stinks," Ted said, wiping his hands on his jeans.

Carter patted his stinky hands on Ted's back. "It'll take a few washes to get it out of your clothes. Sorry, man." He walked away and signaled for me to come with him. Ted picked at the shoulder of his shirt and tried to sniff how bad the odor was while he made his way to the driver's side of his truck. Gary, with sand still stuck to the back of his pants, caught up to him, while the girls all went to Regina's car.

"We'll follow you," Regina said before sitting down and closing her door.

Once we got into his car, Carter leaned close to me and said, "I could lose her in a second and let them drive around the rest of the morning with that dead porpoise. Can I? Please?" I took in his devilish grin and bright blue eyes. I absolutely would love to find a way to rid myself of the Student Council posse and have some time alone with Carter. But I wriggled my nose at him and sighed as my only response. Carter straightened up and put his hands on the wheel. "Oh, fine. I'll be good." He started the engine and led the pack away.

I took his joking as an invitation. "So, you're not mad at me anymore?"

He shrugged. "Oh, I wasn't really mad at you. Just disappointed."

"I said some stupid things last time we were together…"

"Let me put it this way," he said, interrupting me. "I think you're right about not wanting to follow in your parents' footsteps. Go to San Diego. Become a Marine Biologist like you want. You know why?"

I'm not sure I wanted to hear the answer. Was it because he hated me? He didn't want me around? I got on his nerves?

"Why?" I said through the knot in my throat.

Carter tilted his head toward me just a touch, flicking his eyes at me for a moment before looking back at the road. "Because you are a terrible activist."

"What?" I hit him in the shoulder.

He laughed. "I'm serious. You are awful. I watched you on TV this morning. Stiff. Uncomfortable. Almost impossible to hear. I mean, seriously. Your mom hasn't taught you form."

"She just takes over," I said. "She never gives me a chance."

162

"Well, that's probably a good thing," Carter said, "because you'd muck it up."

"You are so not nice right now."

Then I watched his grin slowly fade as his thoughts changed direction. "You know what you are good at? I mean, really good at?"

"Making an ass out of myself?" I asked.

Carter turned onto the main highway. He checked through the rearview window to see if the others followed. Then he said, "You're good with the animals. The way you handled the porpoise just now was perfect. You weren't squeamish at all. You helped put away all those animals the Affron guys brought without needing any help. And then there was the way you handled being in the tank with the mermaid. You're a natural. *That's* what you should do."

I swallowed hard at the compliment. "Thanks," I whispered. I was quiet for a moment. "I don't suppose they could start having a Marine Biology major at your school?"

His expression didn't change. His hands stayed on the wheel. Not a sound rose from his lips, and his breathing stayed the same. But there was just the slightest, almost imperceptible nod of his head. Was that a "Yes, we could push for a Marine Biology program," nod, or a "Yes, you're interested in sticking around?" nod? Either way, I took it as a good sign.

Carter changed lanes. The others followed.

I couldn't leave the conversation dangling on that edge, so I rambled, "It doesn't really matter right now, though. I mean, I haven't even applied to colleges yet, let alone been accepted anywhere. I've still got most of my senior year ahead me. That's a whole lot of time to… to…" To what? Build a relationship with Carter? I couldn't say that. I didn't know how to finish what I was saying.

Carter did it for me. "To find out."

Yes. To find out.

Chapter Sixteen

Up ahead was the parking lot for the center. Carter put on his signal and slowly pushed through the crowd of people gathered there. There weren't any parking spaces, so he just pulled up in front of the door and popped out. He guided Regina to stop right behind him and Ted to pull up behind her. The moment I got out of the car, cameras started flashing in my face. People recognized me from the video. They shouted questions at me about the mermaid and what we were doing while Carter and I rushed to the truck and climbed into the bed.

I lifted up the tail before he had a handle on the torso. This was a mistake, because the sight of that thin, long tail sent the crowd into a frenzy. They pushed up to the truck with their cameras and made it impossible for us to move. Ted and Gary couldn't even open their doors to get out of the cab.

Ted rolled down his window and yelled, "Come on! Back off!"

Regina's high voice screamed over the crowd, "It's not a mermaid! Calm down and back up! It's not a mermaid!" Marlee and Haley joined in. I saw them jumping up and down on the periphery of the crowd. "It's not a mermaid! It's NOT a mermaid!"

Carter lifted up the porpoise's head as high as he could so everyone had a clear visual of it. A collective "aw!" of disappointment rose up, and the cameras lowered.

"Let us through," Carter said. "We need to get it inside."

This mob was a mixture of mermaid watchers and press. They wanted inside the building, so they didn't give up space easily. We had to lift the porpoise up over our heads as we squeezed through the wall of people. Ted and Gary had finally managed to get out of the truck, and they pushed their way toward us. We let them take the porpoise while Carter unlocked the door. The girls were having a heck of a time getting through, and I didn't want to hold the door open long enough for them to make it.

"Don't close it," Regina shouted at me as I stepped inside the building.

"Hurry up!" I shouted.

"We can't get through," Marlee screamed back at me.

I only had the door open a couple inches, just enough to see the girls. People tried to yank the door out of my grip to get inside. Some money was thrown in my direction. Finally I yelled back at Regina, "I've got to close the door!"

"No, June. Don't do it." The fire in her eyes was intense.

"Get yourself on TV," I shouted. *"You guys are my best friends,* after all." I really milked that. I saw reporters' heads snap back at the girls and a murmur of "best friends?" rumbled through the crowd. I felt a little guilty, like I'd just hung meat in a piranha tank. I closed the door and locked it behind me as the savage crowd, hungry for whatever fresh news it could get, devoured the girls.

All the lights were off in the front room. Carter flipped a switch so the guys wouldn't walk into the tide pool tank in the middle of the room and led them toward the double doors. Ted shook his head like a dog to get some of the rain water off. "Are they going to be okay out there?"

"Regina can handle herself," I told him.

He didn't argue, so I figured he knew I was right. He hefted the porpoise up a little higher and led Gary through the double doors into the main room of the center. All the lights were off in there, too, and it was strangely deja-vu-ish.

"Where's Schneider?" I asked Carter. He took the porpoise from the guys and put it on one of the metal tables.

"I was just wondering that myself." He threw a few towels over the porpoise and then gestured to the bathroom in the back hall. "You guys can clean up back there."

Gary and Ted headed back, grumbling about how they'd never get the stink out of their shirts. On any other day I might have laughed, but I wasn't finding anything funny at the moment.

"Do you think something happened to him?"

"I don't know," Carter said, exasperated. "He was here yesterday. I mean, he just stayed in his office all day with the door closed. When I tried to talk to him he told me to finish up with the care of the animals so I could leave. I stayed longer than I had to hoping I might get him to discuss what to do about finding the mermaid. After a couple hours, though, he came out of his office and ordered me to go home. 'There's nothing for you do!' he shouted at me." Carter sighed. "I could tell he was really stressed, but what could I do about it? I left."

Meek fidgety Dr. Schneider yelled at Carter? The guy who couldn't keep up with a truck on the freeway because he probably couldn't drive past fifty miles an hour? This nerdy, wiry old guy who sort of apologized to us, a couple of kids, that he let his phone battery die out the other day? This was not a guy who yelled. What was going on?

I walked over to his office. Over my shoulder I said, "You ought to put that thing on ice or it's going to stink."

Carter scooped up the porpoise by himself and started toward the examination room where the mermaid cadavers had been just days ago. "What are you going to do?"

"Poke around some more. We found something last time. Maybe we'll get lucky again."

Loud banging started at the front door of the building. Ted and Gary burst from the restroom, drying their hands on their shirts.

"You think that's Regina?" Ted asked. "Can we let her in?"

I held off responding to that question. I really liked *not* having her in here.

Ted looked past me and called after Carter. "Dude? Can we?"

Carter swung around with the porpoise and the guys backed away a couple feet to avoid it. "I'm about to cut this thing up into pieces. If you don't want to see that, then maybe you should go out there with them."

"Uh," Ted said, trying and failing not to look grossed out. "I think we'll skip that. Just got cleaned up and all."

Gary had already started toward the double doors when suddenly he stopped and looked around at all the tanks lining the walls. "Where are the mermaids?"

Carter shot a fast look at the big tank and then gasped in mock surprise. "They're not here! Oh no! June! The mermaids aren't here!"

Gary frowned. "I knew there never were any mermaids. You're such a liar, June."

"Oh, there were mermaids," Carter said. "They're just missing. You ought to go tell Regina. That'll be something she can tell the reporters. Get her face on camera, right?"

"Whatever," Gary said. He stomped away.

Ted followed, looking back at us with a very confused expression. He tapped his buddy on the shoulder and said, "So which is it? There never were mermaids or that they're missing?"

Gary shoved his friend away. "I knew I should have stayed at school. I missed a cool pep rally for this."

Then there was an explosion of noise as they opened the front door and pushed out into the crowd. The door closed behind them, and the noise was blocked again.

I dashed into the office while Carter set the porpoise in the right place to be taken care of later. Dr. Schneider's office was in shambles, much worse than it was two days ago. Folders stuck up and papers spilled out of open file cabinets. Scribbled-on notepads and opened mail covered his desk. Wads of paper filled the trashcan to the brim and spilled over. What had he been investigating in here?

I shifted through all the papers on his desk and found a number of printed Internet pages about mermaids. I recognized some of them as sites that I looked at the other night. They hadn't been any more helpful to him than me, apparently. I turned on his computer and logged online. The past couple sites he'd visited were also about mermaids. Why was a scientist like him looking at this stuff? Was he hoping it might clue him in to where he might find more of the creatures?

I was about to give up, figuring he'd come back in a little while, frazzled and holding a coffee cup from Starbucks, and wondering why there was a crowd out front. It was silly to think anything had happened to him. Affron already had the mermaids, what would they want with Dr. Schneider?

I stood up to leave and something white caught the corner of my eye. Hanging on a hook by the door was the lab coat Dr. Schneider always wore. Instinctively, I reached for the coat. I rifled through the pockets and at last found something that might help: a phone number with an unfamiliar area code scribbled on a scrap of paper. Without a pause that would give me time to doubt, I sat down at the desk and dialed the phone number on the Center's landline.

"North Shore Rehabilitation Aquarium," the receptionist's voice answered. "How may I direct your call?"

"Hi. Yes," I stammered, my mind desperately trying to catch up with my voice. I didn't actually expect a person to answer, nor did I have any idea who I was calling, so I hadn't thought through what I would say. "I am a student at Washington State University, and I am interested in doing some intern work with sea animals. I was wondering where you were located so I could send in my resume."

"We aren't in need of any interns at this time," the receptionist answered crisply. "I can recommend another aquarium."

"Oh," I said. *Think. Think.* "You are a facility operating under Affron Oil's philanthropic plan, aren't you? I was told by my professors that Affron was very open to volunteer interns."

"We are funded by Affron, yes," she said, rather snippily. I pictured this little woman with a tiny nose and a bob haircut, sweater buttoned up to her neck and irritated that she couldn't get back to her Facebook newsfeed update. "But we are a small research facility, and we don't use interns or volunteers here."

Okay. That was something, but I needed more information. I bit my lower lip and tried to come up with something.

"Is there anything else?" Snippy Secretary asked.

I took a sharp breath. "Well, I'm surprised you say that because Dr. Carl Schneider called me yesterday afternoon and told me that he'd keep a position open for me there."

There was a pause on the other end. Now I was making her think of what to say. Why? What was it about Dr. Schneider's name that kept her from ticking out another edgy comment?

"Ma'am?" I asked. "Did you hear me about Dr. Schneider?"

Without an ounce of her former snippiness, the receptionist spoke in a very quiet, almost respectful voice. It was almost like she wasn't sure if she should be saying anything at all but her mouth was unable to stop itself. "Would you like to be transferred so you can speak to Dr.

Schneider himself?"

He was there! That turncoat! That creep! He ran off to go work for Affron. I bet he was with the mermaid. I felt the heat rise to my face, but I tried not to convey it in my voice.

"No, I don't want to bother him at this moment. I need to send him my resume. He requested it, but he left before I could deliver it to him personally. Could you please give me an address?"

"Oh no," the receptionist said too quickly. "I think it would be fine if you wanted to fax it to us. Here is the number."

I wrote it down, but that didn't do me any good at all. I thanked her for the information. She asked for my name, but I hung up instead. I'm sure it was a last ditch effort to save herself from having given away too much information. She would have told Schneider I called, and then he'd know I was on to him. Can't have that.

I flipped on the computer as Carter walked into the office.

"Whatcha looking up now?" he asked.

"Dr. Schneider's at a place called the North Shore Rehabilitation Aquarium. You heard of it? It's funded by Affron."

"I don't know it."

I typed the name into the search engine but got nothing. I looked up the Affron web page again but couldn't find it on their list of charities. I then looked up the area code of the phone number and got the northeast corner of Washington State.

"There's nothing up there but a national park and the islands," Carter said. "I can't think where there would be an aquarium. Not a substantial one, anyway."

Islands? I flipped around to Carter. "Which islands?"

"The San Juan Islands."

My heart started to race. Juarez Peña had talked about those islands yesterday. He grew up there with legends about mermaids and killer whales. They had that *Potlach* event where they threw shell jewelry into the sea during the summer. My mermaid was wearing a shell necklace when we found her.

"That's where the mermaids are from," I nearly shouted. I told Carter all about Peña's stories. He nodded more enthusiastically with each detail I remembered. "There is an aquarium up there somewhere on one of those islands. There has to be." I felt my eyes grow wide and my heart lurched right up into my throat. "Oh my God, Carter."

He nodded at me, his eyes as large as mine felt. He knew what I was going to say. "They know all about the mermaids," he choked out. "They're collecting them."

"You don't think Schneider knew about this, do you?"

Carter winced and then shook his head. "No. I don't. He's been genuinely surprised at every turn since you guys showed up with those mermaids on Tuesday morning."

"Well, he's caught up in it now," I said. "I wonder what they've got him there for."

We heard a loud bang come from the front room of the center. Carter and I both dashed out of the office and toward the double doors to make sure no one had snuck in and knocked over something. Coming from the other direction was Regina and her crew. Her blond hair was snagged out of its barrettes, and her lipstick had been licked away. Marlee and Haley looked equally frazzled. The boys came in behind them, slouched and beaten.

"They. Are. Gone," Regina announced dramatically as we skidded to a stop in front of her. "Please tell me you have a Coke machine and a chair."

"We have a chair," Carter returned.

She rolled her eyes and followed him to a folding chair by the large cabinets. "All the reporters and weirdos have left."

"I still don't understand why we can't go too," Marlee said. "There aren't any mermaids here."

Gary snorted, "And there never were."

"That's right," I said. "There are no mermaids here. So you guys can head on back to Olympia and not worry about it anymore."

Regina sneered at me but didn't say anything. The boys sat on the big tables while Marlee walked around and looked at fish in the aquariums. Haley approached me just as Marlee squealed "It's so cute!" over the sight of the sea otter. "It's like a puppy!"

"What are you going to do now?" Haley asked. "Go back to the beach?"

What I wanted to do was call Juarez Peña and ask him if he knew

170

where we might find an aquarium in the San Juan Islands. However, I couldn't do that with Miss Nosy and the Nosettes around.

"I don't know, Haley," I told her. "I'm kind of done with the interviews today. I think I might just go home."

"But where *are* the mermaids? Do you know?"

I grabbed her elbow and led her toward the office door. I whispered, "Look, Haley, I have some suspicions, but I don't know anything for sure. I don't mean to sound rude, but it would really be a lot easier for me to find them and take care of all this without you and your *friends* around."

"I can get rid of them if you'll let me stay."

I flashed my eyes over to Regina who was staring at the two of us, clearly unhappy about being left out of a conversation. We had seconds before Her Highness interrupted, so I tugged Haley into the office and closed the door. "Do you really think that Regina will do what you ask?" I paused, trying not to say it, but it blurted out anyway. "I'm pretty sure it's the other way around."

The hurt in Haley's eyes was instant, but it was brief before the anger chased it out. "You don't understand anything. If you want to be unpopular and picked on for the rest of your life, go right ahead."

"I'm not going to be unpopular for the rest of my life. Only for eight more months. Then guess what? I'll be out of high school. Hopefully, I'll take off halfway through the summer for California and get ready to start college. Regina won't be popular there. No one will have ever heard of her. So, I don't really care if she likes me or not."

"Well, I care," Haley said weakly. "We've both wanted this since elementary school."

I shook my head. "No. I haven't. Just you."

"If we're so different, then why have we even been friends?"

Now I was the one hurt. "Because I like *you*, Haley. I wanted to be friends with *you*. Only you. Not them. And I thought you wanted to be my friend too. If I'd known you would dump me the second Regina offered to include you in the Use and Abuse Club, I'd have done things differently."

Her voice dropped to a crackly whisper so quiet I could barely hear her. "They don't use and abuse."

171

"Really?" I asked. "Then how did they get here? Do you think I invited them? When this mermaid thing is over, they'll be done with you and you'll be nothing to them again. Go back home and forget about it. Tell them the mermaids are gone and we have no idea how to find them."

A spark flashed in Haley's eyes, a kind of intensity I've never seen before. She took a step toward me, and I took a step back, stumbling over Dr. Schneider's office chair. "But if we found the mermaids it would be different, June. If we found them, we'd be popular and famous as a whole group. We'd have a stellar senior year. Go out as Queens of the School, leaving a legacy behind us. Come on, June. We've been losers our whole lives. Do this for me. Please, I'm begging you."

"I don't want…"

And just like that the flash was gone. Her eyes filled with that sadness I've always known in her. That hopelessness at being permanently on the bottom rung of the social ladder. She plopped onto the upholstered chair in the corner, right on top of all the papers and files.

"I'm not going to California," she said. "I'll be stuck here going to the same college they'll probably go to. I'll have to deal with them for a long time. And I won't have you anymore. Please. I need this. Let me be part of the rescue or whatever it is that you have to do to find the mermaids."

I didn't know what to do. Haley had been the center of my life for so long, and I didn't want to let her down. Carter was new to me, and I didn't want to let him down either. He would be furious with me if I dragged Haley and the high school crew along with us. It would be one more mark on my "too immature for him" list. Then, of course, there was my mermaid. I had to consider what would happen to her. Would seven teenagers barging into the building up there be effective or stupid?

"You're not going to let me join you, are you?" Haley said, her voice cracking and tears forming in the corners of her eyes.

Carter opened the office door a crack and stuck his head in. "Time is slipping away from us, June. We've got to get moving." He looked at Haley and saw that she was crying. I caught the very quick irritated sigh he gave, but I also watched him stifle it as he stepped fully into the room and closed the door behind him. "You two all right?" He pulled a tissue from a box on a shelf and handed it to Haley.

"Yes, thanks," Haley said, her eyes wide with adoration for this guy who had in one gesture treated her better than any boy she'd ever met in her life. "We're fine."

"She wants to come with us," I said. "I know you probably don't want that."

Carter smiled that charming smile at me that I loved so much, and I knew he was about to make everything work out. "Actually, I think we're really going to need that blond dude's truck. If we find our silver girl, how are we going to get her away from that place?"

"I hadn't thought of that." We both smiled at Haley. She looked from Carter's face to mine and back again trying to understand what we were saying exactly. When the clarity popped in, she practically flew toward me for a hug.

"Really? Thank you! Thank you, June! Oh my gosh! I love you!" Then she hugged Carter, who kept his face toward me as he laughed. "I love you too," Haley said. "I hope you and June fall in love and get married and have little perfect babies."

Regina slammed the door open. "I am so tired of sitting out there. It stinks, and I'm bored." She looked at all of us hugging and laughing. "Did I miss something?"

Carter pulled away from Haley. "Call your parents to get permission. We're all taking a road trip north." He pushed past her and walked over to Ted and Gary to discuss using the truck.

"Is this some kind of joke?" Regina asked.

"Nope," I answered. "We're going to try to find the mermaid. You're going to help."

"That is what I wanted to hear," she replied. She threw her most winning popular girl smile at Haley and thrust out her arms for a hug. "You are such a great friend, Haley. I don't know what I'd do without you."

Haley grabbed my hand and said, "I think you're a great friend, too," while pulling me right past Regina and out the door.

Chapter Seventeen

Ten minutes later we were loaded in the cars with some fast food and every cell phone in use as everyone called their parents to announce we would be getting home pretty late. Haley chose to ride in the back seat of Carter's car. Regina and Marlee followed in their car, and the boys rode in the truck behind them. We all decided squishing five of us into one car was not going to be fun for anyone, even though Regina was pretty ticked off that she was going to be out of the conversation for the next three hours.

Haley didn't actually tell her mom where she was going specifically, just that she was still helping my parents and me. It wasn't a total lie. She knew her mother would never be okay with her driving all the way up to the islands just below the Canadian border. The others didn't have any problem getting permission for whatever stories they made up. They were the stars of the school, after all, and that made for trusting parents. I don't know that they would have been so enthusiastic if they'd known I was dragging their kids to a secret aquarium to barge inside and perhaps get us all arrested for trespassing. That knowledge might have garnered a different response.

I called my own mom to let her know what was going on. She picked up the phone after two rings. "No comment," she said before I could even get out a hello.

"Mom! Wait! Don't hang up!" I shouted into the phone. I could sense my mom raising the phone back up to her ear.

"June? Is that you? I'm so sorry, honey. If I made you feel bad. I didn't mean to do that." It was an unusually panicky tone for her, so I figured she meant what she was saying. Still, I didn't say anything when she paused for a response. "Where are you? Your father and I have been worried sick."

"Look," I didn't have time to ask permission or deal with parental issues. "Carter and I are going to the San Juan Islands up near Vancouver to find Dr. Schneider and the mermaids. I don't have an exact address, but when I get it I'm going to send it to you. When I call you I want you to immediately send that address to every news correspondent on our list. Don't do anything until then but have it ready to go. Let's give those mermaid seekers out there a target. That target is going to be Affron. Got it?"

My mom started in with all her usual criticisms and suggestions. I was too young. Maybe she should go with me. Or instead of me. I didn't have time for all that. I still had to get hold of Juarez Peña. I told her I had everything under control and hung up on her. I'm sure that put her in a snit, but what else could I do? She'd get over it one day. And if my whole plan bombed, as it very likely could, she'd have this moment to pick at me with for the rest of my life.

I pulled up Peña's number on my contacts list. He was thrilled to hear from me. I told him what I suspected about Affron having a secret aquarium, that Schneider was there, and that we thought they knew about the mermaids.

"You know that your story gets more outlandish every day, right?" he said to me. "Especially after the porpoise thing this morning and you taking off right afterward. Everyone's been calling you a fake and a liar. Your mom's going nuts trying to keep your story fresh, but she has no new details to add, and your dad's screaming at anyone who talks to him because all the mermaid seekers are out in rented boats stirring up all that oil. The traffic is out of control along the whole coast, and now you want people to believe that Affron Oil is collecting mermaids in a secret tank up near Canada?"

"I know it sounds farfetched, but I thought if anyone believed me it would be you. You're the one who told me about all that mermaid tradition stuff up there."

"Oh, I believe you, June. I might be crazy and the only person who really does, but I definitely believe you." Then he gave me a plan to follow. He said to stay on the 5 freeway all the way past Mount Vernon and then to Anacortes where he'd meet us at the ferry station and go with us to the aquarium. "I'm pretty sure that if it is anywhere, it is probably on the Orcas Island. I know San Juan Island pretty well and can't think of where it would be hiding. Orcas Island is the next biggest island, and its name is so cleverly coincidental."

I laughed and agreed to meet him.

When I got off the phone we flipped on the news radio station and listened for updates on my parents. It was hard hearing all those reporters say such awful things about my parents and me. A couple times I punched the button to turn it off, and we'd all sit in the car silently for a few minutes. Then, because I couldn't stand not knowing more, I'd creep my finger back and turn the damn thing on again. The reporters made me out to be nothing more than a clever prankster. They flat out made fun of my mom and all her efforts. They laughed at her attempts to make Affron the bad guy in this whole mermaid/oil scheme. They said she and my dad needed to get their hippie liberal noses out of big business and go live in a tree house somewhere.

"That would be best for the Sawfeather family," the talk show host quipped, "because they wouldn't have any electricity to make their computers work. You love your redwoods and screech owls so much? Go live with them."

I felt really guilty for not being back at the beach to help my folks fend off these horrible insults, but I would have been useless to them. Finding the mermaids was the only thing that would help now. It would help keep my mom's reputation and integrity intact, my dad's mission from failing, and the mermaids alive.

Before we knew it, we were past Seattle and heading toward the mountains. The trees were lush and beautiful. All our cell phones were dying because we hadn't been able to recharge them, so I turned mine completely off to save what I had left for that emergency call to my mom. We finally got to Anacortes and parked side by side in the ferry lot. Everyone got out stretching after being cramped up for so many hours.

"You guys drive slow," Ted said. "I could have shaved half an hour off our time if I'd been in front."

"You'd have gotten lost if you were in front," Regina snapped. Ted looked like he was about to snap back at her, but at a glance from her he dropped his head and stared at his feet. Gary smacked Ted and walked away. I guessed what they had talked about during their ride and I wondered how long it would take before Ted listened to Gary and broke up with Princess Regina. I knew another pretty blonde girl who would treat him a lot better.

Her Royal Highness looked at me, "So what's going on?"

"We're meeting a reporter here," I told her.

"Just one?" She seemed disappointed. "Where are the rest?"

"Still bugging my mom and dad at the beach. Haven't you been listening to the news?"

Marlee sneered. "News? Ugh. Boring. Who listens to that?"

Carter just threw up his hands and laughed. "Really? Haley, I don't get what you see in these people."

Haley mumbled only loud enough for me to hear, "Me either."

I smiled but didn't let on that I'd heard her say anything. "Let's look into the ferry schedule and get some tickets." I ushered everyone toward the ticket window.

The lady behind the glass peered over her bifocals at me. "Shouldn't you all be in school?"

"We're in college," I lied. Carter waved his college I.D. at her.

"And it's after 3:00 in the afternoon," Regina informed her.

The ticket lady snorted. Maybe everyone under forty looked like a kid to her.

I asked, "Do you know of an aquarium on one of the islands?"

"There's a zoo in Vancouver," she replied. "I think they have a small exhibit there of some tropical fish and amphibians."

"No," I said. "That's not what I mean. I'm talking about something more like a place where marine biologists take care of and study sea creatures."

"I don't know anything about that," she answered plainly. "You still want tickets?"

I paused, not really sure how many tickets to get. Did we need to take all three cars? "We need at least one for the pick-up. How long does it take to get to Orcas Island?"

"An hour and a half."

I turned around and bit my lip as I shook my head at Carter. "That's pushing it. What if they close before 4:30?"

"*We* never close at 4:30."

"I don't want to have come up here for nothing."

The lady leaned closer to the window. "Do you want the tickets or not? The ferry will be here in about fifteen minutes."

A loud whirring filled the air, and wind began to whip at us. The Channel 4 News helicopter lowered into view and prepared to land in the empty end of the parking lot.

"Ah! My hair!" Regina screamed, frantically trying to grab her blonde hair with her fists to keep it out of her face. Marlee screamed too. Gary laughed at the girls, and Ted turned his back to Regina and also burst out laughing.

I loved it. My hair blew wild like Pocahontas. I almost broke into a rendition of "Colors of the Wind", but Carter grabbed my hand to pull me toward the helicopter. Juarez Peña stepped out. He was all smiles when he saw me. Chuck Emory was right behind him, waving.

"Bet you thought I wouldn't make it," he said, patting me on the shoulder.

"Never entered my head," I lied.

"Well, let's do this."

"Do what?" I asked.

"You're coming with me on the helicopter," he informed me, "so we can get there as quickly as possible. The rest will have to ferry it over."

Carter raised his hand and pointed at himself. "Can I come with you?"

"Not enough room."

He shook his head and blew out some frustrated air. But just as quickly, he overcame that with his fabulous smile combined with a wink to me. "You *so* owe me for this."

"Whatever you want!" I shouted at him as he took off toward the others. When I felt certain he was out of earshot, I added, "I love you!"

But he turned back toward me one more time, both his arms wide open as if to offer me the world as he walked backward, and then he brought his hands into his heart before pivoting back to my high school crew again.

Cry of the Sea

Despite the breeze from the helicopter blades, I felt hot all over.

"That guy seems like a good one," Juarez Peña said to me. "You should hang on to him."

"I plan to."

I boarded the helicopter and seconds later we were over the water. There were a lot of islands; I didn't know there were so many. So much for paying attention to state geography in 4th grade. Peña had the pilot fly us over San Juan Island just to be sure we were headed to the right place. The rain from this morning had finally moved out, making it a fairly clear afternoon for Washington. We had a good view. He pointed out most of the buildings he saw along the coastline and told me what they were. Nothing struck him as unfamiliar or new.

Orcas Island is nearly cut in half by East Sound, and at first I thought it was two separate islands, each as large as the other. Both halves were equally covered with forest and not terribly populated. A gorgeous resort area marked the shore on the southeastern corner of the island, and I really wanted to be on the ground to check it out. I daydreamed about having a honeymoon with Carter there.

I had a particularly nice image forming in my mind of Carter stepping into the hot tub to join me on our secluded deck, when Peña shouted, "There!" He pointed at something in the distance, and the pilot swerved the helicopter that direction.

Nearly hidden by trees on one side, a flat, one-story building jutted into the water as though at least half the building was floating. I'd heard of a public aquarium in Monterey, California that had some of the tanks built right into the ocean, basically cutting off a real slice of Pacific for show. They had kelp forests and all the indigenous water creatures in them. What I saw below looked like it might be built in a similar way, with views that looked straight out into the water. I wondered how deep the structure went.

"That has to be it," I agreed.

Peña had the pilot fly the helicopter back to the resort where we could land it. There wasn't any place for us near the aquarium—too much woodland. Plus, the noise of the helicopter would have brought a lot of attention. Some quick phone calls were made back to the local news station, and resort staff met us quickly and provided a van for us to use.

Chuck drove this time while Peña and I kept an eye out for a sign or driveway that might lead us to that building we'd seen from the sky. We found ourselves on a two-lane road that wound along the coast. It was quite thin but well paved, like it wasn't terribly old and hadn't been used too much. We didn't see any mile markers or signs for tourists at all.

The two-lane road dead-ended at a small parking lot for the aquarium, the kind only big enough for the staff and no guests. It didn't have any signs on the front of the building to announce itself, and there hadn't been anything on the road for the tourists like "Aquarium" and an arrow pointing the way to tell of its existence. Most aquariums have murals painted on them or some flashy architecture to draw the eye and make the place inviting. Not this place. The building was square, flat and white. It could be any office building anywhere in the world. This place was a secret and not meant to be visited. I did catch an address, however, and I asked Peña to text it to my mother but to let her know not to do anything yet.

I wished Carter was here with us, but I figured the gang was still a good forty minutes out. I turned on my phone long enough to text him our location, so they'd know where to go after they landed. Then I shut the phone back off again, hoping my directions were enough to get them to the right place.

As I got out of the van, Chuck reached for his camera.

"No," I said. "Don't come in with me yet. I'm still going to try my Invited Intern routine and see if it can gain me some access. I need you guys to wait out here for the others or until I call for help."

"I think we should go in there guns blazing," Chuck said. "Don't give them time to hide anything."

Juarez patted Chuck on the knee to calm him down. "We'll wait, June, but not for long. We'll be right outside the door. If we don't hear from you in a reasonable time, we're barging in."

I agreed, hoping that a reasonable amount of time was more than a minute or two. I didn't have any idea what I was getting into.

Two thin windows flanked the unremarkable front door of the building, and I couldn't see much through them. The beauty of the interior instantly took me aback when I stepped inside. The hardwood floors shined between ornate floor rugs; the walls were painted in gorgeous sunset colors with tropical fish aquariums built right into them. Compared to the drab and nearly invisible exterior of the building, the colors and richness of this front lobby was vivid and unexpected. The lobby ran the entire width of the building with a receptionist desk smack dab in the center, featuring one lone woman who put down her novel when I came through the door.

She looked exactly like I imagined with the bob haircut and sweater. I had it right except her nose was much bigger.

"Yes, you've missed the hiking trail by a couple miles," she answered as though certain that was my question because she'd been asked a hundred times before. "All you have to do is go back down the road and watch for the small brown marker sign. It'll be on the right hand side of the road. You kind of have to look for it, because it is too low down, in my opinion."

Honestly, I almost said "Oh, thanks. I'll be sure to look for it" and walked out. My tongue felt thick in my mouth as it hit me that I really didn't have any idea what the heck I was doing. But I didn't turn around and leave. I kept walking toward her.

"I'm uh… not looking for a hiking trail." Her eyebrows went up with curiosity, but her chin plopped down on her hand as though there was nothing I could say that would be something she hadn't heard before. "I'm here to see Dr. Carl Schneider."

The boredom fled as alarm filled her eyes instead. I wondered if the receptionist knew who I was. Could she remember my voice as well as I remembered hers? Had she told anybody about the call?

"I'm afraid Dr. Schneider is busy at the moment," the receptionist said too smoothly.

I didn't want to look like I didn't know what do next. I placed my hands on the front of the desk and leaned in to the receptionist. "Look," I commanded. "I am Juniper Sawfeather. You may have heard of me. I have a news crew outside from Channel Four, and they really want to get in here to see if I'm right about some secret research Dr. Schneider and your people are doing. If you don't want me to call them in this very second, you will direct me to Dr. Schneider or whoever he works for right now."

The receptionist craned her head past me to look through the thin windows beside the front door. Juarez Peña stood there with a news camera in his hands and waved at her.

The woman's fingers trembled as she pushed the intercom button. "Sir? A Juniper Sawfeather is here to see you and Dr. Schneider. She's here with Channel 4 News television." She paused to listen. "Yes sir. I'll send her right down." The receptionist took her finger off the button and slipped both hands under the desk where I couldn't see them fidget. "Mr. Cortlandt will see you in his office."

A door opened down toward the far left of the lobby, and another woman that I guessed was Mr. Cortlandt's personal secretary motioned for me to follow her. She led me through a curving hallway of closed doors and steps that went ever downward. Not a sound emanated from any of the offices we passed, making me wonder if anyone was here. I noticed that the place was devoid of any music. A deep silence filled the air that made me too aware of how fast I was breathing. The secretary opened the last door at the end of the hall for me and gestured for me to step inside. I did and she closed it behind me, leaving me alone with Mr. Cortlandt who sat at his desk facing away from me.

Chapter Eighteen

An eel in its cave. That's what I thought as I stepped toward the heavy desk. The wall behind Mr. Cortlandt's desk was made entirely of glass, but instead of being a lovely island view, it exposed the cloudy strait waters. The busy water reflected on the blue walls of the office, making the whole room take on the effect of an underwater cave.

I felt like spooky sea monsters of the deep were lurking about me, ready to snap out and gobble me up at any moment. My feelings were justified when Mr. Cortlandt spun around in his chair to greet me. Brown spots were scattered across his balding head. His teeth seemed almost too big for his mouth, giving him that evil, leering look that is so common to eels. His eyes were small and beady too, as if the absence of direct light to this room had caused him to slowly go blind.

Naturally, I hated him on sight. I tried to imagine him with a wife. Somebody out there in the world might actually think he was quite cute and charming. Ugh. The thought made me shiver.

I thought of the person I considered cute and charming. Carter. No one could describe him as being like an eel. I held his smile in my mind and let it calm me as the slimy voice of Mr. Cortlandt filled the eerie room.

"Miss Sawfeather. I knew it was a matter of time before you found us. Although, I have to admit I didn't expect you to arrive so soon." He gestured for me to take a seat, but I continued to stand.

"Guess you underestimated me. Before I do the same to you, how about you tell me who you are exactly? Are you in charge of this aquarium? Are you a scientist? Are you Dr. Schneider's boss?" I did a quick pause and added. "Or do you just work for Affron Oil?"

"Please sit, Miss Sawfeather," Mr. Cortlandt said, gesturing to the seat again. This time, I took him up on his offer, but I sat very straight, ready to get up quickly if I needed to. "The answer is yes to all of those questions. I am the leading marine biologist at this facility. Dr. Schneider now works directly under me here, but his center downstate is also under an umbrella of several marine rehabilitation centers that all report to me. All of these centers are funded in part by a grant from Affron Oil, so I do work for them in a manner of speaking. I am hardly what you could consider an Affron employee, however." He tried smiling at me, but it just made him look creepier.

"Mr. Cortlandt," I said as business-like as possible but cutting right to the chase. "I am here because I know that you have the mermaids I discovered on Grayland Beach. Dr. Schneider and the mermaids have been missing from the Sea Mammal Rescue Center, and I know that they are here. I suspect that there are other mermaids here as well."

His grin evaporated immediately. "Yes, I know all about your escapades with the press, trying to convince them of real mermaids. I have to say, Miss Sawfeather, that there are no mermaids. What you discovered were three rare mutant fish."

"Nice try," I said. "I know what I saw." He shrugged like he didn't care. "Since you know I'm right," I continued anyway, "and you know that the press is outside, are you going to take me to the mermaids?"

"No."

Not a pause. Not a thought. His answer was definitive. A man used to saying no.

But I wasn't done yet.

"If you have watched the news at all lately, then you know that there is a lot of interest in these mermaids. Whether or not you have them here, people are going to be interested that I think you do. One report from that news team outside is going to bring thousands of people crashing through the doors of this place and scuba diving past your lovely window here."

Mr. Cortlandt seemed to growl, his lips pulling back from those enormous teeth. "Again, I tell you, there is nothing here for your news team to report. There are no mermaids."

"Then why is Dr. Schneider here?" I asked. "Why would he

abandon an entire rehabilitation center full of sea animals rescued from Affron's latest screw-up to come up here?"

"Dr. Schneider is here to do valuable research."

"On the mermaids. Who do you think you're fooling here?"

Mr. Cortlandt cleared his throat. "I think I'm talking to a dumb kid who is getting involved in matters way beyond her."

I couldn't stand this anymore. "Do you know who my parents are, Mr. Cortlandt?" I didn't give him time to answer. "My father is one the most famous activists in North America. His fight for our Chinook people and the environment are legendary. My mother, Natalie Brenner Sawfeather, is the leading environmental lawyer in Washington State. She is currently working on getting your company taken down for destroying the entire western coast of America with your oil spills. They are powerful people, my parents." As I ranted, I realized for the first time just how important my parents were to the world. "They have home phone numbers for nearly every member of Congress in the United States. They have numbers for many Canadian government officials as well. With one touch of the button on my cell phone here, I can send your address to my mom, and within an hour you'll have press and government officials from both countries swarming in here to see what you've really done with these mermaids." I pulled out my cell phone and turned it on. As it chimed to announce its power, I said, "Your company is so proud of their mission to 'make the world better'. So, what do you think will happen to Affron when people find out that you're hiding or perhaps even killing mermaids?"

The eel-man slammed his hands down on his desk. "Enough of your threats!" he shouted. "What does it matter if we have mermaids or not? In my opinion they are like fish! They breathe through water. They don't think. They don't communicate. None of our tests have shown otherwise." He stood up. "And what makes you presume we are doing anything harmful to them at all? We are simply studying them to prove whether or not they *can* be considered as part human—which we have definitely proven by now that they are *not*. Have you heard enough?"

From behind me, I heard the familiar voice of Dr. Schneider at the door. "No she hasn't," he said. "Not by a long shot."

Dr. Schneider walked toward the desk, and I stood up beside him.

He nodded at me but didn't smile. I wasn't sure if he was glad I was there or not. "Where is Carter?" he asked.

"He should be here any time."

Mr. Cortlandt spoke through gritted teeth. "Carl, remember, the tests we are doing on the mermaids are for the good of the environment and for mankind. It is important to know what we're dealing with before we let the whole world know about them. We've discussed the importance of this mission." He pointed at Dr. Schneider accusingly. "And you agreed with it."

"Yes, Bill," Dr. Schneider said, his tone equally confrontational. I was ready for them to launch over the desk at each other. If they weren't both old, crotchety men, I bet they would have. "And some of what we talked about makes a lot of sense. At the same time, though, you're leaving out the part where we discussed how my mission here is to prove without a doubt that these creatures are indeed *fish*. That they can be discarded just like trout or salmon. How they aren't any more important or valuable to the world than tuna, maybe even less so, since no one will want to eat them. You aren't talking about how I am to formulate these opinions no matter what the cost is to the mermaids."

"Carl," the man seethed. "You're out of line."

"No," Dr. Schneider said, "I'm finally on track for the first time since this began." He focused on me, and I'm sure I looked like a complete dork considering how dumbfounded I was at this heated exchange between the two men. "I need you to come with me."

"Carl," Mr. Cortlandt warned. "Don't do it."

Dr. Schneider ignored him and led me out of the office. He whispered to me, "I'd hit that button on your phone now." I nodded and did as he said.

"I'll call the police!" Mr. Cortlandt called after us.

"Do it!" Dr. Schneider shouted back over his shoulder as we headed up the hallway back to the main lobby. "I'd love to see what the news team outside does when the police show up."

Mr. Cortlandt's secretary popped out one of the doors in front of us, blocking our way. I heard Mr. Cortlandt scream for her. There was a moment where she was uncertain whether she should chase us or go back to the cave. He screamed her name again, and she left us.

"What's he going to do?" I asked Dr. Schneider.

"I'm not sure, but I don't think we have a lot of time."

We entered the lobby to find a huge commotion at the front door. The receptionist stood with her back to the door, using all her weight to keep it from being opened by the several sets of arms reaching through from the other side. I could see Marlee peering through the window with her hands cupped around her eyes. She saw me and waved at me excitedly. I saw her mouth move, and Regina's face appeared beside her.

I left Dr. Schneider's side and ran to the front door.

"June, we don't have time!" he shouted at me.

I pushed the receptionist out of the way and my friends tumbled inside. Carter, Ted and Gary fell over each other. Stepping over them were Juarez Peña and Chuck Emory. Peña had his microphone at the ready, and the camera was firmly on Chuck's shoulder already rolling. The girls strode in behind the reporters. Regina nudged Ted with her shoe to get out of the way, and he rolled to the side instead of standing.

"Dr. Schneider!" Carter gasped, leaping to his feet and bounding toward his boss. It was almost as if he hadn't truly believed his mentor was really a traitor until this second.

"Carter," Dr. Schneider said, motioning for him to follow. "Come with me. Hurry." Carter grabbed my hand, and we ran back to Dr. Schneider, who was already nearing the doorway at the far right of the lobby.

Regina shouted, "Where are you going?"

"Just stay here, Regina," I said.

"No! I'm done missing out."

I let go of Carter's hand and nodded that he and Dr. Schneider needed to continue on. "I'll catch up." I walked back to Regina. "Look, I don't have time to play this stupid game with you right now. Will you stop being such a power freak and realize that this has nothing to do with your stupid high school popularity. This is real life, and it's serious."

She sneered at me. "I know it's serious, June. I want to help. Really. What can I do that will help?"

Go away, I thought.

But right then Mr. Cortlandt and his secretary exploded into the lobby. "What the Hell is going on here?"

The receptionist skittered toward him. "I'm sorry, sir. I couldn't keep them out."

The news camera swung toward him. Peña raised his microphone to catch every word of what was going to happen.

I put my hand on Regina's shoulder. "Here's your golden moment. Keep that man here and keep him busy." She raised her hands to her hair. "Don't worry, you look beautiful as always." Regina smiled gratefully at me. "Go get him," I told her.

With that, Regina barged toward the eel-man with a thousand questions about mermaids and what this building was supposed to be used for. Between her and Peña, and the other Student Council team members blocking the way, Cortlandt would be held up for a few minutes at least.

I crooked a finger toward Haley to get her sneak away and follow me while the attention was off her. She backed away from the crowd and hurried with me through the door where we quickly caught up with Dr. Schneider and Carter.

The building was set up like a honeycomb, each octagon pod designated to a different sea creature or region of species. From what I could see as we passed the open doors, the tanks were completely enclosed, but a handful of the laboratories featured windows that had an ocean view like in Mr. Cortlandt's office. A single hallway connected all the pods and wound downward like a corkscrew, making each floor deeper under the water.

Near the bottom Dr. Schneider stopped, unlocked a door, and held it open for us to step inside. I noticed he kept his head hung low, not looking any of us in the eye as we passed him. He shut the door behind us. I barely registered it clicking into place because what I saw in front of me took away every sense as my body filled with rage and sorrow. The reality of what was before me was so much worse than I could have ever imagined.

A wall of glass stretching from floor to ceiling separated the mermaids from the laboratory. Even though the lights were kept extremely low in the tank, it wasn't hard to see that there were too many of these human-fish in there. I couldn't begin to count them all, but there had to be close to a hundred. They were so crowded together in the tank that they could barely move.

I walked over to the tank, crouched to the floor and pressed my hands and face against the cool glass, unable to speak. Maybe when I opened them again the sight would be gone.

No luck. The vision remained. The mermaids were crammed so tightly into the tank they looked more like oversized sardines than the beautiful creatures I had carried from beach. Some of them whimpered in their strange voices. Most of them trembled. All of them looked as though they might die at any moment.

Carter came over and helped me to my feet. Haley hung back by the computers, her mouth agape at the sight of the mermaids. "I can't believe there are so many," she whispered.

"What's the matter with them?" Carter asked.

"They're suffocating," Schneider answered. "Fish need to move to be able to get oxygen into their gills. They can't move in there."

I remembered what the mermaid had looked like when we first brought it to the center. Her skin was a deep navy blue from suffocation. Most of the mermaids in the tank were that color now. I stood up and faced Schneider.

"Don't look at me like that," he begged. "I asked to have some of them moved into different tanks but was given nothing but negatives. This is the only lab in the facility that locks, and it has the biggest tank. Affron couldn't afford to put the mermaids anywhere else. The risk of exposure was too high.

"So I dared to suggest, 'Why don't we stop collecting them?' Bill—Mr. Cortlandt—just laughed at me and said, 'Have you seen the madness out there? They'll be discovered before too long.' I reminded him, 'They've been discovered. The Sawfeather family has seen to that.'" Schneider sighed. "He didn't think you and your family were too much of a threat. 'It'll blow over,' he told me, 'if no one finds any more of them.'"

"Why didn't you let them go?" I asked. "If you thought it was wrong, why didn't you do something about it?"

"I couldn't," he said desperately. "They threatened my job."

"You can get another job," Haley said.

"Not without references and not after my name has been slandered as the crackpot who believes in mermaids."

"They threatened to shut down the center, too, didn't they?" Carter asked.

Schneider nodded. "I was ordered to study the mermaids like lab animals, and if they died, so be it. This was not what I expected when I got the call to come up here and work. I sincerely thought they wanted me to, oh, *make the world better*. That is their slogan, isn't it?"

Haley's voice came from behind Dr. Schneider. She was standing at his computer pressing buttons. "What is this graph showing?" I got up and moved with Carter over to the computer. Dr. Schneider wiped his forehead with a handkerchief and joined us. I noticed how his hands shook as he took the mouse from her and guided the cursor across the screen. He sat down and refused to raise his eyes to us as he found the work he wanted to show us. The man was truly wrecked.

"Don't think this was easy for me, kids," he said quietly. "When I first got here all I wanted to do was find our mermaid to make sure she was okay, but a lot of them wear the necklaces, and I couldn't pick her out."

He was right. The overpowering frailty of them had taken all my attention, but now that I looked closer, a lot of them wore the shell jewelry that Juarez Peña had told me about. I'd have to study the mermaids for a long time to find my girl, and I didn't have that kind of time. All I could hope was that she was in the tank, and that she knew I was here to help and not hurt her like Dr. Schneider had.

Dr. Schneider was still talking. "By the end of the first day all I'd managed to will myself to do was read the files about what they like to eat, discover that there were indeed male mermaids, and establish that they were dying. I kept putting off the autopsy of the dead mermaids, leaving them packed in ice. I didn't have the heart to pull any living ones out of the tank to study their reflexes or behaviors either.

"According to the papers I'd gathered from the other scientists who had been working on this project, the first mermaid had been discovered less than two years ago off Port Alberni just above Vancouver. Since then they'd popped up randomly, usually beached from oil spills or pollution. Most of the time they were in pairs or threes. Maybe they didn't like traveling alone. Or maybe the others got trapped while trying to rescue the first oil spill victim."

Carter interrupted, "Which is evidence that they are social creatures. Do you know any fish that would help each rescue each other?"

"Only people do that," I said.

With a sheepish grin, Haley said, "The fish do that in *Finding Nemo*."

I hit her and she mouthed "Sorry."

Dr. Schneider nodded and went on, "I wondered how long these creatures had existed. If they've been out there all these years, why were they starting to show up now? And why weren't they going away now that things were dangerous for them?" He pointed to a map that showed where the majority of the mermaids had been found. "It's almost like they're coming here on purpose to look for their missing relatives."

I walked over to the tank, searching the eyes of the mermaids for the one that might recognize me. "I'm kind of surprised you didn't jump into the biology and experiments, Dr. Schneider. Weren't you curious?"

"Sure I was curious," he said. "But I didn't want to do what they were asking of me. This work for Affron won't get my name written up in history. Who remembers the debunkers? When would there ever be a class taught in a college or university where the professor would ask, "Tell me the name of the man who proved that mermaids were nothing but over-sized halibut?"

"True," Carter said.

"Juniper Sawfeather's name is all over the news for discovering mermaids. You have fame now for that little thing, and if Affron hadn't taken the mermaids away, I could have expanded that discovery all the way to the cover of *Scientific American*. My name would have been in the annals of history. But that's all been taken away!"

He stabbed a button on the computer and a horrible squeaking and groaning came from speakers around the room. It sounded like whales. I covered my ears because it was so loud.

Dr. Schneider stood up, yelling over the noise. "This morning I was told that I had to start the experiments or think about flipping hamburgers for the rest of my life. I started with sound sensitivity and recognition. Whale and dolphin soundings. Mating calls and nursing coos at first. I got a reaction from them, but it wasn't significant. Then I switched it up and tried cries of distress. The mermaids reacted immediately and with much more demonstration. Watch them."

I had been staring at Dr. Schneider and the speakers, so I pivoted to take in the vision of the mermaids. Their heads were all up on stiff necks, and their strange, black eyes were open as wide as possible. They squirmed around as if they wanted to back away from this horrible sound. Some of them began to make their own calls, as if they were answering the voices they heard.

"Interesting, right?" Dr. Schneider yelled. "They're behaving like fish now, aren't they? Does this mean they don't think? No. But it does mean that they may not necessarily think like a human."

He switched off the noise. Tension fled from their bodies immediately and the relief in their demeanor was clear. Though now sadness filled the tank. Their heads drooped, and they brought their hands to their faces as though ashamed or devastated that they couldn't do anything to help the creatures they had been hearing.

I thought of my dad's Chinook tale of the killer whale and the mermaid's attachment to it. I recalled the legend Juarez Peña told me about the drowned sailors becoming killer whales. The island I was on was called Orcas. Now I know those weren't just silly legends or made up folklore. They were true accounts. The mermaids and the killer whales were linked in love and history. And they were linked to my people, the American Indians of the Pacific Northwest.

"Do you have a recording that is specifically of killer whales?" I asked. Honestly, I didn't want to hurt them, but I had to know if I was right.

"Yes, I do." Dr. Schneider hit a button and a horrible keening came out of the speakers.

All at once the mermaids began thrashing about. Slamming into each other. They frantically searched for a way to get out of the tank but couldn't find one. Some of the mermaids smashed their tales against the glass so hard I worried the five-inch thick glass might crack and jumped away.

"What's happening?" Haley screamed. "Why are they doing that?"

"Turn it off!" I shouted to Dr. Schneider.

"Fascinating," the scientist said, moving away from the computer and walking toward the tank. "Even more dynamic than last time."

"Hayley, turn it off!" I shouted, but she was panicking. I saw Carter push her to the side and frantically search for the way to end the recording. More slamming against the glass caught my attention. I shifted to look at the chaos and squeezing through the silver bodies was a face I recognized—my mermaid. I knew her big eyes, and I could tell she knew me. She pressed her hands up against the glass, and stared at me.

Noise crowded around me. The whale calls, the mermaids slamming against the glass, the sloshing of the water, Carter and Haley yelling at each other, and Dr. Schneider having some weird epiphany. I tried to tune it all out and focus on my mermaid. I locked eyes with her and stepped forward to put my hands over hers. All the noise became dulled, like I had stuffed cotton in my ears. What came through clearly was a voice that I couldn't understand at first. I focused harder. Nothing but the mermaid.

"Help them."

It wasn't quite words like that, but somehow I understood what she was telling me. I tried to respond to her with my mind, but I didn't know if I could send my thoughts to her the same way. "These whale cries aren't real. It's just a recording."

"Help them!"

"Ah ha!" I heard somewhere behind me—Carter's voice. The whale sounds stopped and the silence buzzed in my ears. I tried to stay concentrated on my mermaid.

"See? It stopped."

She nodded at me, but her eyes were still so sad.

"Help us."

"I'm trying."

"Is that her?" Haley asked, walking toward me.

"Yes."

"She's beautiful."

"Oh my God." That was from Carter. I tore my eyes away from the mermaid to find out what was upsetting him. "Did you know this would happen?" he yelled at Dr. Schneider.

"I… yes," the scientist stammered. "I tried it once before."

"Then why did you push that button?"

That's when I realized that there was something wrong even though the panic had stopped. Inside the tank several mermaids had been pressed so hard against the glass they were smothered to death. Five more were floating at the top of the tank lifeless.

"This is my fault," I said weakly.

"No, it's not," Haley said, putting her hand on my shoulder. She pointed at Schneider. "It's his."

I ran over and pushed Dr. Schneider in the chest. "So you knew that they would freak out like that? Why didn't you say, 'No, June, we can't play those sounds, it'll kill them'?"

"It wasn't so extreme last time. I didn't think."

I screamed at him. "You never think! You are the stupidest scientist I've ever met!"

"June, look!" Carter yelled over me. He yanked my hand and pulled me away from Dr. Schneider. He wrapped his arms around me tightly as we faced the aquarium. It wasn't until I felt the pressure of his arms around me that I realized I had been shivering. I leaned my head back against his chest and took in the sight in front of me.

Inside the tank, the mermaids were now rushing up and toward the back where part of the top of the tank was opening up. I got as close to the glass as I could to be able to see what was happening. Four men in wet suits and scuba gear were there, pulling the mermaids up and over the top of the tank out to the open water. Mermaids hoisted their torsos up with their arms and flipped over the top, with a push from the men to get them going.

"What's happening?"

Dr. Schneider laughed. "They're being released. Cortlandt must really be in a jam up there with the reporters you sent."

"That's good, right?" Haley checked.

"Of course it's good," I said. "For the mermaids. But now there won't be any evidence that they were here or that they exist. When the reporters get down here, they'll all be gone. Right, Dr. S.? Guess you really won't be in *Scientific American* now, will you?"

My mermaid banged with her fist on the glass. I went back to her and put my hands over hers again. Her eyes were much brighter, and she had a wisp of a grin on those thin lips. I could almost see that dimple in her cheek. "You'll be safe now," I thought to her.

"Come with us," she shared with me.

"I can't."

Her silver forehead wrinkled. "You—in the water—with me—before."

"I can't live like that."

The brightness in her eyes fled again. Nearly all of the living mermaids were out of the tank now. She had to go.

"I will find you again," she thought to me.

"I will be looking."

She swam away from me and hauled herself over the opening. Then the two men dove into the tank to start removing the dead mermaid bodies. They lifted them up and over the glass and dropped them far enough away that the murky water obscured them from vision. All this happened in minutes.

As the last mermaid vanished with a diver, I heard a commotion in the hallway outside. A lot of voices. A key turned in the lock, and a second later Dr. Cortlandt entered followed by his secretary, Peña, Regina, and a whole lot of other reporters and cameras. Mr. Boyle, the thug who stole my mermaid from the Center in Aberdeen stepped in behind the crowd and made his way to Schneider's desk.

I motioned to Carter to keep an eye on the man, and he nodded.

"Juniper Sawfeather," Mr. Cortlandt said, approaching me with an outstretched arm and a smile. "Here you are. We have been looking all over this building for you."

A dozen microphones poked toward me.

Juarez Peña asked the first question, "So, where are the mermaids, Juniper?"

"They're gone," I answered. "There were close to a hundred in that tank until two minutes ago. Mr. Cortlandt ordered them released before you could get down here to see them."

Cortlandt laughed his fake, eely laugh. His secretary joined him, and I decided she was similar to a barracuda. "A hundred mermaids in a tank that size and then extracted in a just a few short minutes? Does that even seem plausible?"

The reporters muttered about how this didn't make any sense at all. A profound disappointment crossed Peña's face too.

"We all saw them!" Haley shouted out. "Some were dead, even."

Marlee screeched, "You saw the mermaids?"

Regina pushed toward Haley. "A loser like you gets to see the mermaids while I'm stuck up in the lobby with all these stupid reporters and this ugly, weird man."

Ted grabbed his girlfriend's arm and yanked her back so that she lost her balance and fell back into a desk chair. "Leave her alone, Regina. You're just embarrassing yourself."

I stepped between Haley and Regina as the popularity queen struggled to regain her balance with no help at all from Ted, who had moved over to his snickering best friend. "I let Haley come see them because she's my best friend. You are the loser today."

Regina's eyes turned to thin little beads. If they could shoot lasers, they would have. "I think this whole thing was a hoax, June. And I'm going to make sure everyone at school knows you're a fake."

"Fine!"

She grabbed Marlee's hand and pulled her out of the laboratory. Gary followed while shouting, "I told you it was fake. I can't believe you made me miss practice for this." Ted lingered an extra moment, passing a final apologetic glance at Haley before walking out too.

Cortlandt stepped up to me, gesturing to the empty tank. "So, now you've lost your popularity and your credibility. Anything else you want to say, Miss Sawfeather?"

"Yeah." I faced the reporters. "I wish you all had gotten here faster. You let Affron win again."

At that, I pushed through them and headed for the door with Haley and Carter close behind.

Chapter Nineteen

College catalogs and application forms littered the living room. My mom and I pored through each one that looked interesting. So far (and we'd been at this for forty-five minutes) neither of us had raised our voices or looked cross-eyed at each other. It was truly a miracle.

"Now, what about San Diego?" Mom finally asked. I know she'd been avoiding it. "Isn't that where you said you wanted to go?"

"I've thought about it," I confessed. "I thought really hard. Part of me still wants to go there because I know they have the best program, but another part of me thinks I should stay in this area."

Mom grinned as she ran her fingers through my long, black hair. "Could it have anything to do with a young college student majoring in Biology?"

I felt my cheeks get hot. "Maybe," I answered. "It also has to do with something else."

Mom nodded, but the grin changed to something more sincere. "You know the chances of seeing another mermaid are slim."

"Oh, I know," I said too quickly to fool her. "If they've got any brains at all they're probably far, far away from here." I knew that wasn't true, though. They've lived out there in our waters for hundreds of years, and I didn't believe they would abandon their homes or their killer whales. Every couple weeks I headed out to Grayland Beach to see if maybe my mermaid friend was swimming around by the buoys keeping an eye out for me.

I flipped through the pages of a Humboldt University catalog slowly, but I wasn't looking at the pictures. I remembered all the effort it took to get the reporters to finally stop harassing our family and go away.

There hadn't been much point in defending my story any longer. No one believed me anyway. Plus, someone at Affron nicely retouched my video for me, messing with the image, brightening it too much and setting the contrast way off. It looked ridiculous. Not even worthy of the tabloid rags. Somehow, when this new image got spread around the Internet, the old one was forgotten.

Haley was angrier about it than me. She came over on Saturday afternoon, the day after our adventure, to show me what had happened and how quickly. "I worked hard on that video."

"I know," I said. "I think that Boyle guy wiped out all Schneider's research, too. Carter said he was messing with the computer the whole time Regina was wigging out. So, there's no proof of anything."

"Well, I wouldn't say *no* proof," Haley said. She reached into her jeans pocket and pulled out a flash drive. "A good nerd always has one handy."

I grabbed her up for a big hug. "You're the best."

"I'll keep it safe. Who knows when it might come in handy?"

Over the next few weeks, Haley and I gradually went from being teased and hassled around campus to being ignored and forgotten once again. Glad to know things could get back to normal. We did manage to recruit six members to our Recycling Club, and we were already making a difference around campus. I promise that I wasn't hijacking backpacks for water bottles. Actually, most of the support came from the many friends of the newly single Ted Cowley, who had become our most enthusiastic member and attended every meeting.

The stories about the whole mermaid sighting being a scam made all the crowds disappear. All that remained were the die-hard conspiracy freaks. There's not much you can do to stop them once they get a hint that something supernatural is out there. My parents had to do a lot of work explaining how their daughter had tricked them as well—the only way to save their reputations. It hurt to hear them bash me, but none of it was how they truly felt and we'd all agreed telling lies was the only option.

Eventually though, the whole thing went away. Just another urban legend.

I had worried that disregarding the mermaids would wind up helping

Affron. Luckily, my parents, the world's greatest environmental activists, knew what to do. They used the footage my dad and I shot of the oil-coated sea life (absent of mermaids) and took it right to the governments of both countries. Armed with laws about oil tanker retrofitting and signed promises from Affron not to roll that fateful night, my mother had a case that knocked Affron on its butt.

According to legislation in both Canada and the United States, Affron had to cease operation until all their tankers were redesigned and inspected by government officials. On top of that, they were hit with heavy fines and forced to put a much larger percentage of their profits into the condition and staffing of their rehabilitation centers.

I raised my eyes over the college catalog and gazed at my mom with admiration. She really was a powerful and wonderful person.

"The other reason I was thinking of staying close to home is that I think I kind of got a taste for this activist stuff," I told her. "I thought I'd stick around and help you and Dad out."

Mom pulled me in for a squeeze and tossed the Humboldt catalog on the floor. "You can do whatever you want, June," she said. "I'll be proud of you no matter what you choose or where you choose to do it. I've raised the strongest, most incredible girl in the world."

We decided to call it quits for the night. Too many decisions to make with Dad out of the house. So, while Mom made dinner, I headed up to my room.

I dropped a bit of food into the goldfish bowl on my dresser and watched the tiny creature swim around and gobble up the flakes. Then, as slowly as I could, I dipped my finger into the bowl. At first the fish backed away from me, but I was persistent. I held my finger absolutely still and waited. Curious, the goldfish approached my finger and seemed to be sniffing it. After a moment the goldfish must have sensed that the finger would cause it no harm, so it swam around, pressing its little body against the finger, enjoying the sensation of touch.

The phone rang. Wiping my wet finger on my jeans, I picked it up. "Hello? Dad? Are you okay?"

The line was scratchy, but I was pretty sure I heard my dad say, "Plantation Lumber is creeping into Chinook protected land. They want to rip down the cedar trees here and use them for rabbit cage linings. We could use some people to stand with us out here. You and your mom want to join us?"

"Yeah," I said. "We'll be there as soon as we can."

I hung up the phone and shouted. "Mom! Cedar trees falling! Dad needs us right away!"

Not waiting for my mom to answer, I jumped into gear. As I changed my clothes into more rugged attire and gathered up the necessary tools, I found myself feeling happier than I had in weeks.

Anything could happen, I thought giddily. *I saw a mermaid on my last mission. Maybe today I'll see a unicorn or a dragon.*

And if not, if a certain college freshman could be persuaded to come along (and I felt confident that might be the case), I would at the very least have a night of holding hands, chanting in protest together, and cuddling close to stay warm. It could be as romantic as my dad had hinted once upon a time. That delicious thought in mind, I followed my mom out the door and headed toward another adventure.

Acknowledgements

This novel would not have happened if not for the Society of Children's Book Writers and Illustrators-Midsouth Region group. I'm particularly grateful for the editor critique session I had at their annual Fall Conference five years ago and the novel revision workshop led by author Helen Hemphill, events that helped me figure out how to get this novel going in the right direction. It is a great group of people. I also really appreciate the members of the Teen Lit Authors listserv who all are ready with advice and support.

I'm immensely thankful to the group here at Fire and Ice Young Adult Novels. Thank you to Nancy Schumacher and Denise Meinstad for accepting my novel. Caroline Andrus, I couldn't imagine a better cover design. Megan Orsini, your editing and advice were perfect, and I appreciate the great care you gave to my story.

Above all, I want to thank my family and friends. It has been over a decade since this story began in my brain, and deciding to start the whole thing over again from scratch three years ago was hard to do. You kept me from quitting and are there for me still.

About the Author
D. G. Driver

D. G. Driver is a member of SCBWI and Author's Guild. She grew up in Southern California only 30 minutes from the beach. As a girl, she used to dream that magic would change her overnight into a beautiful mermaid. Alas, that never happened, but her love of the ocean never diminished. Even though she is landlocked in Tennessee now, she still only needs one whiff of sunscreen to bring her imagination alive. Thanks to the support of her husband and a sweet drawing of a mermaid done by her daughter that was taped on the wall above her desk to keep her motivated to finish, Cry of the Sea is her first published Young Adult novel. A dragon picture hangs there now, so we'll see what happens…

www.dgdriver.com
www.facebook.com/donnagdriver
www.d-g-driver.tumblr.com
@DGDriverAuthor
www.instagram.com/d_g_driver#
www.pinterest.com/dgdriver
www.wattpad.com/user/DGDriver